DARKWHISPERS

DARKWHISPERS

A

BRIGHTSTORM

ADVENTURE

VASHTI HARDY

Illustrated by GEORGE ERMOS

NORTON YOUNG READERS

An Imprint of W. W. Norton & Company
Independent Publishers Since 1923

Copyright © 2021, 2020 by Vashti Hardy
Illustrations copyright © 2021 by George Ermos
Map illustrations by Jamie Gregory
First American Edition 2021

First published by Scholastic Children's Books

For information about permission to reproduce selections from this book, write to Permissions, W. W. Norton & Company, Inc., 500 Fifth Avenue, New York, NY 10110

For information about special discounts for bulk purchases, please contact W. W. Norton Special Sales at
specialsales@wwnorton.com or 800-233-4830

Manufacturing by Lake Book Manufacturing
Book design by Christine Kettner
Production manager: Julia Druskin

Library of Congress Cataloging-in-Publication Data

Names: Hardy, Vashti, author. | Ermos, George, illustrator.
Title: Darkwhispers : a Brightstorm adventure / Vashti Hardy ;
illustrated by George Ermos.
Description: First American edition. | New York, NY : Norton Young Readers, 2021. |
Audience: Ages 9–12. | Summary: Twins Arthur and Maudie set sail in their
sky-ship to find noted explorer and author Ermitage Wrigglesworth, but their
newly-discovered aunt, Eurora Vane, is also seeking him—and a secret
he had just uncovered.
Identifiers: LCCN 2020041258 | ISBN 9781324015956 (hardcover) |
ISBN 9781324015963 (epub)
Subjects: CYAC: Brothers and sisters—Fiction. | Twins—Fiction. | Missing persons—
Fiction. | Aunts—Fiction. | Airships—Fiction. | Voyages and travels—Fiction. |
Adventure and adventurers—Fiction.
Classification: LCC PZ7.H22165 Dar 2021 | DDC [Fic]—dc23
LC record available at https://lccn.loc.gov/2020041258

W. W. Norton & Company, Inc., 500 Fifth Avenue, New York, N.Y. 10110

www.wwnorton.com

W. W. Norton & Company Ltd., 15 Carlisle Street, London W1D 3BS

2 4 6 8 0 9 7 5 3 1

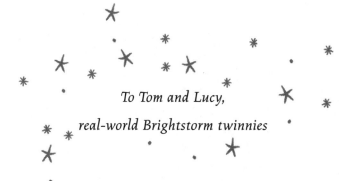

To Tom and Lucy,

real-world Brightstorm twinnies

PART ONE

CHAPTER I

A KNIFE THROUGH WATER

ABOVE AN ENDLESS OCEAN, in a place where thoughts faded like the setting sun, there was a far-reaching mist as gray as death's shadow. In the depths below, no fish swam or whales vented, and the seabed remained desolate and hushed as a lost memory.

The immense cloud folded and billowed soundlessly, and within the inky gloom, on a craggy island, creatures waited. They knew that the flash and snarl of sky-burn was coming. They could feel it in the prickle of their leathery skin, and every cell of their body could sense the electrical charge building.

The darkness was broken by a radiant blaze and, in the blink of an eye, they took flight.

* * *

Arthur and Maudie Brightstorm were both unusual yet usual children. For one thing, they had no parents and their family home had been taken from them unfairly, yet they had each other and had found an unlikely family in the crew of a sky-ship. For another, at thirteen years old they had already traveled to the farthest point humans had ever been in the Wide, frozen South Polaris, driven by the desire to find the truth and clear their family name.

Maudie was pragmatic and considered—it was one of the things that made her an exceptional young engineer—while Arthur, although a bright, bookish boy, had a history of acting before thinking things through. At times this meant that the twins would find themselves in risky situations, such as now as they skulked through the streets of Lontown in pursuit of a tall figure who slipped through the night like a knife through water.

Arthur had caught sight of him not ten minutes before as he'd stared thoughtfully out of his bedroom window at the midnight-quiet Archangel Street. The man had come from the south end and had hurried north, looking around nervously and fumbling with something small in his hands. Finding his manner suspicious, Arthur had resolved to follow and find out what this particular man was doing out so late. Maudie went along, mostly to stop Arthur from being too reckless.

Their quarry stopped and looked over his shoulder.

Maudie pulled Arthur to a standstill beside a tall wall. "What's he up to?" she whispered.

They watched as the figure turned in front of a grand, white-stone house, perfectly symmetrical in its arched windows and pillars, then ascended marble steps that glistened like polished bone.

Arthur squinted into the darkness and murmured, "Who lives there?"

"I'm not a walking Lontown address book, Arty."

"I was just thinking out loud. I mean, it's Montague Street, so it's surely someone important."

Their muscles became rigid as the man, lit by a street pitch lamp, turned to look over his shoulder again and scanned the street. They pushed their bodies against the bricks, hearts thudding.

"This was a bad idea," Arthur whispered.

"*Your* bad idea. It was *you* who woke *me* up."

"You didn't need much persuading; your feet were in your shoes before I could even find mine!" he hissed.

The figure they were pursuing was Smethwyck, devoted assistant of Eudora Vane—the eminent explorer and the woman who was responsible for their father's death.

But they were far enough away, and well hidden in shadow, so Smethwyck looked away and fumbled with the object he was holding, cursing as one of his sleeves became momentarily hooked on it.

"Unnecessarily flouncy," Arthur whispered.

Maudie stifled a snigger and strained to see what it might be. "It looks like some sort of lock pick."

There was a *clonk*, then the door opened. After one last brief look over his shoulder, Smethwyck disappeared inside.

"He's broken in. Come on, let's get closer," said Arthur.

They rushed across the street to stand behind a laurel hedge close to the door.

After several minutes Smethwyck reappeared, grasping a bundle of what appeared to be books. He clicked the door shut, glanced around, then headed back down the street.

When he was a safe distance ahead, Arthur and Maudie moved from behind the hedge and followed him through several streets until he turned and crept up the path of a large, detached house.

Arthur whispered, "Quick, let's get across the lawn. There's a light on."

Maudie nodded. There was only a thin sliver of moon that evening, so she felt confident they wouldn't be seen.

They jumped the ornate railing and hurried toward the great house like a pair of foxes scurrying in the night. They stopped behind a voluminous rose bush, just short of the huge windows that were open to the warm night air, snow-white drapes blowing softly outward in the breeze. The glow of pitch lamps inside lit the grass with an orange glow.

The room was sumptuously decorated with elaborate gilded mirrors, plump kingfisher-blue and ruby-red cushions, gold cornices, and lush plants, the likes of which, Arthur noted, were not from anywhere near Lontown.

"Do you think that chandelier is crystal and diamond?" he whispered.

"And I'm betting that's real gold. The luxury is actually hurting my eyes, Arty."

A man they didn't recognize walked to the fireplace, looked at his pocket watch, then adjusted the mantel clock. On the sideboard beside him, although it was difficult to see clearly from the distance, there appeared to be photographs of individuals in various locations: mountaintops, snowy plains, jungles—and one rather horrible picture of a man holding up the

head of a dead animal, possibly a North Polaris bear, Arthur guessed. When the man had finished with the clock, he turned and stood in thought. There was something familiar about him, but Arthur couldn't place what it was. He was elderly with a pin-sharp look about his eyes, white hair cropped short. The wrinkles of age were concentrated around his eyes and the bridge of his nose as though formed by many years of very careful and calculated thought. He was immaculately dressed in a double-breasted suit, with diamond cuff links and a pale pink shirt. One hand held a bejeweled cane, although he appeared to have no weight bearing on it, and the other hand was tucked into his jacket pocket, the thumb resting outside. His chin was slightly tilted upward. He oozed superiority.

The door opened, and Eudora Vane walked into the room with the force of a strong gust of wind, looked at the clock, then dropped into a chair.

The twins exchanged a glance, something like a roll of the eyes mixed with horror, as they both recognized the similarity.

Maudie whispered, "He *must* be her father."

"You know what that means." Arthur took a breath. "He's our . . . *grandfather*."

They had no memory of any of their grandparents. On the Brightstorm side, their grandfather had died many years before they were born, and their grandmother had passed when they were very young, although in the photographs they'd seen, their Brightstorm grandfather had their father's kindly eyes and their grandmother his infectious smile. Eudora Vane, they learned not long ago, was their mother's sister.

"Waiting is tedious," Eudora huffed.

"For goodness' sake, stop slouching." Her father's voice was as trimmed and precise as his appearance.

"There's no one here," she complained, but she sat up straighter nonetheless.

"Forget yourself within your own four walls and forget your standing in society. It's a slippery slope, especially in these times . . . as well you know."

Eudora narrowed her eyes. "Do you really believe that he was on to something? The tiresome Eastern Isles are only good for one thing and that's the pomerian puffback and . . ." She paused and shrugged, looking to the pink fur cuffs on her jacket. "The Eastern Isles are not good for anything now."

Arthur and Maudie glanced at each other. This probably had something to do with Ermitage Wrigglesworth. Notable explorer and the author of numerous books on exploration, Wrigglesworth had gone missing in the Eastern Isles. They'd seen it reported in the *Lontown Chronicle* when they'd returned from South Polaris. The crew they belonged to, the Culpepper crew, was planning to set off in search of him next week. There wasn't much reward money, it would barely cover their costs, but the call to adventure was too irresistible for all of them.

Eudora's father strolled toward her. "I've no doubt he was on to something. Wrigglesworth couldn't help but put his sniveling nose into everyone's business. He was the most annoying lickspittle at the universitas, always snooping and listening in on conversations, jotting things incessantly in his journals. He was useful if you wanted to know something, but if he hadn't been born into sovereigns, I would've squashed him like a fly—in fact, I think I did on a few occasions." He stared into space as though reliving a memory, a small grin on his lips. "Speaking of flies . . ."

Footsteps echoed loudly beyond the door. Smethwyck stepped inside and dipped his head to each of them. "Thaddeus. Eudora."

"You took your time," said Eudora bluntly.

"There's something different about Eudora, but I can't put my finger on it," Arthur said, his voice almost silent.

Smethwyck put the pile of books he'd taken from Montague Street on the table.

Without a word of thanks, Eudora and Thaddeus began looking through them eagerly.

Arthur leaned in toward Maudie and whispered, "From their conversation just now, I think we can assume it was Wrigglesworth's house he broke into. I wish we could see what's in the books."

"It must be good, because that grin on Eudora's face is getting bigger by the second."

Eudora and Thaddeus continued keenly flipping pages and exchanging narrow-eyed looks and raised eyebrows while Smethwyck stood on the outside like an excluded child.

Then Arthur realized what was different. "Where's that vile insect of hers? Miptera."

Maudie squinted. "Probably out bullying all the smaller insects."

At that moment, they both heard the *clack-clack* of mandibles and the furious flicker of wings. Eyes suddenly wide, they looked down as a gust of wind blew the curtain to reveal the huge silver insect sitting on the window ledge looking their way.

"Clanking cogs—run, Arty!" Maudie hissed.

But before they could kick their legs into action, Miptera flickered her wings ferociously and sped in their direction.

The twins dropped and Miptera missed, flying into the rose bush. They both leaped up and pelted across the grass away from the house. They couldn't hear Miptera chasing them, so they caught their breath behind a tree for a moment then risked a look back. As they did, Miptera zoomed back inside through the open window, knocking it in her urgency with a sound like a glass being hit by a metal spoon. She flew hectically toward Eudora, but before she reached her, she was batted away by the swift hand of Thaddeus Vane.

"Can't you get yourself a proper sapient? That creature is a disgrace."

Eudora flinched but didn't move to pick Miptera up. She stood, and her gaze moved to the garden. "Something's made her uneasy."

The twins held their breath as though somehow it might make them invisible. But then Thaddeus suddenly called Eudora excitedly, pointing at one of the books, and she hurried back obediently.

Arthur and Maudie saw their chance and rushed away into the night.

$* \quad * \quad *$

On the doorstep of number four Archangel Street, Welby took his watch from his dressing-gown pocket, tutted, and raised his large V-shaped eyebrows at Arthur and Maudie.

"We were putting the rubbish out?" Arthur suggested.

Maudie pursed her lips to contain what threatened to be a smirk at Arthur's feeble excuse.

Welby's eyebrows edged up another half inch. "How very thoughtful of you. Perhaps we can make this your responsibility henceforth, as you are so very eager?"

"Actually, Parthena wanted a midnight stroll,"

he tried again. Parthena was their sapient hawk, a hyperintelligent creature of the Wide with the ability to understand humans.

Welby gave an exaggerated yawn. "Parthena is in the dining room with Queenie. Next?"

Teasing Welby had become one of Arthur's favorite occupations since moving into Archangel Street. But before he could try another silly excuse, Maudie pulled him along the staircase and said, "Sorry we're home late. We'd better get to bed."

Welby shook his head and shuffled back toward his downstairs bedroom. "You'll be updating Harriet in the morning then," he called over his shoulder.

Once upstairs, Maudie said, "Arty, you shouldn't joke too much. Remember, he's got moves!"

They both grinned. It was true. They'd been totally amazed in the sand dunes near the Citadel on their expedition south when they'd been ambushed. Welby had displayed quite an array of martial-arts moves.

"He probably had training at whichever Uptown school he attended," Arthur said, narrowing his eyes. "Perhaps he had a private defense tutor," he added in a Welby well-to-do way and made several slice movements with his hand. He liked Welby, but Welby could also be a bit judging of them. Actually, now that Arthur thought about it, it was mostly of him, not Maudie. Welby liked ingenuity, and Maudie always had a tool in her hand of one kind or another, while Arthur often had what Welby referred to as "a glazed look."

They both laughed and sat on their beds.

"He probably still has lessons; he's been out every morning since we got back from the last expedition. I bet that's where he goes." Arthur flopped back onto his pillow. "At least we know whose house Smethwyck broke into. I wonder what was in those books?"

"Before you suggest it, I don't fancy going back to find out. Thaddeus Vane didn't seem particularly welcoming." Maudie wrinkled her nose. "I actually felt a bit sorry for Miptera."

"Sorry for the creature that made us crash in the Everlasting Forest?"

"Well . . . maybe not. I can still hear the splinter of wood." She shivered.

"Let's see what Harriet thinks in the morning."

CHAPTER 2

ARMADA

AT BREAKFAST, Felicity Wiggety, the *Aurora*'s cook and the person who would always defend the twins with her lucky spoon and her life, bundled into the room. Her wild red hair was up in a baggy bun, her silver spoon hooked over an apron that barely covered her voluminous skirt. Her large feet were shoeless, which was her preference around the house on account of the lack of "styles in my size to my liking." She smiled at Arthur and Maudie and put a rack of buttery toast on the table. "You're up late this morning, twinnies. Were you both burning the candle to its nub in the library again?"

Welby coughed loudly.

After peeking briefly over the top of the morning

Lontown Chronicle to observe the situation, Harriet went back to her reading.

"It's tiring work planning an expedition," Arthur said. "And Maudie's been flat out, doing all the modifications to the top floor and . . . stuff."

"Stuff?" Maudie began retying her hair ribbon. "It's complex engineering."

Harriet smiled to herself.

"Not as complex as mapping the Eastern Isles."

"Or as interesting as late-night Lontown excursions," Welby said loudly.

But Harriet was now engrossed with reading and didn't seem to hear.

Maudie exchanged a look with Arthur and leaned in to whisper, "We should tell her before he does."

Arthur scooped jam onto his toast and nodded, but he thought the moment wasn't right.

Felicity poured tea into their cups. "That jam is Uncle Elbert's recipe. I've never felt such a tingling in my toes as the day I first tried that!"

Arthur took a bite and smiled to himself. Felicity had a tingling in her toes about something on most days, and she was rarely wrong. The jam was sweet as a summer day and tasted unlike any berry he could recall. "It's lovely. What's it made from?"

"Elbertberries."

"You're making that up," Arthur said in between bites.

"It's true as the chime strikes on the Geographical clock. It's a cross between a bramble berry and a red rubus. Uncle Elbert mixed the two and here you have it. He's quite the taste fusion genius."

"There's an article in the *Chronicle* about us," Harriet said suddenly.

They all paused and looked at her.

"What does it say?" Maudie asked.

Harriet gave a small cough and began reading:

Intrepid young explorer Harriet Culpepper, who daringly captained her sky-ship, the *Aurora*, to become the third group to reach South Polaris . . .

Arthur noticed her cheeks blush a little.

. . . has successfully persuaded the Geographical Society to formally recognize the official names of the Continents in all their documents, publications, maps, and correspondence forthwith. The land masses commonly referred to as the First, Second, and Third Continents will now be singularly and routinely referenced as Vornatania, Nadvaaryn, and the Ice Continent, respectively.

Welby gave Harriet a tap on the shoulder. "Excellent work, Harrie."

She smiled. "It's a small change, but a huge advancement. Even the Eastern Isles is problematic—Eastern for whom?"

"What do the people who live there call them?" asked Arthur.

"There are many languages there, but the people of the islands call them the Stella Oceanus in their common language, which means the stars of the sea," said Harriet.

Arthur thought that sounded much more poetic.

"But I'm pleased the Geographical Society have accepted the continent name change, at least; it's a big step for them."

"I expect it met with some resistance from some of the families?" said Felicity.

Arthur knew one family in particular that wouldn't have liked the change. One that put themselves at the top of everything.

"I bet the Vanes tried to block it." Maudie scowled.

"Indeed," said Harriet.

"Good to see you having more influence after your achievements." Welby nodded.

"Shame about the Ice Continent though," said Arthur, wrinkling his nose. "I mean, it's not the most original name. I bet the thought-wolves have a much better name for it." His heart burned at the memory of meeting the wondrous creatures on their expedition south. They had the ability to communicate directly through thought. Tuyok, their pack-leader, had become a true friend, and Arthur missed him, as though a piece of him had separated and would remain forever in the frozen continent with the wolves . . . and his father.

Maudie looked at him, and he could see that she felt the same way.

Harriet's attention had now been taken by something else in the newspaper, which was making her frown intently.

The twins noticed. "What is it?" they said in unison.

Harriet put her hand up for a moment, finished reading, then folded the *Lontown Chronicle* and placed it on the table. "There's a meeting this afternoon at three chimes at the Geographical Society. All esteemed explorer families are invited to attend; apparently there's a highly important matter to discuss."

Arthur leaned in. "What else does it say?"

"Little else."

"Are we going?" Maudie asked.

"Of course we're going," Arthur said keenly, then looked at Harriet. "Aren't we?"

"We're meant to be setting off for the Eastern—I mean, the Stella Oceanus—in less than two weeks," said Maudie, "and we've still got the transformer valve to connect, the upper roof mechanism to restore, and the balloon pumps to clean, let alone my new project."

"Maud, stop talking; you're making me want to go back to bed."

She pushed Arthur's arm playfully.

Harriet grinned. "We're perfectly on schedule; we will be finished on time. I've got the rest of the crew arriving in two days to help with any final touches. Welby, if you and Felicity can stay behind and continue preparations for their arrival, we'll update you when we get back from the Society."

"Certainly, although I have to go out on some business first," Welby said.

Arthur glanced at Maudie and did a subtle martial-arts hand twist.

"Have you finished collating all the maps, Arthur?" Welby asked.

"I'm almost there."

"Pah! I took the liberty of checking, and you still have much work to do."

Arthur blushed under his freckles.

"If you think you've even scratched the surface with the few maps you've collected, well . . . the Stella

Oceanus are in their hundreds and scattered like a bucketful of Parthena's birdseed."

With a swoosh, Parthena flew into the room, landed beside Arthur, and turned her head to regard Welby—even for a hawk, the look of bemusement was clear.

Arthur stroked her head. "Don't worry, he knows you don't like birdseed really, Parthena."

Queenie, the oversized, fluffy, sapient cat sitting on Harriet's lap, gave a soft meow from under the table as if to say, "me neither."

"You've perhaps researched only two or three of the commonest maps at most."

"I'm being thorough." Arthur turned to Harriet. "So that's really all it says about the meeting?"

Harriet paused. "It does say something else. . . . It says that Eudora Vane is chairing it."

Queenie poked her head above the table and Parthena outstretched her wings and ruffled them. Maudie and Arthur exchanged a glance.

"Harrie, last night we followed Smethwyck," said Maudie.

She frowned. "Why did you do that?"

"I was restless—" Arthur began.

"As usual," Maudie added.

"—and I was at the window, seeing if Parthena wanted a night flight, when I saw him walking down the street suspiciously, so we followed him."

"I don't suppose there's any point in saying that perhaps you should've told me?"

"Sorry, but he would've been gone by then. Anyway, he broke into a house on Montague Street, then went to the Vanes and gave them some books he'd taken."

"You went to the Vanes?" Harriet said slowly, as though helping it to sink into her brain.

"We didn't go *inside*."

"Just to the window," Maudie confirmed.

"But what if you'd been caught?" Harriet shook her head. "Which house did he break into?"

"Er . . ." he looked at Maudie, who shrugged. "We forgot to look at the number, but we are pretty sure it was Ermitage Wrigglesworth's."

"Do you think this meeting might have something to do with what they found?" asked Arthur.

Harriet thought for a moment. "I'm sure it will, but all the explorers must log their detailed plans before travel with the Geographical Society, and nearly everyone has copies of Wrigglesworth's by now; they're available to anyone who asks. Eudora must suspect he was up to more than he revealed to the Society." She tapped the newspaper. "Well, one thing is for certain—if Eudora Vane is involved, there's bound to be trouble."

* * *

As the watchtower approached the chime of three, Maudie, Arthur, and Harriet turned the corner to the Lontown Geographical Society. The square bustled with people making their way toward the Society building. Arthur felt a cold shiver run through him as he thought of the first time they'd come here and been told the lie about what had happened to their father at South Polaris—how their father had been wrongfully accused of stealing fuel from a rival sky-ship. The false story had been that their father and his crew had perished because of supposedly vicious creatures, which had turned out to be the peaceful thought-wolves, and really it had been Eudora Vane behind it all, because she'd hated their father for marrying her sister. To Eudora Vane, it was unthink-able that a new-blood explorer could marry someone from a respected heritage explorer family.

Maudie looked across at Arthur. "Are you all right?"

"I'm just remembering, you know . . ."

"I know."

"Scraggleneck scratchings, two for a sovereign!" came a call.

Maudie and Arthur looked over to where the sound had come from: a stall in the square.

"I don't believe it," Arthur huffed.

It was Mr. Beggins, one half of the vile couple who had bought the twins from their governess, Mistress Poacher, after their father's death. They'd been taken to live in the Slumps of Lontown, in a leaking attic room with a soggy mattress and hardly any food before they managed to escape and join the Culpepper crew. Mr. Beggins stood behind a hand-pushed cart. He ran a hand through his greasy hair, then noticed Harriet and the twins.

"Oi! You owe us for those two ungrateful little blighters!" Mr. Beggins called, storming over to them.

Harriet put her hands up to hold Arthur and Maudie back. "Leave this one to me."

"Mr. Beggins, how interesting to meet you properly. I had rather hoped Felicity's lucky spoon knocking you out would be the last vision I would have of you. Alas, here we are."

His face blushed crimson, with both embarrassment and fury. He opened his mouth, but Harriet's calm yet forceful demeanor and her absolute mountainlike resolve were formidable, and although the two stood perfectly even in height, she seemed to tower over him.

"I would hate to think you were operating here without an Article 561," she said.

"I . . . well . . . Of course . . ." he bumbled.

"Is it two- or three-years' imprisonment, Arthur? Arthur is very well read on Lontown law these days. What was it you were telling me about the law on paying for children, then forcing them to cook and clean for you without a sovereign in compensation, and making them sleep in a filthy room with holes in the roof and no food?" She said it with a bright airiness, but her sober undertones were clear as the Lontown afternoon sky.

"We took in those ungrateful urchins out of the goodness—"

Harriet simply raised a finger to silence him. "Ah yes, that was it. *Twenty* years' imprisonment: plenty of time to reflect on your actions." She leaned in toward him. "I hear there's a sapient rat who is most perturbed by cruelty and makes it her life's business to torment such prisoners. She'll steal the paltry amount of food you're given and just when you try to sleep, she's there, quick as lightning, nibbling your ear, your toes, your . . ."

Mr. Beggins had turned quite green.

Harriet laughed brightly. "I daresay a 561 is the least of your problems, Mr. Beggins. Those three-day-old scraggleneck scratchings you sell are unlikely to pass Lontown health standards." She squinted and whispered, "Aren't they made from illegal bird poaching?" Then she slapped him on the shoulder. "I'm sure you've got a handle on it all. Although, didn't we pass the police only a moment ago on Langley Way?" She shrugged. "Come along, twins. That's enough rats for one day."

As Mr. Beggins rushed to pack away his stall, looking around frantically, the twins smiled broadly and followed Harriet up the stone steps of the Lontown Geographical Society, through the carved doorway, and into a grand hall. The majestic pillars and gilt-framed maps still took Arthur's breath away, as did the statues of the great explorers.

They pushed through the double doors that led to the auditorium. It was a vast room beneath the enormous dome, which was the iconic landmark of Lontown. The ceiling was elaborately decorated with gilded, repeating patterns, all leading to the pinnacle of the dome, where an enormous compass was painted in the shape of a blazing sun. Around the room, chandeliers hung from the outer ceilings between pillars, and a half circle of red velvet seats pointed at a large stage. Many of the Lontown explorer families were already in there—Arthur recognized Azalea and Dryden Bestwick-Ford; Rumpole Blarthington; Evelyn Acquafreeda, the sea-ship explorer; Samuel Fontaine; Eldrid Nithercott and his eldest daughter Beatrice, who must have been getting ready to captain their sky-ship; tall Hilda Hilbury in her ribboned flowerpot hat; and many others.

Harriet, Arthur, and Maudie sat at the back.

"We can see everything from here," Harriet whispered. "Sometimes the tiniest nod of the head, or glance, between explorer families can be very telling."

Officials from the Geographical Society were seated on the platform, including Madame Gainsford with her sapient stoat resting on her shoulders like a fur collar. But she wasn't in her usual central seat; this time it was occupied by Eudora Vane. As usual, Eudora was dressed from head to toe in a pale shade of pink, and on her jacket was Miptera, looking for all the world like a piece of jewelry. Although Eudora's external beauty was still undeniable, Arthur and Maudie knew only too well the charred heart that existed within.

Madame Gainsford banged her gavel, then stood up. "Esteemed society, you will all be aware of the reports that one of our very own, the eminent explorer and author of numerous expedition accounts, Ermitage Wrigglesworth, has gone missing in the Eastern Isles. We were informed in the early chimes by Madame Vane that she received word from sources in the east that he may have gotten into danger. Where exactly, we do not know."

Arthur leaned in toward Maudie. "Sources in the east? What rubbish."

"Madame Vane, perhaps if you would now address the esteemed families with your proposal."

Eudora Vane stood up and spoke, her voice soft and sweet as sugar, as though she wouldn't harm even the smallest insect. "The news I received yesterday late in the evening suggests that he may be in some peril. Details are sparse . . . but I have a proposal." She smiled. "As we all know, these islands are in the thousands, and for one sky-ship to presume they can tackle them alone is futile." She scanned the audience and paused when she reached Harriet Culpepper. It was no secret that Harriet had been planning to head off in search the following week. "And would be rather self-indulgent."

"How dare she," Maudie hissed.

Harriet put a gentle hand on her arm. "Don't rise to it." She looked straight back at Eudora without any change to her expression.

Eudora Vane walked the length of the stage. "I propose an armada of First Continent explorers to venture east and search for him."

Madame Gainsford gave a little cough and tapped her gavel lightly on the table. "Do use the correct names for the continents please, Madame Vane."

Maudie leaned in toward Arthur and whispered, "What's she up to? Armada?"

Eudora gave Madame Gainsford a veiled smile of acceptance and continued. "An armada of *Vornatanian*, Lontown explorers will venture east. We recently lost one explorer due to a tragic mistake, a cook's error; we shall not lose another one!"

Arthur and Maudie glanced at each other with gaping mouths.

"Tragic mistake?" Maudie said, shaking her head.

"The nerve of the woman!" said Arthur. They knew the truth: that she had been behind the poisoning of their father's crew. But they had no evidence, and her status in Lontown enabled her to get away with it.

Around the hall, the heads of the various explorer families nodded in agreement with Eudora.

"We must hurry, for dear Ermitage's sake. We leave on Friday." She dipped her head to Madame Gainsford, who then took the floor.

"On behalf of the Geographical Society board, I

am pleased to inform you that the reward has been increased to one hundred thousand sovereigns so that all participating families may share the fund. Please, could the heads of the families willing to join the Lontown Armada stay behind. You have much planning to do."

Feet shuffled as many of the audience began to leave the room.

Maudie stood up. "Come on, let's get out of here."

"Too right," said Arthur, jumping up beside her. "We don't have any time to lose if we want to get ahead of Eudora Vane and the others, and . . . Harrie, why aren't you moving?"

Harriet looked pensive. "I want to find out more. For a start, why does she really want to find Ermitage Wrigglesworth so much? It's certainly not a rescue mission in her mind."

"The reward?" said Arthur.

Harriet shook her head. "She has more sovereigns than she could desire. The best way to find out what she's up to is to stay as close as we can. That means playing along and being part of her plans, for now."

The hall was emptying, other than a dozen or so explorers who were making their way to the stage to join Eudora Vane.

"We'd better get going," said Maudie, tugging Arthur.

"Hold on a moment." Harriet took a pen from her belt and scribbled down an address. "I want you to go here. Ask for Octavie and say I sent you. I want you to find out—"

"Just the heads of house to remain!" bellowed someone from the stage front, obviously aimed at them.

"Off you go. We can update each other when we get back."

Arthur took the piece of paper. It read:

18A Montague Street

CHAPTER 3

OCTAVIE

WHEN ARTHUR AND MAUDIE arrived at Montague Street, they realized the place Harriet had sent them to was just across from the house Smethwyck had broken into the previous evening.

"How strange," said Maudie as they walked up the steps.

"I wonder what we're meant to find out here?" said Arthur as he knocked on the door.

A woman with short, graying, wavy hair answered the door. She had a quiet, curious smile, determined eyes, and a youthful face despite the wrinkles. Her white sleeves were rolled up, and she held a small piece of machinery in one hand.

"Is that an injector pump?" Maudie asked.

The woman smiled. "What an interesting way to introduce yourself."

"Sorry. We're looking for Octavie. We're . . ."

"The Brightstorm twins. You're rather famous in Lontown and the subject of quite a lot of closed-door explorer gossip. I'm Octavie; do come in."

"I'm afraid we're not entirely sure why Harrie, that's Harriet Culpepper, our . . ." Arthur realized he didn't know what to call her. Their captain? Their friend? Their sort-of stand-in parent? He wasn't sure what to say, so he just said, "She sent us to you. She didn't have much time to explain why."

Octavie led them inside. "Well, you've come to the right place. Come into my study. I have some tea in the pot, and I baked a lovely spiced-fruit loaf this morning."

They followed her into a brightly lit room full of books, odd mechanisms, and tools. Octavie put the machinery on the table and looked at them, a sparkle in her eyes that was somehow familiar to Arthur and Maudie, even though they had never met this woman before. She put her hands into her trouser pockets, which were baggy to the knees and tighter at the bottom, just like . . .

"Harriet," they both said.

"We mean, you must be related to her. Are you?" asked Maudie.

She nodded and turned her wrist to them to display her Culpepper bird tattoo. Each explorer family carried their mark proudly; the Culpeppers had two swallows dipped in flight. Arthur and Maudie had just gotten the Brightstorm moth—a rare, highly resilient species of gold and red, which their father had discovered in the volcanic islands of the north—tattooed on their arms on returning from their expedition to South Polaris.

"I'm Harriet's great-aunt—her late grandfather was my brother. I'm very pleased to meet you at last." She shook Maudie's hand, then paused and swapped to her left hand to shake Arthur's.

Arthur was sure he remembered Harriet mentioning a great-aunt at some point . . . then it came to him. He'd been at the Last Post with Harriet when he'd found the secret writing in Wrigglesworth's diary revealed by lemon juice, and they'd had a conversation in which Harriet mentioned she'd had a great-aunt who had known him well. "You were good friends with Ermitage Wrigglesworth!"

"Ah, tea, I almost forgot." She went to a side table, where a teapot rested on a stand above a gentle, flickering flame. She saw how Maudie was peering at it and said, "It's often the simplest things that are most effective." Then she took two fresh cups from the tray.

As she lifted the pot, Arthur noticed that she had some more tattoos above the Culpepper swallows. Some triangles . . . Her sleeve shifted down as she put the pot back on the stand.

Octavie served them their cups, then sat and clasped her hands together. "I'm sorry I haven't been by to say hello. Harriet has been to see me, of course, but I know how busy you've all been with the rebuild since you got back from South Polaris, and I didn't want to trouble you."

"So you know Ermitage Wrigglesworth, the missing explorer? Harriet mentioned it," Arthur pressed.

"Indeed." She sipped her tea and observed them, with that Culpepper twinkle in the eye that was going to make them work hard for information rather than gift it freely.

"You must be ever so worried about him," said Maudie.

Octavie squinted a mild frown. "How long has he been missing?"

"His expedition left over a year ago and he's been reported missing for several moons. Apparently the Geographical Society just stopped receiving letters."

She shrugged. "My dears, I was friends with Ermitage an awfully long time ago. You could say that we drifted apart."

"But you live on the same street?"

"Yes, I believe we do." She smiled. "So, the great Madame Vane is leading a Lontown armada in search of him."

Arthur wondered how she already knew that, as it had only just been announced.

"Whispers and rumors." Octavie winked, reading his thoughts. "I still like to keep my ear to the ground. And Harrie wondered if I can tell you anything else?"

They nodded.

"We believe that Ermitage Wrigglesworth's house was broken into last night and something was stolen," said Arthur. "Something that may help us learn what Mr. Wrigglesworth was looking for."

She sat back. "I'm afraid I've no idea what that could be. Ermitage Wrigglesworth is the obsessive, inquisitive sort. He wants to know everything about everybody; it's why he wrote so many books about the explorer families—their histories, where they went, what they did, what made them tick. But for him . . . Well, let's just say he always felt something was missing. The east held much fascination for him—it's somewhere to get lost in the spiral of discovery. There are hundreds of islands. Personally, I'm not sure he intends to be found. He's a very old man who lived for exploration and probably wants to live the last part of his life on a small island in peace. The armada will go and spend copious amounts of time and money looking for Ermitage and they will likely return empty-handed."

It made sense to Arthur, the idea of escaping, running away from the past. He too had felt this way at times since losing his father.

"They'd be better off investing their sovereigns in other ventures."

Maudie coughed. "But excuse me for saying, Eudora Vane isn't the sort to waste her time on things that aren't in some way beneficial to her, whether financially or otherwise. Usually otherwise."

"She would certainly be held in esteem if she were the one to find him. And if it were another sky-ship in the armada, she would still be held up as the hero because she took charge of the project," said Octavie. "Quite clever, really."

"Yes . . . but."

Octavie had a wry grin on her lips. "But that's not enough for a Vane?"

"With her it's not just about the acclaim," said Arthur. "Perhaps Mr. Wrigglesworth was seeking something in particular, perhaps something new to control in the Stella Oceanus? Undiscovered pitch mines?" Maybe Octavie was right and he'd just gone there to live out his last days and not be bothered. Yet Arthur couldn't help but feel that something didn't fit.

"Do help yourself to fruit loaf," Octavie said, gesturing to the cake on the table.

Arthur looked again at the symbols above her family tattoo: triangles, but all slightly different and . . . She clasped her hands together softly and they were hidden once more.

Maudie took a piece, but Arthur explained he had an egg allergy. Octavie opened a decorative tin painted with large leaves and offered him a short-bread instead.

"What should we tell Harriet?" Maudie asked.

"Tell her not to waste her time with this armada. They will likely be back within six moon cycles, all the poorer for it."

"Are you sure he never mentioned anything he might have been looking for there, even long ago? Jewels, maybe? Gold?"

Octavie shook her head. "I'm afraid not."

She seemed a bit too certain, and Arthur couldn't shake the feeling that there must be more.

"Now, do tell me all about South Polaris." She deftly

steered them away from Ermitage Wrigglesworth, and after asking many questions about their last expedition quizzed them on the improvements they were making to the *Aurora*. Arthur suspected she was purposefully avoiding the reason they'd come to see her. He sat quietly while Maudie obliged with enthusiastic details.

They finished their tea and Octavie showed them to the door.

"Sorry you couldn't help us," Arthur said, making sure he made eye contact. Dad had always said if you looked someone square in the eye, the truth shines back.

She looked away and opened the door, but it was only open an inch or so when she closed it again and said, "I have some engineering books that may be of use to you, Maudie. Wait here a moment." She disappeared into the room off the hallway and returned with an armful, which she handed to Maudie.

"Thanks!"

Arthur frowned. He was sure she was keeping something back. As though she half wanted to tell them something.

They opened the door and were about to step back out into Montague Street when Maudie said, "Oh, you left something in here." She pulled out an envelope that had been tucked into one of the books.

Octavie put her hand out and stopped her. "It's meant to be there. . . . Forgive me, but I wanted to get to know you a little, before . . ." She paused for several seconds, then smiled. "Never mind. Enjoy your trip east, and I hope you have luck finding Ermitage— although I suspect otherwise."

Arthur and Maudie gave each other a swift glance of confusion as Octavie ushered them out. "It really was delightful to meet you both—give my love to Harrie."

The door shut behind them.

"That was odd." Maudie shrugged.

"Very."

CHAPTER 4

THE RING

BACK AT NUMBER FOUR Archangel Street, they waited for Harriet in the dining room.

Maudie tapped the envelope on the table. "We should wait for her to get back before we open it."

Arthur pressed his fingers over the envelope. "It's something hard."

Felicity walked in bearing a tray of marsh cakes. "What have you got there, twinnies?"

"Octavie Culpepper, Harriet's great-aunt, gave it to us," said Arthur.

"Well, why are you playing with it? Open it and see what's inside."

"Felicity!" Maudie laughed.

She waved her hand. "Oh, Harriet won't mind."

Arthur tapped the envelope on the table. "She

didn't specifically say to give it to Harriet, and she did hand you the books, Maud." Parthena jumped up on the table and nudged the envelope with her clawed foot. "See, even Parthena agrees."

In a moment, Maudie had ripped it open. She tipped the contents onto the table.

It was a gold signet ring. Arthur examined it. "It looks like some sort of bird engraved on it." He turned it over. "And one on the underside."

A soft clunk sounded as the front door closed, and moments later Harriet entered the room, her brow furrowed, and a bundle of papers clutched in her arms.

"What happened at the meeting?" Arthur asked eagerly.

Welby joined them and sat down at the table with Harriet.

"Each family within the armada has been assigned islands to search. It seems like Eudora had expected most of us to come on board. How did you get on at Octavie's?"

"She didn't know what could have been taken, and she said not to hold out much hope. She thought Mr. Wrigglesworth had most likely gone to live out his days and not be disturbed. That he probably didn't even want to be found."

Harriet exchanged a glance with Welby. "Curious."

"She gave Maudie some engineering books and one contained an envelope with this in it."

Arthur passed her the signet ring, and she examined it.

"We thought you might know what it was."

"I'm afraid I have no idea."

"It means nothing to you?" Arthur pressed, disappointed.

"Sadly not. And Octavie didn't wonder about the books taken from his house? I thought she would at least be able to speculate what it was about."

"She said she hasn't spoken to him in years."

Harriet sighed. "Well, we don't have time to ponder. The Lontown Armada sets sail on Friday and we have to finish the *Aurora*, which means one week's work in two days, so I've sent word to the rest of the crew to arrive early tomorrow morning. The Acquafreedas are already setting sail by sea this evening, as they'll be slower than the main fleet."

"Then I'd best get some supplies sorted," said Felicity.

"Would you mind if I keep Arthur here to assist me for a moment?" asked Harriet. "Welby can help you instead, if that's all right?"

Welby gave a nod.

"Of course," Felicity said, patting Arthur on the

arm as she left the room with Welby, then she called back, "Queenie, if you can pop a note to Balfour's Pantry Supplies?"

Queenie jumped up with a *"prrwt"* and followed Felicity out of the room.

"I need to finish the weather canopy," Maudie said, and hurried away.

Arthur was curious about why he wasn't helping Felicity.

Harriet looked up and smiled. "I've been thinking about your skills and strengths, Arthur. This will be your second lengthy expedition, and I want to recognize all that you achieved at South Polaris and the work you've done so far assisting Welby with the maps."

Arthur frowned. He hadn't done that much at all, really, and now he felt a bit guilty.

"I'd like to make you assistant navigator in the Stella Oceanus expedition."

"Oh!" Arthur said. Something like a warm balloon swelled inside him. He hadn't expected this, because Welby was second-in-command and assistant navigator to Harriet. Perhaps Welby was going to focus on his other duties more? He supposed he *was* getting fairly old . . .

"I'd still like you to help Felicity from time to

time, but I think some more responsibility will do you a world of good. Would you like the role?"

He nodded eagerly. "Yes, thank you!" This would also mean he'd work more closely with Harriet.

"Excellent. Then you will report to Welby."

His heart sank. "Welby?" He tried hard not to let the disappointment show in his voice, but it didn't work.

"Is there something wrong with that?"

He shook his head and imagined how many times a day Welby's judging eyebrows would rise in his direction. "No, of course not."

"Good." She smiled. "You're ready for it." Then she took the map that she'd received from the meeting and spread it on the table. "We'll start by cross-checking this map against those you've gathered so far and plan our navigation. We should look for extra opportunities to search for Wrigglesworth on the way."

Arthur thought for a moment. "And we should probably see if there's anything peculiar about the islands Eudora Vane has assigned to herself."

"Indeed, good thinking." Harriet frowned and tapped her pencil rapidly while scanning the map. "OK, read out the list of main island groups and I'll mark them off."

He took the flyer Harriet had brought back from

the meeting. "The Portendorfers are first; they will be searching Ishia and Florinni."

While Harriet scanned the map, Arthur's mind drifted back to Octavie. "Your great-aunt had some interesting marks on her forearm."

Harriet glanced up. "Her swallows?"

"No, the strange triangles above. Are they part of the Culpepper tradition?"

"She's had them ever since I've known her. Some club she belonged to at the universitas, I think." Her voice trailed off as she focused back on the map and wrote "Portendorfers" next to the appropriate islands.

"A club?" Arthur persisted.

"Hmm? They were young and—who's after the Portendorfers?"

"They were young and . . . ?" he tried again.

"Just a silly club. I forget now what she said it was called."

"What about the ring? Do you think that was part of the club?"

"Perhaps she didn't realize it was in the envelope?"

Arthur shook his head. "She meant us to have the ring."

"The ring is curious, but Octavie loves interesting objects. When I was a girl I was fascinated by her various trinkets. But I don't think it's significant.

She's getting old, Arthur. She probably used it as a bookmark and forgot. But keep hold of it in case. Now, who's next on the list?"

Octavie didn't seem forgetful to Arthur. He scanned the list. "The Nithercotts are next. They've got Pontia and Heilettica—oh, and Pelastria."

While Harriet was searching the map, Arthur picked up her magnifier and examined the ring closely. The bird was unlike any other he'd seen, yet was familiar. It had a proud long neckline, plumed feathers on its head, and a huge sweeping tail, wings arced. "What type of bird do you think is on the ring?"

"I don't know," Harriet said, without looking up. "Octavie explored a lot around the Citadel of Nadvaaryn—perhaps it's something from there."

Again, it was unlike anything he could recall.

"Arthur, are you going to assist, or should I send you to help Felicity?"

"Yes, sorry." He went back to the list. "The Bestwick-Fords are Florentina and Targi. Wait, they were one of the other sky-ships trying to get to South Polaris, weren't they?" He recalled them turning back because their sky-ship couldn't get through the rough snowstorms of the frozen south.

"Yes. Now, who's next?"

He looked back to the paper. "The Catmoles . . ."

He carried on reading the list of islands while Harriet checked them off, but after a while his mind drifted back to the ring.

Harriet tapped her pencil on the map. "There is a time for dreams and a time for focus. Which family is next on the list?"

"Er . . . the Temples have Vivaro and Dulcie," he said, but his mind was still on the ring.

CHAPTER 5

THE WELBY WAY

THE FOLLOWING DAY, the remainder of the crew arrived: Gilly, Meriwether, Barnes, Forbes, Cranken, Forsythe, Keene, Wordle, Hurley, and Dr. Quirke.

Number four Archangel Street was filled with sawing, banging, tapping, sparking tools, and laughter, all fueled by Felicity's endless supplies of tea and snacks. And with so many other tasks to complete, there was barely time to draw breath.

Before anyone could blink, it was Friday, and the cannon sounded at the Geographical Society, signifying the start of the challenge. The roar of ten sky-ships firing their engines in unison filled the air around the sky-ship yard as the Lontown Armada rose into the sky. The Jones's sky-ship with its two montgolfiere balloons, the Blarthingtons, Hilburys,

Nithercotts, Bestwick-Fords, Catmoles, Portendorfers, Temples, Fontaines (with their sky-ship imaginatively named the *Fontaine*), and lastly the Vane sky-ship, the *Victorious*.

But the bulk of the crowds gathered in front of number four Archangel Street.

No one wanted to miss the transformation from house to sky-ship, especially those who had missed the *Aurora*'s first, surprise launch to South Polaris.

The ground rumbled. Everyone gasped. Then the house began its utterly extraordinary metamorphosis— the front folded inward, great pistons and cogs whirred and crunched until the edges of the house and the door disappeared inside. Shutters opened beside the windows and small propellers sprouted from the house, unfolding and turning.

Being inside was a different experience for Arthur and Maudie. The crew hurried to the attic space, and with the scrape of metal and the sound of a great mechanism clunking and grinding, the roof began lifting backward. A thick beam of daylight illuminated the floorboards, which would soon become the deck, and as the roof folded in a huge accordion behind them, they were bathed in warm sun. Balustrades took the place of the walls and a panel slid back in the center of the floor. The great fabric balloon started to emerge.

Harriet released a lever and the huge steering wheel rolled from beneath the deck into view. She flashed Arthur and Maudie a smile, and with a sparkle in her eye she grasped the wheel. Her short hair waved in the breeze; she wore flying goggles, a white scarf and shirt, her characteristic trousers that were baggy to the knees then tucked into leather boots, and a large belt from which hung her compass, uniscope, and various other tools. Welby was close by, pointing and ordering the others gathered on the deck. Felicity Wiggety rushed to the side, her cheeks red and her giant spoon in hand, waving at the people below.

The crowd gasped as the house lifted from the ground. Finally, a section of wood creaked and revolved. Arthur and Maudie rushed to look over the edge. It had revealed a shining brass plate that read *AURORA,* and a new addition—the Culpepper symbol in bronze emblazoned beside it.

"Everyone, to your posts!" Harriet called, looking over at Arthur and Maudie with a wink.

The great fabric balloon blossomed above.

Eudora Vane's sky-ship, the *Victorious,* was the largest sky-ship and was above the docks a short distance away, rising powerfully, its wings spread majestically wide.

"Arthur, your cog!" Welby shouted.

Arthur realized everyone was already at theirs, so he dashed to the port side and began turning his cog.

Harriet Culpepper stood at the wheel, her hair and scarf flowing messily in the wind. "We need lift, fast!"

"Put your backs into it," Welby bellowed.

They all turned their cogs furiously, until there was a loud *click* and a shudder. "Good work," Harriet called.

Parthena took flight above them, leading them onward. The *Aurora* lifted, the crowd's cheers faded on the wind, and suddenly they were flying high, wings extended, balloon taut, Felicity hurrying to make a celebratory brew, duty notes being handed out by Welby.

The domes, spires, and ordered rooftops of Lontown disappeared, and they passed over the crooked buildings of the Slumps, where a permanent gray haze seemed to settle. Then the houses petered out to fields and tracks; everything became greener. They ate marsh cakes and talked and laughed as they sped above countryside and villages, taking off their sweaters as the midday sun shone down on them, and all the while, Harriet Culpepper kept her eyes on the horizon and her hands on the wheel.

Not being a race, the sky-ships of the armada all

stayed within sight of one another, and after several chimes the land became jammed with dreary-looking hills.

"Look, it's the pitch mines," said Arthur, calling to Maudie who was tinkering with what appeared to be a lever and chain on the deck. "Some of the sky-ships have already landed to fill up."

Maudie joined him. "I'm glad we don't have to stop there. I feel filthy just looking at it."

"To think we could have ended up there as forced labor," Arthur said.

"Did you ever have a pitch engine, Harrie?" Maudie called over to Harriet.

She nodded. "There wasn't much choice, but I always hated it, which is why I began developing the water engine at a young age with the help of the Citadel kings' technology."

As sunset bloomed in the west like colored ink spreading in water, Arthur and Maudie stood with Felicity and Gilly at the aft end of the sky-ship taking in the view of hills, rising and falling like gentle waves, crisscrossed by farm fields and wild woodland patches with full, blousy trees. It felt good to be under the wide sky again, the *Aurora* drifting almost soundlessly into the evening.

"It warms my soul being up here," Felicity sighed.

"I can't wait to get deep into the islands," said Gilly, the curly-haired botanist. "I've visited several dozens of them, and what always amazes me is the sheer diversity, how no two are ever the same."

"Do you think that's why Mr. Wrigglesworth liked going there?" asked Arthur.

"It's an explorer's paradise."

"How about the last one we've been assigned to? Nova?"

Gilly smiled. "I've never been there; it's the farthest one out, but I hear it's quite beautiful."

It seemed a little peculiar to Arthur that Eudora Vane had sent them there. It was probably because she wanted to make things as difficult for Harriet's crew as possible by sending them to the farthest reaches of the Wide.

The next day, they stopped off on the edge of a forest of great oaks not far from the coastal cliffs. In the distance they could see some of the other sky-ships landing close to another hilly area of small pitch mines where they could refuel before the long trip over the sea. The crew collected wood, and Harriet pulled Arthur and Maudie aside.

"Here." She passed them both thin ropes with a short rod of metal extending from a small attached case. They had the Culpepper symbol engraved on the metal. "It's a strike-fire." They had seen Harriet use something similar before to get fires started swiftly. "My parents always gifted me something useful on each expedition, so I thought I'd carry on the tradition. I've adapted it so that you can create a spark one-handed; simply hold it like so, and press the rod in with your index finger." She demonstrated. "Or you can press it down on a hard surface and create the sparks that way."

"Thank you!" they both said. Arthur put his in his pocket, and Maudie added hers straight to her tool belt.

The crew made a campfire, with Arthur and Maudie testing their strike-fires to get it going, then ate vegetable pies followed by berry buns. After their meal, Maudie excused herself, saying she needed to work on something behind a tent on deck for a while and declaring that no one was allowed to see what it was. Arthur got up to follow her, itching to know what she was up to.

"That includes you, Arty."

"What? But you said you'd show me once we were on the expedition and—"

"And I'm not quite ready to, so you'll have to be patient."

Arthur wasn't good at patience. He huffed.

* * *

The next morning everyone was on deck bright and early to set sail. Today they would be leaving their home continent and traveling over the sea to the first of the islands: Ephemeral Isle.

It would take three days just to get to this first island, and that was if the wind was in their favor. Meriwether, with her golden hair waving in the wind and her slightly unscientific method of licking her finger and putting it to the sky, assured them it would be.

Maudie vanished back into her mysterious canvas work space straight after breakfast.

"I take it that's not a new iron arm you're working on behind there," Arthur called. The arm Maudie had made him had been rather bashed up on their last expedition, and she'd promised to make him a new one—although in truth he was more than happy without it. While it was useful when they were climbing the rooftops back home, and sometimes it stopped stares in Lontown, it could cause chafing around his shoulder and strain on his neck. So he didn't miss wearing it; he enjoyed more seeing Maudie create better versions of it.

"I'll get back to it soon, I promise," she called.

That afternoon was to be Arthur's first navigation lesson with Welby, so he went to the library after lunch, his explorer's journal and pencil ready.

Arthur laid the map Harriet had been given by Eudora Vane out on the table. There were hundreds of islands. He scoured the shelves for any books on the Stella Oceanus that might include a clue as to what Ermitage Wrigglesworth had been looking for. After a while he found one called *Going East—A Myriad of Isles to Discover,* written by Wrigglesworth himself. There were many maps inside of various islands. "Brilliant!" Arthur said to himself and continued looking for similar books. Next he found a book by Zora Acquafreeda. The Acquafreedas had explored the Stella Oceanus fairly thoroughly in their sea-bound ships. When he compared the two books, he found the Acquafreeda maps to be more difficult to work out and inconsistent in their portrayal of the islands, but as they were viewing from the sea rather than from above, perhaps this was to be expected. But there were intricate drawings and measurements of the channels and seaways and rivers, which he thought might be useful.

Arthur suddenly became aware that Welby had

crept into the room and was looking over his shoulder. He put a book as thick as a brick and a small leather case on the table beside Arthur's map.

"You need to work on your surveying skills. Finding Wrigglesworth may be the purpose of this voyage, but an expedition is never just about the main reason you are going."

Arthur looked at him as though he was speaking backward.

Welby raised his eyebrows. "Arthur, if you want to captain your own ship one day, you will need the full range of skills."

Captain his own ship? Arthur had never imagined such a thing, but as Welby said it an undeniable tingle ran the length of his spine.

"If you are focused only on the mission in front of you, you may achieve it, but you will not better your skills and knowledge. That takes extra work and commitment."

"I have been reading lots," Arthur said in an effort to impress. "Look, this is *Going East*, written by Wrigglesworth. I'm trying to find a pattern in his routes."

Welby raised his eyebrows. *Was he impressed?* It was hard to tell.

"Your eyes are always on the goal, Arthur, and I mean that as a compliment."

The warm glow Arthur began to feel was swiftly extinguished when Welby continued. "However, you need to also take time to study the full range of calculations in depth, even though you won't use your entire armory in a single expedition. For example, this book here." He tapped the huge book he had put on the table. "*Navigational Complete* is the most comprehensive navigation book in the Wide."

When Arthur flicked through the pages, he saw so many symbols and numbers that it made his head spin and he shut it again.

Welby tutted.

"I'm sorry. I will try, Welby, it's just that numbers and working it out is a bit more Maudie's thing."

Welby tutted again. "When Harriet was a young girl, she hated all the working out too. She just wanted to 'do it,' to get out there and explore the Wide in a sky-ship of her own. But she quickly realized that in order to achieve her dreams, sometimes you have to learn things that may seem difficult and irrelevant at first, but they end up playing a part. What she does when she's steering the *Aurora* might look instinctive to you, but behind it are years of careful study and, yes, some hefty calculations. The most fruitful learning often comes with a bit of hardship." Welby opened the lid of the metal case.

"This is for your studies. Some of the equipment we use in navigation."

It was full of strange-looking tools. He'd seen similar ones at Brightstorm House in his father's office, but tools were more Maudie's area of expertise and he couldn't say they excited him as much as Wrigglesworth's books.

"Thanks," he said.

"Finish chapter one by the morning. I'll be testing you on the contents tomorrow afternoon."

"Test?" Arthur said in horror.

Welby nodded and left the room.

Parthena hopped across to Arthur and butted her head consolingly on his leg.

"I bet you don't have to work out loads of calculations in order to fly." He sighed and opened *Navigational Complete* at chapter one. It showed how to put together a piece of equipment, something called the Campbell verniere, but the diagrams were complicated and after half an hour of fiddling he had created something . . . that looked nothing like the picture.

After an hour of trying he sighed and looked at Parthena. "Do you think Felicity will have me back in the kitchen?"

CHAPTER 6

EPHEMERAL ISLE

LATER, HOPING for a bit of sympathy, Arthur told Maudie about Welby's test and how much he'd tutted at him.

She laughed. "Oh, Arthur, you'd think he was asking you to eat worms!" She opened the great book and read silently for a minute, then took out his attempt from the box and swiftly pulled it apart. "Look, this chapter is only telling you how to put this together. Twist this in here, line up this part with this, bolt this on . . . and it's done." She passed it back to him.

"Can you do all of my Welby work?"

"I've got quite enough of my own to do, thank you." She looked over at the mysterious tented area. "I have to finish my project, and I have at least ten engineering books that Harriet has recommended on the go."

Not knowing what was under the tent was becoming torturous. "I'm your brother, your twin; can't you at least—"

"No. Now help me with this loose end, because the wind is picking up."

They had always tied Maudie's hair ribbon together, as Dad had said it would be good for Arthur's coordination when he was young, and it had now become habit.

The initial rush of adventure petered away the next day as the land disappeared behind them and the sea below became endless and flat. The skies turned a uniform gray of cloud that neither let the sun in nor brought rain, as though the day was quite bored with itself.

As Maudie had put the piece of equipment together, he decided he'd leave it in one piece and maybe not correct Welby if he assumed Arthur had done it. Instead, he spent some time reading *Going East*. He also gathered every other book by Ermitage Wrigglesworth, and it was evident that Wrigglesworth had explored more in the east than anywhere else, his trips becoming more and more frequent up until his disappearance. He also had a fascination with history.

Before Arthur knew it, the morning had almost gone, and when he looked at the chime, he realized Welby would be there soon for Arthur's navigation lesson. So he put the books away and sat ready with *Navigational Complete*.

✳ ✳ ✳

The following days brought a welcome shift in the weather, so Arthur brought his books up onto the deck. He hadn't seen Maudie that morning, but clangs and bangs were sounding from somewhere, so he assumed she was working on her project. They were due to land on Ephemeral Isle by early afternoon, where, if all went according to plan, every sky-ship in the armada would land as well.

From her place at the wheel, Harriet glanced over to where Arthur sat, surrounded by books. "Would you like to take over for a while?"

He frowned. "Me? At the wheel?"

"Yes," she said, as though she had no idea why that would be a strange thing to ask, when really everybody knew it was only ever Harriet or Welby who steered.

"But . . . Welby . . ."

"Welby is assisting Dr. Quirke with preparing the vaccination program and new tropical weather kit, so he'll be a while yet."

Arthur approached the steering wheel. Queenie was sitting on the top. She eyed Arthur uncertainly and gave a muted hiss of disapproval.

"Oh, don't be silly, dearest," said Harriet.

Parthena, who had been flying happily alongside the *Aurora* all morning, descended a little to see what was going on.

Harriet let go of the wheel and gestured toward it.

"But . . . what do I do?" He suddenly noticed that the wheel had several levers and switches built into it. It was far more complex than he'd realized.

"Just hold on and get a feel for it. We're cruising at the moment; the weather is fine . . . simply take it."

Queenie jumped down and wound herself around Harriet's ankles.

Arthur stepped forward, reached out his hand, and grasped the upper left side. Instantly he felt the subtle vibrations of the *Aurora* rippling through his fingertips, his hand, his arm, through his body to his chest, so that he felt part of it, as though they were one. It was unexpected, incredible.

Harriet was watching his face intently.

He looked ahead; he was lined up with the prow, the Wide laid out before him. He had the ability to go anywhere. It was so vast, so astonishing, so full of possibility. Dad must have felt that too, and at that moment he felt a connection, as though his father was somehow back with him.

Parthena landed on the top of the wheel and squawked happily.

Arthur noticed that Harriet was grinning widely. "How about one day soon I teach you about the levers and switches?"

He nodded.

"Of course, there are manuals in the library, but this ship has many quirks, and I'd very much like to teach you myself."

All he could do was continue to nod and smile because his happiness threatened to choke him if he tried to speak.

"Ah, look," Harriet said, whipping her uniscope from her belt. "The Acquafreeda sea-ship. We've caught up."

The deck beneath Arthur's feet suddenly rose.

"Hey! Move, I need to get out!" a muffled voice shouted.

Startled, he stepped aside. A hatch in the deck opened, and Maudie peered out. "I've finished the captain's weather shield, Harrie!"

"The what? And what the clanking cogs are you doing down there?" asked Arthur.

"It's a weather shield for the captain, or whoever is steering the ship," she said, suddenly realizing he must've been standing at the wheel. "You pull the lever there, and the panels rise around you. They're positioned so that they slot together automatically. The front one has an extra part so that it becomes the roof. If you are in a storm and it's not safe to land, you can still steer, because the panels have windows."

"Impressive!"

"This one isn't my design, it's Harriet's. But she's letting me work on it. She said the more experience I can show in my engineering journal the better when it comes to the universitas."

"And the panels stay hidden beneath the deck?"

"Yes, there's a compartment just below that houses them. If it needs maintenance, then you put your fingers into these small slots on either side of the deck here and pull them aside. It connects to the engine room and the wing mechanism in what was part of the attic."

"Nice work! Although I'm not sure it'll get much use," said Arthur. "Mr. Wrigglesworth wrote that the skies to the east are clear as a diamond."

"Harrie thinks we might be able to approach the Geographical Society with it, don't you, Harrie, and roll it out to other sky-ships."

"Along with your other project, you're going to be the most impressive candidate they've seen in a long time," Harriet said as she reattached her uniscope to her belt.

"Ah, the secret project."

"Arty, you really have no patience."

"I tell *you* everything! I've shown you my Welby work."

"Only because you wanted . . . *help*," she whispered. "Anyway, the surprise is for your own benefit. It'll be more exciting that way. Speaking of Welby, here he comes."

It was time for Arthur's next lesson in the library. With a heavy sigh, Arthur obediently followed Welby below deck, wishing he could stay at the wheel.

* * *

The temperature had been increasing as they headed southeast and the climate was balmy but pleasant. Later, after they'd all had a late lunch on the sunny deck, Harriet declared that Ephemeral Isle was in view. A cheer broke out, and the twins rushed to the front to see it with Maudie's uniscope.

The *Victorious* looked to be the first sky-ship to reach the island. The armada was set to land on Ephemeral Isle and come together for a final briefing before heading off on their separate routes.

When Arthur got a turn on the uniscope, what he saw quite surprised him. He'd read in one of Wrigglesworth's earlier books that it was a lush, green island, but there was barely a patch of green anywhere. Instead, it appeared to be a vast huddle of shacklike buildings.

Gilly the botanist was standing beside Arthur, sketching the clouds in a tiny notebook. "Very light-weight, so I can always have it on hand to draw any new creatures I find." He smiled and pocketed the pencil and book in his linen vest. "Not that I'll need it on Ephemeral."

"Why not?" asked Arthur.

"It's rich in pitch and has been mined to within an inch of itself. The reason it's been chosen as a meeting point is because the pitch sky-ships all need to refuel here." He gave a shiver. "Rather horrid place, really. Vornatanian exploration and the demand for pitch has a lot to answer for. Not much wildlife left at all. Apart from the *scaribeaus mettallium*."

"The what?"

"A tough insect. The gradual destruction of this island became its gain. It thrives on metal and dying trees."

"I can't wait to see what that looks like," Arthur said with a twinge of sarcasm.

"You've already seen one," said Gilly.

"I don't think so," Arthur said, confused.

"Back on the last expedition, and in Lontown. A sapient one, in fact."

It dawned on Arthur in a silver flash. "Miptera's from here?"

Gilly nodded. *This was where Eudora had found her sapient.*

They landed at the docks. The island was stone gray and full of ramshackle buildings that looked as though they'd been put up temporarily, only to become permanent. The town bustled with small trade sky-ships and noisy crew members covered in soot using the sort of language that Felicity often let slip.

Everyone had been invited across to the *Victorious*

for refreshments. The idea of going back on that ship filled the twins with dread.

"I'm not going," Maudie said.

"Me neither," Arthur added.

Harriet nodded. "I totally understand, but I have to go, and Welby can join me. But I'd very much like to take you both to show her that . . . well, that you won't be intimidated by her, quite frankly."

Arthur and Maudie exchanged a glance that said they absolutely didn't want Eudora Vane to think they were in any way scared of her. Plus, another thought suddenly struck Arthur: it might be their only opportunity to find out what was in the journals Smethwyck took, as they were bound to have brought them along.

"We'll go," they both said.

"I'll come too," said Felicity. "For moral support and to inspect their culinary offerings."

After making their routine checks, the *Aurora* delegation made their way across the docks, feet shuffling along the planks, which had the black soot of pitch ingrained in them. Their route took them past salt-weathered shacks and stone dwellings with crumbling mortar and wooden shutters with flaking paint.

The armada had attracted much local interest,

and the cobbled streets bustled with people selling trays of seafood, machinery, and painted shells.

Arthur caught sight of a silver insect gnawing on the edge of a shack, and at first his heart skipped an uncomfortable beat as he thought it was Miptera. Then he realized there were dozens of them on the building. A man came out of the shack and started thwacking them with a broom until they all flew away.

Soon the group were walking along the jetty that led to the enormous hulk of the *Victorious*. The deck was already full of many of the other explorer families laughing and chatting while members of Eudora's crew offered trays of expensive-looking canapés to passing guests.

Harriet strolled confidently through the mass and began talking with Evelyn Acquafreeda, who had made it on time, and Welby took Maudie to introduce her to Samuel Fontaine, a useful person to know because he was on the engineering board at Lontown Universitas, while Felicity started speaking to one of the crew about the food they were serving.

Arthur found himself alone on the deck. It was a balmy afternoon, so he loosened the necktie that Welby had insisted he wear. Everyone seemed to be keeping up the pretense of being fine in their formal clothes in the ever-increasing heat of the day—apart from Harriet and Maudie, who had worn loose cotton shirts. Not knowing what to do, Arthur went over to a table laden with exotic foods.

"Does this have egg in it?" he asked a member of the Vane crew stationed behind the table. The man simply shrugged. Arthur decided it would be safe to go for a small pink fruit. "Typical. Even her canapés are pink," he said under his breath, then popped it into his mouth. He almost spat it out again, such was the unexpected sickly sweetness of the fruit, which wasn't a fruit at all, more a sugary, gritty concoction.

Smethwyck was not far away, issuing instructions to a crew member. He looked over and grinned snidely at Arthur's stifled choke.

Felicity joined Arthur at the table. "I see you've discovered marchpane! Not to my liking either, far too sweet, but very popular among some of the uptown families." She pulled her lucky spoon from her apron and fanned herself with it.

The heat appeared to be getting too much for Smethwyck as well, who took off his stiff, neat jacket and looped it over his arm. That was when Arthur noticed the small journal in Smethwyck's jacket pocket. He squinted, and although he couldn't be sure, he thought he caught a flash of the initials *EW* on the spine. Could it be a journal stolen from Ermitage

Wrigglesworth's house? Of course Smethwyck would keep it on him; he wouldn't want to risk someone snooping around while they were on the *Victorious*!

Felicity was busy tasting and examining the foods on the table, so Arthur sidled closer to her and whispered, "Do you think you could cause a distraction somewhere near Smethwyck?"

She studied him curiously. "I don't know what you're up to, young Brightstorm, but I think I like it." She grinned widely then picked up a plate of the marchpanes and drifted away toward the group Smethwyck was with.

Arthur edged farther behind them.

"These really are quite exquisite; you must all try them. Oh my! Isn't it a swelter of a day though? I feel rather . . . overcome . . . in fact, I think I might . . ." And with that, she fell back on the deck in Smethwyck's direction, sending the tray of marchpanes and her lucky spoon skittering across the deck.

People close by rushed over, and although Smethwyck made little attempt to help Felicity, the distraction was enough to focus his attention, so that Arthur could swipe the journal unseen from his pocket.

Arthur ducked beneath the table and swiftly flicked through the journal: there were sketched maps, islands, some in detail, many with question marks. There was a small piece of paper folded inside, blank apart from the Vane symbol on it, an insect clasping a ring held by a winged serpent, but he didn't care about the loose piece of paper—on the marked page was a drawing of the same triangle symbols he'd seen on Octavie's arm! Beside the last symbol was written an unfamiliar word: *Erythea*. He repeated it over in his head; he was sure he'd never come across it before. What did it mean? The next page had a drawing of an island marked "Nova," but as Felicity gave an exaggerated groan, he knew he was pushing his luck and sneaked back out.

"Oh, deary, it must've been the heat that overwhelmed me. Mr. Smethwyck, would you be a treasure and fetch my lucky spoon?"

As Smethwyck tutted and bent to retrieve the spoon, Arthur eased the journal back, unseen, into Smethwyck's pocket.

"I'll take that," Arthur said, putting his hand out for the large silver spoon.

Smethwyck thrust it forcefully into Arthur's hand. "Always making some sort of exhibition of yourselves, aren't you?"

Arthur scowled. Felicity brushed herself down and winked at Arthur.

The rest of the assembled crews hadn't seemed to notice the commotion, as they were enthralled in their own discussions. A large group was gathered around the helm where Eudora Vane was handing out posters with Ermitage Wrigglesworth's face on them, to help in the search. Maudie was some distance away engrossed in conversation with Welby and Evelyn Acquafreeda, her hands wildly describing something.

"What are you two up to?" Harriet asked, approaching Arthur and Felicity narrow-eyed.

Arthur pulled Harriet over to the edge of the ship with Felicity and pretended to point out something over the side. "I saw one of Wrigglesworth's stolen journals in Smethwyck's pocket, so I took it and had a look . . . temporarily."

"So that's what you were doing!" Felicity whispered. "I just went along with the tingling in my toes."

Harriet rolled her eyes. "Arthur, there's risky and there's ridiculous. This errs on ridiculous. Smethwyck could easily have caught you."

"But he didn't. And I did see something interesting."

They leaned in closer.

"I saw the triangles, the same as Octavie has on her arm, the secret club you told me about. And beside one of the triangles was the word *Erythea*."

Harriet frowned. "I've never heard that word before."

Maudie bounded over to them. "Evelyn Acqua-freeda is fascinating! Do you know she's building a sub-ship for exploring deeper in the oceans than anyone's ever been before? And she was very interested in my—" She quickly stopped herself, seeing their serious expressions. "Never mind. What have you all been doing, and why are there canapés all over the deck?"

"I'll fill you in later," Arthur said quickly, as Smethwyck walked past, squinting at them in a hot glare.

CHAPTER 7

THE VOTARY OF FOUR

THE FOLLOWING MORNING the crew of the *Aurora* set sail early; Harriet said it would be wise to travel as far as they could before the midchime heat. She was right, because even by nine chimes the temperature had increased suddenly, almost as though a great dial in the sky had been spun. The clouds disappeared and sunlight danced on the waves below in a scatter of radiance. On the *Aurora*, the rays reflected off the great balloon and scorched the deck. Dr. Quirke handed out tinted eyeglasses with leather side protectors, like an adapted version of Harriet's flying goggles; she'd been working on them since their expedition south to protect from sun glare. Maudie thought they were ingenious and labeled them sun-blinkers.

Arthur sat on the deck and opened his journal to a list he'd made: Octavie's ring, the Bestwick-Fords, the triangle symbols, the word *Erythea*. Maudie had suggested that perhaps Eudora was mistaking the symbols for an indication of further lucrative pitch mines somewhere in the Stella Oceanus, as they did look rather like mountains, but he wasn't convinced. After updating his journal he flipped back to his list, which he couldn't get off his mind. He was about to cross out the Bestwick-Fords—he couldn't remember why he'd put that there—when Harriet called over to him.

"Why don't you come and take the wheel again? The wind is picking up and it'll be good for you to feel the difference in control. It's still over a week's travel to our first official search island of Montavo, so plenty of time to practice."

He stood beside her and grasped the wheel.

"Each sky-ship has unique controls and mechanisms, but you'll learn that to be a good captain goes beyond the mechanics," she said.

"What do you mean?"

She glanced at him with eyes that seemed curious about how he might take her next words. "Each sky-ship has a life force. A personality. There's a unique vibration, a heartbeat of the engine; it's something that goes beyond the physical appearance. When you grasp the wheel, you become one with it. Do you understand what I'm saying?"

He nodded. He'd felt it just now as he'd grasped the wheel, that magical tingle of being more than himself, being part of the Wide.

Harriet gave a soft smile. "Sailing a sky-ship isn't simply about mastering the controls, it's about working together with it. You have to know the mechanics inside out, but there is so much more. Some captains get it, some don't. Take the Bestwick-Fords. Sometimes they fly blindly without listening to their ship's needs, like when they pushed her beyond her capabilities in the winds of the Silent Sea."

Arthur remembered seeing them turn back on the last expedition with a broken mast. "The name of the Bestwick-Ford's sky-ship—it's the *Fire-Bird*, isn't it?"

"That's right," Harriet said. "Named after the mythical bird."

He looked at her, an idea exploding in his mind. "Harrie! Do you think that could be the bird on Octavie's ring? Do you think that's what Ermitage Wrigglesworth was looking for?"

She thought for a moment. "I suppose it *could* be what's on the ring, but the fire-bird is a myth, Arthur."

"But thought-wolves are real. Why not a fire-bird?"

She smiled but shook her head. "I'll tell you why. It involves the story of how the Bestwick-Ford sky-ship got its name. The fire-bird myth was essentially created by Eleana Bestwick-Ford two generations ago. Eleana traveled extensively in the Stella Oceanus at the same time as Ermitage Wrigglesworth and Octavie when they were first setting out as the next-generation heads of the families. You could say that they had something to prove and there was a certain element of friendly competition between them. Eleana had heard a story about a fire-bird that supposedly existed on the last island, Nova, and she convinced them all to race there. When they reached it, they found no such creature, and Eleana, still fiercely competitive, so the story goes, sailed farther east, even though there are no more islands and the sea is endless and she'd likely run out of pitch. Of course, when she'd gone far enough to realize there was nothing but water after all, she turned back. But she got disorientated in the sea mist and was shipwrecked. Many of the crew lost their lives, and the crash was so bad that those few who washed up on Nova's shores had a lot of injuries—including brain injuries. Eleana had no memory of who Wrigglesworth or Octavie were, who she was, who her family were, even why she was there. Except for one thing—she kept repeating 'fire-bird.'"

Arthur was hanging on every word. "Maybe she saw it?"

Harriet shook her head and took her uniscope from her belt. She looked to the horizon.

"Perhaps she had that ring made after all the fuss?"

Harriet glanced back. "Her memories eventually came back to her, but the fire-bird became something of a sensation in Lontown for a brief period of time, with various stories made up about it. However, it turned out to be a small red bird native to the last island of Nova. It was what the people of that island called it. Quite amusing, really! We'll likely see some of the birds when we eventually land in Nova."

Arthur felt the heavy rock of disappointment land in his stomach. If this was true, then he would have to cross it off his list of possibilities.

A warm breath of wind ruffled Harriet's choppy hair. She studied him for a moment. "Look, if you're really interested, Welby keeps an archive of *Lontown Chronicles* and you may be able to find something in there about it. I'm sure he'll let you look, *if* you work hard on your studies." She paused. "He says you are finding it hard to focus."

"I'm not!" Arthur protested, making an effort not to shuffle his feet uncomfortably, because he knew it was true: his brain wouldn't stop buzzing with all the other questions that were demanding answers.

So, in his lessons that afternoon, Arthur tried to concentrate as hard as he could.

"An improvement, I must say," Welby said, arching his white eyebrows high. "Although you will need to show consistency if you are going to achieve."

"I will."

"Why be satisfied with scraping through when you could excel, Arthur?"

Arthur imagined that Welby had found it easy to do everything since the moment he was born into his privileged Uptown life.

"I think that's enough for today."

Arthur coughed. "Harriet mentioned that you have some old *Lontown Chronicles* I could look through. I thought there might be something we've missed about Ermitage Wrigglesworth in there."

Welby thought for a moment. "I'm sure there won't be, but I suppose it won't do any harm as you've worked hard today. Follow me."

They walked down the hall to Welby's room. It was well organized and modestly decorated with a small oak desk and several framed pictures on the dark-green papered walls.

"Is that Harrie as a child?" Arthur asked.

"Yes, her first day at school." Welby smiled wistfully. "Her mother and father were very busy at that time, so I looked after Harriet a lot."

Welby opened a cupboard door and revealed a stack of boxes.

"These are the papers I've held on to. I've kept each of them for a reason, perhaps an interesting article on navigation, or about the Culpeppers, or a significant moment of discovery. Leave them in the order you find them, please."

Welby left Arthur in his study. Arthur took the first batch of papers and laid them on the table.

After a few chimes he had been through the first box. Some newspapers were extremely old at around seventy years, and when Arthur touched them he thought they might crumble to dust. He was about halfway through the second box when a picture on one of the front pages made him stop in his tracks. The headline read **CITY CELEBRATES ITS TOP GRADUATES.** Among the group was a woman who looked very much like Harriet except the year was long ago. He read the picture caption. **Left to right: Eleana Bestwick-Ford, Octavie Culpepper, Ermitage Wrigglesworth.** Arthur's heart gave a little jump. He picked up the magnifier from Welby's desk and looked closely. They all had the triangle tattoos on their wrists! He read the article:

... The three friends have been inseparable since they started at universitas and graduated with the three equal highest grades. They put their success down to a rigorous study pattern together.

The outcome was a surprise to those who had hotly tipped the prefect Thaddeus Vane as the likely high-score champion. Griselline Vane, esteemed explorer and mother of Thaddeus, who graduated fourth highest in the year, said, "Of course the achievements of an individual who has succeeded by his own merit rather than the dilution of teamwork, is in my eyes the winner of the year."

Arthur shook his head and muttered, "Typical Vane."

When asked of their ambitions following universitas, Bestwick-Ford, Culpepper, and Wrigglesworth stated, "We plan to head east as far as we can go, to the ends of the very Wide." Sources say that the three even have a secret club, formed in their first year, called the Votary of Four. A strange name, one would think, for a club of three, but the four refers to the peculiar tattoo they each sport with four slightly different triangles. When pressed, the three refused to say any more, except that Lontown should watch their progress in the east with interest.

"The Votary of Four?" Arthur looked at the picture with the magnifier again and sketched the symbols as best he could in his journal.

The symbols matched what he'd seen in Wrigglesworth's stolen journal: a triangle pointing upward, a triangle pointing downward, a triangle pointing upward with a horizontal line through it, and lastly a triangle pointing downward with a line horizontally through the bottom.

Arthur hurried up onto the deck to find Maudie and share his discovery. He could hear her tinkering behind the tent, where she'd been all day.

"Maud, you'll never guess what I've found," he called, sorely tempted to just whip back the canvas.

"Arty, I'm busy. Can it wait? And don't even think about peeking."

"No, it can't wait."

"Well, it'll have to. I want to try this when we land in Mysa in a week, and I still have so much to do and I'm right in the middle of . . ."

Banging resumed.

Arthur huffed.

CHAPTER 8

MANGROVES

AS THE DAYS UNFOLDED, the climate became increasingly humid and the islands farther in the southeast became a lusher green color. There were now hundreds of them as far as the eye could see, like a giant's footprints showing the way. As they traveled toward Mysa, they stopped at some of the smaller islands for food and routinely asked if anyone had seen Ermitage Wrigglesworth. At first there had been very welcoming towns and villages, and Harriet and Welby were good at speaking the common language of the Stella Oceanus, but the farther they went, the warier the islanders became of strangers and of them. In fact, on several occasions Arthur had the distinct impression they were being watched, although Maudie told him it was likely because the residents hadn't come across many from Vornatania and were merely being cautious.

On the island of Montavo, Welby had found a lead: a woman who said that Wrigglesworth had traveled to Mangrove Island, a small island on the map officially marked Salicia. The woman had traded supplies with Wrigglesworth, she said, not more than ten moons previously. She had supplied him with some tools to build a hut.

Arthur looked over the side of the sky-ship as they approached Salicia, which at first glance looked dense and uninhabited. The heat of the sun was on his shoulders and the humid wind drifted across him, warm and salty, giving his chestnut hair a messy, tousled look. Maudie approached him and ruffled it even more.

"Your hair's got a life of its own. You're becoming like Welby: breezier the farther from Lontown you are." She smiled.

"We'll circle the island and see if there's any sight of this hut," Harriet called to him.

The island was small, a land of mangroves, dense foliage, some pools, and a few sandy-looking patches. They all searched keenly below.

"There it is!" shouted Harriet. They could see a

small wooden structure on the island, not too far from the coast. "There's nowhere big enough to land the *Aurora*. Arthur, make a quick sketch of the channel ways so we can follow the easiest route. We'll set down as near as we can—that inlet there—but I don't want to stay here long. Our freshwater drinking supplies are low; Gilly says there is nothing but salt water in these swamps, and I'd rather not use the salt filters for drinking water if I can help it. I'll head for the hut with Gilly, Felicity, Arthur, and Maudie. Welby, I'd like you to remain with the others here."

"Do you mind if I stay and do the final touches to my—" Maudie stopped herself again. "I want to try it in the morning."

Harriet nodded. "Of course."

With an inquisitive squawk, Parthena asked if she was going too.

Arthur stroked her head. "You sit this one out in the shade. Mangroves don't look like a great place for a bird your size to get stuck, and we won't be long."

Wearing lightweight beige trousers and shirts, the expedition group set out in the direction of the hut. They waded through the seagrass toward the mangroves, the water up to Arthur's thighs.

"I'm hoping there might be some new tropical

ingredients to discover," said Felicity. "Sometimes the best herbs and spices are found in the most out-of-reach places."

"It must be practically impossible to live here," Arthur said, struggling to get his leg untwined from a piece of seagrass.

Gilly cleared his throat. "It may not suit humans, but there is plenty of life here, Arthur: fish, crustaceans, migratory birds such as pelicans, even eagles. Then there are the numerous insects and of course the odd crocodile."

"Crocodiles?" Arthur said, aghast, feeling the hair on his arms rise. They didn't have anything like that in Lontown, but he'd seen images in the explorer books. They looked utterly fearsome.

"They've got to eat just like any other creature, and a little healthy fear is a good thing. It keeps us on our toes and is a reminder that we're not actually at the top of the food chain," said Gilly.

"I just prefer creatures that don't think of me as food."

They swished ahead.

"Did you know, their bite exerts a twenty-thousand-pound force? Quite incredible, isn't it? It would be like a sky-ship landing on your chest."

Arthur looked at Gilly and gulped.

Harriet led them onward. "Any crocodiles we meet are likely more scared of us. Stay together, keep your eyes wide, and we'll be fine."

"I once caught a catfish in the Insulae," said Felicity. "Near took my fingers off! Luckily, I had my spoon handy to give it a swift bash." She whomped her lucky spoon against the water to demonstrate. "Maybe we'll find one here," she said hopefully.

"Have you got your sketch of the waterways?" Harriet asked.

Arthur passed her the piece of paper.

"Good work. We'll follow the channel into the bend here, then take the right fork and cut off through the mangroves, then through this short channel, and the hut should be ahead."

They swished on through the water until they reached the tangled limbs of the mangroves. The tropical heat was intense, and they were glad to get within the cover of the trees. The mangroves had great, dense root systems that rose high above the water, giving the appearance that the trees were on stilts.

"Be careful, it's easy to get your ankle trapped in the underwater twists of roots. Get high up if you can and make sure you have a firm hold as you move."

"Will you be all right, Arthur? You've not been wearing your iron arm?" said Gilly.

"It got rather damaged on the last expedition, and to be honest, I'm better off without it."

"Right you are." Gilly smiled.

They began climbing their way through the mess of roots. A putrid smell hit Arthur. "Urgh, it's like rotten eggs!"

"It's the decaying vegetation in salt water," said Gilly. "Fun fact: did you know that in just one pint of this water there will be around ten thousand parasites?"

At Gilly's words Felicity seemed to turn a shade of green. She exchanged a glance with Arthur. "Your facts are not as fun as you think, Gilchrest Nicolby."

"Keep a cool head and keep battling on," Harriet called. "Getting through this is as much a mental battle as a physical one."

It was slow going, and Arthur's arm and thigh muscles burned, but thankfully it wasn't too far to get to the next channel.

Harriet batted sand flies away as the water became muddier.

"It's impossible to swat them when I'm holding on with my arm," Arthur said.

"Here, we're nearly out." Harriet took a handful of mud and spread it over his face then did her own. "That'll keep them away a bit."

They continued to swish through the water, which was up to their knees in the channel, glancing around for crocodiles. After several forks and bends, the hut came into view.

"Imagine if he's in there!" Arthur said, suddenly realizing there was absolutely the possibility that their mission would be over.

"Hello?" Harriet called as they approached the structure.

They waited a moment, and Arthur half expected to hear someone call back, but no one did.

"There's not a person in the Wide who would be able to stand this stink for long," Felicity said, nudging Arthur.

They hurried to the hut and let themselves inside. It was plain, with some cans on the shelves, a few books, a simple hammock, a rickety table with a drawer, and a chair.

"Well, it looks like he was here at some point. Search the books and drawer for anything that might be relevant or has a date written on it," Harriet instructed. "Remember: he has a tendency to hide information, as Arthur discovered on the last expedition with the lemon juice."

Arthur went straight to the desk and opened the drawer. It was empty.

He picked up one of the two books on top, keenly flicking through, while Gilly looked through the other. There were sketches of the mangroves, a detailed drawing of the channel way, some rough sketches of other islands. Most of the book still had blank pages to be filled.

Arthur sighed, disappointed. Harriet was right. Ermitage Wrigglesworth guarded information. If he had been looking for something out here, if it *was* to do with the fire-bird and Votary of Four, he wouldn't have made it easy to find.

Arthur noticed an *E* scratched into the desk. He pushed the book aside; it read *Erythea*. "Harrie, it's that word again."

She looked across. "Perhaps it's a word from one of the island languages, perhaps a greeting? They say that there are over one hundred languages spoken in the Stella Oceanus, especially this far in."

But he ran his fingers over it, certain it meant something important.

"Has anyone else found anything?" Harriet asked.

Nobody had.

Arthur looked at the desk. He opened the drawer again and felt inside. Then it struck him that the depth of the front was more than the inside space by a couple of inches. He felt the side of the drawer and sure enough, there was a catch. He flipped it up and pulled the handle again, and a secret compartment was revealed underneath.

"Look! Another book!" He took it out as the others gathered around.

Inside were curious sketches of some creatures. They were hideous-looking: black, long-tailed, flying creatures with batlike wings and what appeared to be tentacled faces.

"What in all the Wide are they?" Harriet said.

Underneath the drawings was a single word: *Darkwhispers*.

"These strange birds are unlike anything I've seen in all my travels," said Gilly.

"You don't think they're on this island, do you?" Arthur said, looking warily over his shoulder.

Felicity shuffled her feet uncomfortably. "Deary me! They give me an instant tingling in my toes, and no mistaking. I doubt Wrigglesworth was seeking them out!" Felicity laughed.

"Darkwhispers." Arthur breathed the word almost silently.

"Perhaps they do look a bit like a rare breed of bat," said Gilly, studying the drawing. He thought for a moment. "Many of these islands have cave systems, and it's likely these creatures are no bigger than a hand, so not scary at all in real life."

"We should keep our wits about us just in case," said Harriet. "This other book has several weather pattern and pitch calculations for navigating to Nova. I'd bet that's where we'll find him, so it's perhaps good luck that Eudora is trying to banish us there."

"He's probably swinging in some hammock, drinking local brew, having completely lost track of the chime!" Felicity laughed.

"Come on. It's getting late. Bring all the books, and we'll examine them further on the *Aurora*."

They began heading back toward the channel. Dense green foliage bore down on either side of them, and the thrum of unseen insects pulsed in the air all around. Somewhere nearby a bird screeched, and they all froze for a moment, thinking of the strange creatures drawn in the book.

"It's just an eagle," Gilly called.

Arthur directed them around the bend with his map. It seemed muddier than on their way in; perhaps the tidal channels were changing. He almost lost his boot several times.

Harriet called from behind. "Turn your foot out

as you move rather than pull it straight; it'll stop the mud sucking you back in."

After a while Arthur looked at his compass and stopped suddenly. He realized with a terrible twist in his guts that he'd been holding the map upside down!

"Harriet, I'm really sorry, but I had the map turned the wrong way and we need to go back."

"It's all right, Arthur, we've not gone too far," said Harriet.

"Every direction looks similar, so it's an easy mistake to make. We'll be back on track in no time," declared Felicity. "This way, it's less muddy over here."

A flash of green caught Arthur's eye. "Look out!" he yelled as a snake reared up. Before anyone could react, it went for Felicity's outstretched arm like a dart. She dropped her lucky spoon and cried out, her face contorted in instant pain.

In their moment of frozen disbelief, the snake slithered away as swiftly as it had attacked. Felicity dropped to her knees.

"What was it?" Harriet said, hurrying over.

Felicity was now lying among the roots groaning in pain.

"I . . . I . . . don't know. It was green."

"I got a glimpse of it, a pit viper, I think," said Gilly with a panicked expression. "We don't have much time; her arm's swelling already."

"Can we suck the venom out?" Arthur said, his voice high.

Harriet shook her head. "Venom enters the bloodstream extremely quickly; trying to suck it out is ineffective. Arthur, hurry back and fetch Dr. Quirke," she said forcefully. "Tell her we need the antivenom to a pit viper. I'll keep the wound below the heart and keep Felicity calm."

"Wild yam may slow the poison. I'll look around," said Gilly.

But Arthur was already hurtling as fast as he could back to the sky-ship.

In a rapid, hyperalert state, Arthur flew back down the channel and through the tangle of mangroves, moving instinctively and swiftly, pulling strength that he didn't know existed from somewhere deep inside.

"Dr. Quirke!" he yelled as soon as the *Aurora* was in sight.

Welby peered over the edge.

"Get Dr. Quirke . . . Felicity . . . snake . . . pit viper . . . antivenom," he spat out between gulps of air, sweat dripping down his face.

Dr. Quirke soon came running down the gang-plank carrying her small bag of medicine. "Which way?"

Arthur had no breath left to get back, but he had to, for Felicity. He pointed. "This way!"

Then Welby was there, hooking his arm and helping him forward.

When they reached Felicity, she was completely unconscious and gasping for air in small, wheezy breaths. Dr. Quirke quickly injected her with a substance from her bag.

Arthur dropped to his knees, every cell in his body aching to turn back time. "It was my fault! If I hadn't turned the map the wrong way!"

"It's not your fault, Arthur. There are snakes in jungles; it's just a fact. It's no one's fault," Gilly said gently, but Arthur caught Welby's judging eyebrows.

Welby shook his head. "Concentration, Arthur. It's what I've been trying to teach you."

His scorn cut into Arthur's already raging guilt.

"It's an easy mistake to make, Welby," Harriet

said. "None of us realized either, we were too focused on the journals we'd found."

Welby returned to the ship to fetch more of the crew, and they made a makeshift stretcher to bring Felicity back to the *Aurora*. It took longer, as they had to find a way through the crisscross of channels, but eventually they made it.

At the top of the gangplank, Dr. Quirke pulled Arthur to the side. "She's going to be fine. In fact, your swift journey through the mangroves to fetch me almost certainly saved her life," she said.

Despite her reassuring words, Arthur still felt dreadful.

CHAPTER 9

SKY-AK

THAT NIGHT ARTHUR DREAMED he was climbing through the mangroves, but he was surrounded by a thick, hot sea mist closing in on him. He was lost, and Felicity lay alone, depending on him . . .

"Wake up."

He was in his bunk. Maudie stared at him. "You were muttering in your sleep."

"Oh, was I?" he said dreamily, yet sweat was beading his brow.

"You were saying a weird word, something like 'Erith. Erith-aya.' You kept saying it."

"Is Felicity all right?" he asked.

Maudie nodded. "I looked in on her before bed. Dr. Quirke is still with her but says that Felicity will be back to her old self within a few days. Harriet said that if she is well enough, we set sail at sunrise for Mysa. We need to search the island for Wrigglesworth, but it's also supposed to have a large freshwater lake in the middle, where we can replenish our drinking supplies. Go back to sleep."

In the morning, Arthur awoke in another panic and went straight to Felicity's room. He gently tapped on the door.

"Come in," said Felicity in an unusually soft and croaky voice. She still looked pale, her red hair was loose and disheveled, and she had a great bruise on her arm where the snake had bitten her.

"I'm so sorry," he said.

She frowned. "What in all the Wide for? These things happen when you're an explorer. I'm only sorry we didn't catch and cook the blighter!"

"Where's your lucky spoon?"

"I dropped it in the mangroves, and I guess they forgot to bring it back in the rush."

"Oh, no!" Arthur felt dreadful. It was as though a part of her had been left there.

She shrugged. "I think it's clear that its luck has run out anyway."

"But it's your lucky spoon! I'll go back for it this morning."

"And risk you being bitten too? What if there was a nest of them and it was just a parent protecting its babe? No, sir! In the end, it's just a spoon. Now what you can do for me is help Meriwether with breakfast before she burns the muffins . . . and bring me a large cup of tea."

By eight chimes they were ready to set sail again.

"Crew to your posts!" Harriet called.

"Where's Parthena?" Arthur asked, realizing he'd not seen her all morning. He turned to Queenie; she and Parthena were becoming quite inseparable, both preferring to sleep on deck.

But Queenie just gave a knowing *"prrwt."*

"Harrie, we can't go, Parthena's missing!" said Arthur, but at that moment he caught a flash of silver in the sky above and Felicity's lucky spoon dropped on the deck.

Parthena flew a circle around the *Aurora* and then landed beside Arthur.

He smiled. "Clever girl. Thank you."

Parthena dipped her head in response.

"Right! Let's set sail, crew! It's about time we found Ermitage Wrigglesworth."

On the second day, after flying through the night, they reached Mysa in the early afternoon, and not a moment too soon, as their freshwater supplies were almost spent. Felicity was up and about and feeling "brassy as a cooking pot," although Arthur caught her pausing and leaning against the balustrade a few times.

From above, Mysa looked like a great eye with the glistening blue lake at the center. They landed on the northern edge of the lake where there was an open bank of land. When they had secured the ship, Harriet extended the gangplank out over the water, and everybody, without exception, simply took off their boots and jumped in fully clothed, to escape the now-suffocating tropical heat.

It was cool and refreshing, and Arthur floated on his back, kicking his legs like a frog, gazing up at the powder-blue sky.

After drifting happily for several minutes, Arthur looked over and saw Maudie whispering to Harriet back on the shore. He swam over. "What are you two plotting?"

"Patience, Arthur Brightstorm. You're about to find out."

Harriet instructed the crew to sit along the edge of the lake and wait, while she and Maudie disappeared back to the ship.

There was the clank of chains and a hoist rose up

on deck. It swung an oval object the size of a Lontown cart into the air. Arthur squinted in the sun. Was it some kind of sea-ship, like the Acquafreedas'? The shape rotated out from the ship above, then it was slowly lowered. Arthur clapped his hand over his mouth in astonishment.

It was a miniature sky-ship!

By now the crew were all on their feet.

It was beautiful, with a streamlined hull about the size of a canoe, what looked to be two extending wings, balloon fabric, some sort of compact engine on the back, and a fin. It was lowered into the water with a gentle splash.

Maudie appeared behind him. "What do you think?" she said proudly, her face not just glowing from the beating sun but positively shining with pride.

"Maud! I can't believe you managed to keep this secret!" Arthur said. The rest of the crew began chattering and walking around admiring the invention.

"I wanted it to be a big surprise and I was a bit worried I might not be able to get it working. I had the idea back in South Polaris, that sky-ships should have a backup—something that could help you out of sticky situations or be useful for short missions. I mean, there's still some perfecting to do. At the moment it can't reach too high and it could do with more speed and . . ."

"High? You mean . . . it flies?"

"Well, a little. I need to work on how to gain extra lift; there's still things to work out . . ."

"I don't care! It's brilliant." He noticed that on the

side was painted *Violetta II,* and he had to swallow back the immense emotions he had: a heady cocktail of pride, heartache, and excitement.

"Want to know what I've called the invention?" Maudie asked.

He nodded eagerly.

"It's called a sky-ak."

"Clanking cogs, that's amazing!"

Maudie tucked a rag into her tool belt. Her grin filled her face. "Harrie thinks I can refine the engine, patent it, and roll it out in Lontown. It could make sky travel on a small scale more accessible, that kind of thing. And the engine is water-powered, a very basic, reduced model of the *Aurora*'s engine, but the principle is the same. It just needs to make contact with the surface for more frequent uptake of water, and that gives the propeller a bit of a boost for lift, but that's something I can work on over time. It even has salt filters, just like the *Aurora*, so you can use it over sea too."

"How many people does it hold?"

"It's meant for one or two, three at a squeeze."

"Then what are we waiting for?"

They climbed inside. Maudie took the front with the small steering wheel and the panel of switches and levers, and Arthur sat behind her.

"The fabric-covered area at the back is for storage, but you could fit a third person there, perhaps."

To the enormous cheers of the crew, Maudie started the engine. It had a muted, almost soundless chug like a heartbeat, similar to the *Aurora* but softer. The balloon inflated, Maudie pulled a lever to extend the wings, and in a moment they lifted, just the height of a person, but Arthur whooped and Maudie laughed, and they were off. The sky-ak sped forward, rose for a while, then dipped back to the water, then up it went again, something like a pebble skimming in slow motion across the surface.

"This is brilliant, Maud! Brilliant!" was all he could say as they made their way in a circuit around the lake, before returning to the *Aurora* to more applause and cries of "Can I have a go?" and "Me next!"

They continued riding in the sky-ak into dusk, until it was too dark to see and they were all forced back to the sky-ship for bed.

✶ ✶ ✶

Over the coming days they finished searching Mysa, then made a direct route for Nova, stopping along the way at the few small islands, which were sparsely inhabited. Although each inquiry drew blanks as to the current whereabouts of Wrigglesworth, some people did recognize his picture, and there were reports that he had been heading toward Nova as recently as six moons ago.

The weather became even hotter, which Arthur hadn't thought possible, but thankfully it was dispersed with some very sudden and short bursts of warm, refreshing rain that made everyone dance on deck for joy and open their parched mouths to the sky.

With Welby occupied plotting the course to Nova, navigation lessons had been put on hold for the time being. Arthur was getting to spend more time at the wheel, with Harriet never far away to supervise and guide. Even during the rain showers, Arthur loved it.

On one of those rainy days, Maudie was tinkering with the weather canopy. "Are you sure you don't want the canopy up?" she asked Arthur.

"Maud, it's barely raining." He didn't want to feel a barrier between himself and the sky; there was a feeling of oneness when he held the wheel, of being in control yet part of something bigger.

She sighed and carried on adjusting a chain.

Arthur turned to Harriet, who was sitting on the deck beside him writing in her journal. It was protected from the rain by a small book shelter that Maudie had made. "How long until we reach Nova?"

"If the wind stays fair, then tomorrow. Although it's difficult to know how accurate our calculations are with such sparsely explored territory."

"It's strange, don't you think?"

Harriet frowned at him.

"That Eudora assigned us the farthest island. I know it was probably to get rid of us, but everything points to the fact that it actually is the most likely place to find Ermitage Wrigglesworth."

Harriet nodded. "The thought has crossed my mind a number of times during our journey."

"It could just be because of the pitch issue," Maudie suggested. "Supplies are much more uncertain out here and she knows we have the water engine."

"That's what I've been thinking," said Harriet. "Although, something about it still unsettles me a little."

Welby approached and handed some charts to Harriet, then went with Maudie to carry out routine checks on the balloon. Arthur had spent time in the library reading through the chapters of *Navigational Complete* and continuing his search on the Votary of Four. But he'd found nothing. He looked dreamily to the west where the clouds petered out, and peach-rose blended into violet and cerulean as the sun bowed out of the day. He imagined the four triangles floating in the air before him.

"Hey, daydreamer, you're veering off course," said Harriet, gently putting her hand up to adjust the wheel by a few degrees, then continuing with her writing.

"Oh, sorry." Arthur realized suddenly that amid all the drama of the mangroves and the excitement of the sky-ak, he'd forgotten to ask Harriet if she knew anything more about the Votary of Four, which he'd read about in the old *Lontown Chronicle*. She had mentioned that she thought the triangles were some sort of club, after all.

"Harriet, have you ever heard of the Votary of Four?"

She looked up from her notes.

"It was something I saw in one of Welby's old *Lontown Chronicles*. There was an article about Octavie, Ermitage, and Eleana having the highest marks in the year and it mentioned they were all part of a club called the Votary of Four. Only, I can't find any mention of it anywhere in the library."

Harriet put her pencil down. "Yes, I remember you asking. What makes you especially curious about it?"

"The symbols on Octavie's arm were also in the

journal that Smethwyck stole from Wrigglesworth, remember? They had the word *Erythea* written beside them. That word was scratched into the desk on Mangrove Island too."

She thought for a moment. "And you think this is somehow all relevant to Wrigglesworth's disappearance?"

He shrugged. "I just have a feeling about it."

"The Votary of Four . . . As far as I know, it was just a silly club, more a game between young explorers. Octavie told me as much herself. One night they came up with an idea that became a bet. They decided, based on historical myths, that a fourth continent could exist, and they each bet the others that they would be the first to find it."

"A fourth continent?" Arthur said in disbelief. "How could a whole continent exist without anyone knowing about it?"

"Exactly. Here, I'll take the wheel and you go to my study. Somewhere on the shelf there is a book called *Dispelling the Myths*. Go and fetch it."

Arthur hurried below and scanned the shelf in Harriet's study, then pulled a slim, brown leather book from between two much more ample-looking volumes. On the cover it read *Dispelling the Myths of the Wide*. He rushed back on deck with it.

Harriet flicked open the pages. "Ah, here you are." She pointed at a page with the four symbols on it.

"That's their tattoos!" Arthur said excitedly. He read the descriptions. "The triangle pointing upward with a horizontal line through it represents air, which some of the elite of Lontown colloquially refer to as the First Continent but whose proper name is Vornatania. The triangle pointing downward with a line horizontally through the bottom represents earth and is Nadvaaryn. The triangle pointing downward is water, the Ice Continent, and finally the triangle pointing upward represents fire and was created as the symbol of the final lost continent."

"They used fire for the fourth symbol, as they believed the location would be close to the equator."

"But Octavie must have believed it, if she was part of the club?"

"She did, for several years, and they tried hard to find it, but as you will see, if you read the book, there is emphatic geographical and reported evidence that it can't exist. The others in the club were furious with her for publishing the truth. They said it made them look like failures."

"Octavie wrote this book?"

Harriet nodded and turned to the title page where Octavie's name was detailed in small gold writing.

"So that's why she and Wrigglesworth fell out? She told me she hadn't spoken to him in years."

Harriet shrugged. "I guess they never managed to reconcile."

"Maybe Wrigglesworth couldn't let go of the idea."

"Do you know, I'm convinced we will find him on this last island, Arthur. I can feel it somehow."

"May I take the book?"

She nodded. "Of course. Now go below deck for some rest; we should arrive in Nova by morning."

CHAPTER 10

THE ISLAND AT THE END OF THE WIDE

THE WIND TURNED against them and it took longer to reach Nova than anticipated. But by the time they'd set the *Aurora* down on the powdery, moon-bright sand, they were all in agreement that the island was by far the most beautiful they had visited. It was late afternoon, and the sky was a cloudless azure blue, and the palm trees and gently lapping waves of a crystal-clear sea made them all feel that they'd flown into a painting. They'd spied some houses on the central hilly area, but it was easier to set down on the beach and trek their way inland. As the sun was low in the sky and they were all hungry, Harriet said they would wait until the morning to seek out any residents.

Maudie and Arthur lowered the sky-ak to explore

the bay a little, and Felicity insisted she squeeze inside with them to go fishing. They managed to catch a large yellowtail snapper, which Felicity cooked on the beach.

As the crew chatted about the island, they almost managed to convince themselves that they would surely find Ermitage Wrigglesworth relaxing on a beach and could report back to Lontown that all was well.

Except for Arthur, that was. That night he lay awake thinking about the four symbols and the votary, and that word *Erythea*. He'd seen it in the journal on the *Victorious*, scratched into the table in the mangrove hut, and clearly written by the symbol of the mythical fourth continent. The question burned in his brain: *What if this fourth continent is real and its name is Erythea?*

He lit a candle and opened Octavie's book about myths. One chapter was titled *"The Votary of Four."* It listed all the families who had tried and failed to get beyond the last of the Stella Oceanus. Each had returned saying there was nothing but sea until they found themselves out of fuel. Many had died trying. Some talked about an impenetrable bank of sea mist, but so many had tried and so many had come back empty-handed that the evidence was indeed conclusive. There was nothing there. Arthur looked at the fire-bird ring. It was linked, he was sure. He turned it over in his fingers as he thought, then he noticed something different about the bird on the back. Squinting, he held the ring to the light. It *was* different; he'd just assumed it was the same. As he looked more closely, he realized it had wings, but it wasn't a bird. He leaped out of bed and went to the library where they kept the journal from the mangrove hut. He opened it to the page with the drawings of the ominous-looking, batlike creature and the word *Darkwhispers.* They looked remarkably similar.

There was more to all of this, he was certain, and tomorrow when they went to the village, he was going to find answers to his many questions.

Maudie popped her head around the door, her face suntanned and her hair loose and wavy. "What are you up to?" she asked.

He was about to blurt out the news, but he found himself saying, "Just looking for more information on Nova."

He wasn't sure why; he usually shared everything with Maudie. But she'd been getting so much praise and attention for the sky-ak that he just felt he wanted to keep this to himself.

For now.

* * *

The crew gathered on deck early the next morning, ready to head to the village, but to their surprise they were greeted by two unexpected sights. The first was that the *Victorious* had been spotted by Harriet in the far distance, several hours away.

"I wonder how they're doing with their fuel supplies. They must have found a good supply on Sol southwest of here."

Welby nodded. It was rumored that there may be a source of pitch there.

The second unexpected sight was a smiling man who had come to meet them on the beach. He wore cropped green trousers and an olive-colored, loose shirt. His hair was dark brown and wavy. He had a relaxed, easy walk and deeply suntanned skin. As he approached, his hands were outstretched, and he said in clipped Lontonian:

"Welcome to Nova. My name is Gallus. Have you come seeking Ermitage?"

"Is he here?" Harriet asked, surprised.

Gallus nodded. "I'll take you to him."

They all looked between each other. He really *was* here.

"I can't believe it!" said Maudie, following Harriet down the gangplank. "He's here, after all this trouble and a whole armada searching far and wide for him!"

Arthur couldn't wait to meet him. Whatever the reason for him hiding away here and not going back to Lontown, there was plenty to ask him about the votary and the fire-bird ring.

They walked a long but well-trodden path past palm trees and up a steep slope toward a small village. The houses here were different from the others Arthur had seen on the journey; they were more decorative, with pretty arched windows and steps with banisters carved to look like ivy.

"May we offer you refreshments?" asked Gallus.

"Thank you. But if you could show us to Wrigglesworth first, we would much appreciate it." They were all thirsty after the trek, but Arthur knew that Harriet was thinking that the *Victorious* would be here soon and she wanted to be the first to question him.

Gallus nodded, and they carried on past the hut and farther up the hill a little way.

"Perhaps he's sunning himself up here," Maudie

said, and Arthur would've laughed if at that moment he hadn't seen something that felt like being hit in the face by a cold bucket of ice.

On the top of the hill was a grave.

The crew fell silent. The grave was marked by a wooden post that read:

ERMITAGE WRIGGLESWORTH
EXPLORER FROM VORNATANIA, WHO LOST HIS LIFE TO THE SEA.

It was as though someone had pierced the sky and deflated the atmosphere.

For a moment, Arthur was back in the frozen forests of the Ice Continent, seeing the graves they'd found there, and the memories of Dad rushed through him again. He grabbed Maudie's hand and squeezed because he knew she'd be feeling it too.

Felicity was the first to talk. "Well, that's that, then." She tucked her lucky spoon back in her apron.

"That's that, then," agreed Dr. Quirke.

They slumped on the edge of the hill, Harriet beside Gallus. "What happened?" she asked him.

"We recovered his crashed sky-ship in our boats. I'm sorry it wasn't the answer you were hoping for. Like many in the past, he had been deluded about going even farther east. There is nothing out there. Just water and death. Many have searched; all have failed. We warn them not to, to be content in what they have and know, but . . . Well, as you know, the people of Lontown are rarely satisfied with no."

Arthur thought that was a bit cutting, but also true.

"We marked his grave in your language, as we thought it fitting."

"What now?" Felicity said.

Harriet stood up and brushed her hands on her trousers. "There's no point delaying and having fellow explorers wasting time and effort when we know the outcome. Welby, when we're back at the *Aurora*, would you send word by messenger pigeon to the other sky-ships that they should return to Lontown?"

Welby nodded.

"We'll rest here for today, then head for home tomorrow. If that is acceptable with you, Gallus?"

Arthur detected a hesitancy before Gallus bowed his head in agreement. But as he did so, Arthur caught sight of a glint of gold around his neck: a ring on a chain. A ring that, in the brief moment Arthur glimpsed it, looked extraordinarily like Octavie's ring! It disappeared back behind his smock.

"It is our way to celebrate the life of those lost," said Gallus, standing up. "Will you join us tonight to celebrate?"

"We would be honored," said Harriet.

"Our village is yours. You are welcome to explore it today, of course."

"Thank you, but we'll probably head back for now and take stock of our supplies. Perhaps we may do some trade with you before we return?"

"We don't have pitch here, I'm afraid."

"Oh, no, our sky-ship doesn't use pitch."

Gallus looked taken aback.

"Also, one of our . . . comrade ships is on its way."

He nodded.

They made their way back down the path to the village.

Noticing that a man was staring at them through one of the decorative screens covering the windows, Arthur stopped and looked back, and the man ducked.

"Arthur, stop being so nosy," hissed Maudie.

"He was staring at me."

"But it's their island. We're the strangers, so they're allowed to."

He squinted.

"What's wrong?"

"There's someone watching us over there, too, behind that tree."

She looked around, but the person had disappeared.

"You're imagining it. Let's get a drink and go back to the sky-ship."

They accepted a refreshing glass of water with lime and some pineapple, then started down the path. Arthur lingered at the rear, and when they were a little way down, he ducked into the forest and pulled Maudie along with him.

"What are you doing?" Maudie said in an urgent whisper. He put his finger to his lips. "I'm going back to look around. Are you coming?"

She rolled her eyes. "No, I'm going to enjoy the fact that the mystery is over with a trip in the sky-ak before that beastly woman arrives."

"Suit yourself." He shrugged.

Maudie hurried after the others and Arthur dashed through the palms to the back side of the houses. Staying low, he crept to one of the windows and, after listening for a while to make sure there was no one there, he peered inside. There was a strange animal in a wooden cage. It looked rather like a small bear but clung on to the bars with what appeared to be webbed toes. Arthur ducked as the door opened,

then peeked again. The man let the bear out of the cage and said something in a different language that sounded apologetic. He stroked it kindly on the head. Something flickered on the bear's neck, something that reminded Arthur an awful lot of fish gills. The man continued talking to the creature, and then Arthur picked out a word that made his eyes widen like dinner plates—*Erythea*.

The man had said Erythea!

And a thought struck Arthur that felt as though an ice cube had slid down his spine. What if Wrigglesworth wasn't dead? What if there was a fourth continent and he'd made it there? What if these people were purposefully hiding something?

He ran back through the palms to the *Aurora* to tell Maudie and Harriet, but when he got there, he saw that the *Victorious* had already landed farther up the beach and Harriet and Welby were walking toward it.

Maudie stood on the beach like a statue, watching. "Eudora will probably want to take credit for finding out Wrigglesworth's fate," she said.

He pulled her to one side, away from a couple of villagers close by. "There's something not right about some of the people on this island," he whispered.

"Oh-kaaay . . . and by that you mean?"

"The ring on a chain around Gallus's neck—it's the same as Octavie's."

She frowned disbelievingly.

"Well, I think it was. It was hard to see clearly."

Maudie shrugged. "It's highly unlikely. You're just tired; it's been a long journey."

"All right, then, how about this creature that I just spotted in one of the houses? One of the men kept it in a cage. He only let it out once we'd gone! I've never seen anything like it before, not in any of the *Natural Fauna of the Great Wide*—and I've read that cover to cover several times."

"We're at the farthest reaches of the eastern Wide. There's bound to be a few creatures we don't know about. We can't know *everything*."

Frustration bubbled in his throat. "It was a land mammal."

"A mammal?"

"A land mammal with webbed toes and what looked like gills."

She heaved a sigh. "Gills? Arthur, you need to lie down. It's the heat. Dr. Quirke says it can play games with your mind. I'm going to get ready for the celebration. I suggest you have a nap." She turned on her heels and went back to the sky-ship.

Instead, Arthur went to the library and checked

Natural Fauna of the Great Wide. There was nothing there that looked remotely like the creature he'd seen.

After a while, Maudie came into the library, her hair tied up neatly and a clean white shirt on. "Harriet's gone ahead, and the crew have gathered on the beach and are making their way back to the village now. Are you coming?"

He nodded and shut the book. He'd just have to find a way to prove that something was up in the village.

The last of the Culpepper crew disappeared down the path, and Maudie hurried after them. "Come on!"

He jogged after her, his thoughts like a raging river. "I mean, why would a land-breathing animal need webbed toes and gills? And they speak remarkably good Lontonian, which is curious for such a remote island, don't you think? There's something not right. I can't put my finger on it, but it's lots of little things that don't add up."

She stopped and turned. "Arty, we're going home tomorrow. Ermitage Wrigglesworth is dead and our mission is over. There's nothing more to discover, no mystery. Just sea and mist and death for those who try. Yes, I read Octavie's book too. I found it on your bed. But it's concluded; we know the symbols are meaningless now." She sighed. "It was too much seeing that grave, remembering what happened to Dad. Now I just want to go home. Don't you?"

"Dad always taught us to trust our instincts."

"Instincts on what? There's a grave, and witnesses to what happened."

A gust of warm wind loosened Maudie's ribbon. Arthur's hand twitched as he moved to help retie it, but he stopped himself. He had to make her see. "Did you learn nothing about truth and lies in South Polaris?" he said.

"Arthur, the crew is going home. We did what we came to do. We found Wrigglesworth. I know it wasn't the outcome you were looking for, and I know . . ." She paused and looked down at the sand.

"What?" he said indignantly.

"I know that seeing Wrigglesworth's grave is bringing back awful memories."

"It's not that!"

"Arthur. I understand; the crew understands. We're all here for you."

He huffed, grabbed the ring from his pocket, and held it out. "Why won't you listen! This means something."

She took it. "Arty, I'd love to believe there's more to the ring, to the symbols, but the evidence is to the contrary. Even Octavie wrote that there's nothing but sea and mist!"

"Something is wrong here, just like in South Polaris when we knew that there was a huge lie surrounding what had happened."

Maudie glared. "Don't try and use that situation to further your case. We can't just go off on a wild goose chase, we have to look at the facts!" She stuffed the ring into a pouch on her tool belt.

He threw his hand up in frustration. He couldn't understand why Maudie didn't get it. It was so obvious, so clear to Arthur: everything fitted, everything . . . the symbols, the map, the ring. Yes, it was random pieces that might not add up to something conclusive at the moment, but . . . He could feel his temper rising like the tropical heat, the blood roaring in his head. "You just want to hurry back to Lontown so you can show off your sky-ak and get into the universitas!" he snapped.

She put her hands firmly on her hips. "And you're just trying to unexplain what's been explained! Things happen, Arthur; nothing can change the path of what's done. Let it LIE!" she shouted with frustrated ferocity.

Then Maudie's mouth clamped shut. . . . So did Arthur's.

After a moment when they just stared at each other incredulously, cheeks hot with anger, Maudie turned to follow the others along the path to the village.

"Are you coming or not?" she called without turning around, her loose ribbon trailing behind her.

"Not!"

"Fine!"

"Fine!"

CHAPTER 11

SEPARATED

ARTHUR SAT on the *Aurora*'s deck with his back against the wheel column, stroking Parthena and listening to the fading songs of the crew in the distance. Even Queenie had gone. Several times he almost ran after them, but each time the stubborn knot inside him held him to the spot. After a long period of debate with himself, he was about to stand up when he heard talking. They were voices he didn't know.

"Hurry. Check the rooms and make sure no one has been left on guard."

Arthur's heart jumped. They were approaching the *Aurora*. He heard footsteps on the gangplank. Panicked, he assessed the situation. Should he confront them? Hide? He couldn't make it to the hatch, and, besides, they were going to search the rooms. Over the side would hurt, and he wasn't sure if he'd be spotted. His frantic fingers felt the small gap in the deck and instinctively he lifted the weather-shield panel in the floor, jumped inside, and beckoned Parthena to follow, pulling the hatch back down just as the sound of footsteps echoed above.

"There's no sign of anyone on deck," someone called.

"Search every room." Arthur recognized the cold drawl of Smethwyck.

More footsteps sounded, lighter, more drifting. "Hide, and have your guns ready." It was Eudora.

Guns ready? Arthur couldn't believe what he was hearing. Why did they have guns? Then Eudora's honeyed voice spoke again. "Don't forget to weight their bodies before you cast them out to sea. We don't want them to be found this time."

Terror and questions erupted inside him. They were going to kill the crew of the *Aurora*! Harriet, Felicity, Welby, Gilly, all the others and . . . Maudie! He clamped his hand over his mouth in an attempt not to cry out. How long had they been gone? When were they due back? What could he do?

Moments passed as he crouched in the small cavity, frozen by panic. Perhaps he could send Parthena to warn them? But at the moment she was just as stuck as he was.

Arthur's heart hammered. Why was this happening? Why kill the crew of the *Aurora*? He had to do something. But his mind was racing, and he couldn't think. He remembered Maudie saying that there was a small passage to the engine room. He felt around with his hand and found the opening, just big enough to crawl through. But there was no way out from the engine room without going back on deck. He thought frantically—the solution had to lie in the engine room itself. He could fire the engines. If he did that, it would be a warning to the others—they would know that something was wrong and could get away. "Parthena, don't make a sound. Wait here," he whispered.

"Let's hope they won't be long," someone said above.

Arthur scurried on his knees as quietly as he could along the passage. The engine room was less familiar to him. He looked around at the levers, cogs, and cranks, trying to follow the pipes back to anything that made sense. Then he found a crank with one mechanism going out; it looked big, like the start of something. He turned the handle and it vibrated in his hand. Things began clunking and whirring and grinding. Steam hissed and the floor beneath him shuddered. Perhaps it would be enough to warn the others . . . or would they rush to see? Had he drawn them in? He suddenly panicked that he'd done the wrong thing!

Then voices came from nearby in the engine room.

He squatted behind the engine and froze.

"What did you touch, Banks?" said a woman.

"Nothing! It must've been you. You had your hand on that handle!"

"Well, pull it up again!"

A stiff *clonk* sounded.

"Nothing's changed! I don't know this engine; I just came to work it out!"

Shouts sounded above.

"Come on, we'd better get help; Smethers will know what to do."

Arthur thought that perhaps he could escape the ship in the confusion and get back to the others to make sure they were safe. But the loud voices were coming from everywhere; it was too risky, so he scurried back into the vent.

The sound of gunshots rang out from the deck. Arthur bit down on his lip and breathed heavily through his nose as he hurried back to the space beneath the wheel. He braced and put his eye to the gap in the deck; it was only half an inch, but he could see flashes of what was going on above.

"The engines are fired; there's no going back. They've heard us!"

"What fool started the engine?"

"Get the wings open—we're going up!"

Arthur's stomach lurched as the *Aurora* lifted suddenly. This couldn't be happening! He could hear more shouting—gunfire, screams.

"Stop shooting, retract the gangplank, and get to the cogs!"

Arthur heard the rumble of the wings extending and there was another surge as they lifted again. The shouts faded into the distance.

They were well and truly in flight.

Parthena's eyes glistened in the darkness, but she didn't make a sound; she just shook. Arthur scooped his arm around her and pulled her onto his lap, trying but failing to hold in great gulps of fear.

Footsteps echoed above as someone took the wheel.

"Did we get any of them?"

"It was hard to see in the dusk."

It was Eudora Vane and Smethwyck.

"No matter. We're in flight now and they have no way of pursuing us."

"The *Victorious*?"

"Has virtually no pitch left in the store and there's none on the island."

"But . . ."

"We will deal with them on our return; no other explorers were sent within one hundred miles of that island. The Fourth Continent will come to us sooner than expected, but no matter."

Fourth Continent? Arthur's eyes were wide in the dark. So it was true: *the Votary of Four had been right!*

"How many days' travel did the journal estimate?"

"Three to five, which will be easy now that we have this water engine and we don't have to worry about pitch. It's open ocean ahead, then we negotiate the mists and those creatures."

After a while, the engine noise settled to almost nothing and they were gliding somewhere high, the odd pinprick of light indicating the night sky through the small gap above. Arthur held on tight to Parthena, her head tucked into his neck.

* * *

"Arthur's on the *Aurora*!" Maudie yelled, panic choking her voice. How could this be happening? Tears welled, stinging her eyes.

Harriet sprang into action with a stream of orders. "Forbes and Cranken, go to the *Victorious* and check their fuel supply—I'm suspecting they've run it dry, but if not, we'll pursue them as far as is safe."

"Perhaps he got off in time; he's a clever boy," Felicity said frantically.

"Extend the search area," Harriet ordered the remaining crew.

Welby ran from the tree line. "There's no sign of him."

Harriet put her hands to her head. "Keep looking."

"Where are they going? Why did they shoot at us?" said Felicity, waving her spoon in agitation.

"I don't know, but they're not heading back in the direction of Lontown," said Harriet.

"Then where *are* they going?"

Thoughts rushed Maudie—what if Arthur had been right? There was more to all this. She suddenly felt alarmed in the certainty of it all. In between sobs she blurted out everything that Arthur had told her he'd suspected.

Harriet and Felicity exchanged dark looks, then Harriet called to Gilly. "Send a messenger bird to the Acquafreedas. I convinced them to stay close to us at the gathering on Ephemeral as a precaution, so they shouldn't be too far and we have a better chance over distance pursuing the *Aurora* in a sea-ship. Felicity, get Maudie some sweet tea from somewhere; she can barely breathe. Dr. Quirke and Meriwether, I want you to go to Wrigglesworth's grave. I'm very much suspecting it's empty."

Maudie remained rooted to the spot while the crew hurried away. Harriet turned to Welby. "The *Aurora* was the only water-engine-powered sky-ship in the Wide. It can go farther than any pitch-reliant vessel. Eudora must have stolen it because she needs to go farther, and the only possible explanation is that she believed or had some sort of evidence that there really *was* something further to be discovered. And Arthur saw the signs all along." She shook her head. "Welby, find Gallus and insist he come here immediately."

As Harriet hurried away, Maudie heard her curse under her breath and mutter, "How could I have let this happen?"

"There's hardly any pitch," Forbes called from the *Victorious*'s deck.

Maudie looked to the darkening sky, every inch of her taut and a savage ache gnawing inside. She clenched her fists and prayed that the Acquafreedas weren't too far away.

CHAPTER 12

THE DARKWHISPERS

TWO DAYS DRAGGED by for Arthur on the *Aurora*. At nighttime, only one person was left on duty and they remained at the wheel, so Arthur had found that he could crawl through to the engine room, then sneak to food and drink from the stores and use the bathroom. Poor Parthena was getting more agitated with not being able to fly, and Arthur hoped they would get wherever they were going soon, no matter what the consequences were. On the third night, he managed to make it to the library to get a book, but the light was too dim to read in the hold and he couldn't risk a candle. Yet it gave him comfort just to hold it. It was one of Maudie's engineering books. Several times he'd almost given himself up, but the sheer fear of knowing what Eudora Vane and her crew were capable of kept him hidden.

On day four, as Arthur drifted in and out of the irregular slumber pattern he'd fallen into, it seemed to get dark very quickly even though he was certain it had been light for only three or four chimes. Arthur would have thought he was losing all sense of time were it not for the hushed voices above. Something was going on.

The engines became silent as the sky-ship went into cruising mode.

A strange whispering sound filled the air, a soft, hushed murmur.

"What are they?"

"I can't see!"

"They're everywhere!"

"Look! Did you see the size of their claws?"

There was a shriek of wind, as though something sliced through it at great speed. Arthur pressed his eye to the gap where he could see a narrow section of the scene above. A dark shape circled them, too fast to see. Heads whipped around in all directions, searching frantically.

"There's something out there!"

Then he saw it again . . . then another . . . and

another. Some sort of flying creatures circled them, their wings slapping through the air like sodden leather. It was too difficult to see in the thick gloom of cloud, but they were getting closer. . . . Three, no, five . . . no, there were at least ten.

"Get below deck!" someone yelled.

They all ran for the hatch.

"Not you, Smethwyk, you idiot. Someone has to remain at the helm!" That voice he recognized as Eudora Vane's. So much for the captain putting the crew before themselves.

Below deck in his hiding place, all Arthur could see was the rush of shadowy creatures above. He pressed his eye close to the gap, half terrified to watch, half needing to see more.

A *thud*, heavy as a huge bag of grain, sounded as something landed on the deck, followed by the scratch of claws on wood. The strange whispering sound was closer now. Arthur's heart raced. A section of extended leathery wing, then an area of tentacled head and a smoky eye came into his narrow field of vision. It was one of the creatures from Ermitage Wrigglesworth's journal.

The darkwhispers.

He glimpsed Eudora, still on deck, almost frozen between the wheel and the hatch. The darkwhisper was fixed on her. There was a flash of silver as Miptera flew for the hatch, but Eudora remained.

✳ ✳ ✳

Eudora wanted to move, yet somehow, she couldn't. She was back in Lontown, in Vane Manor.

Why was she holding a small sky-ship? That's right— it was a toy. Mother had made it for them, for her and Violetta. Eudora's heart burned with the fire of loss and longing—dear sweet Violetta, her sister. She heard a laugh, close by. A laugh that was contagious, the sort that you couldn't help but get sucked into; a laugh she knew like her own distant happiness. She looked to her side. There was young Violetta, freckled, a ribbon hanging across her forehead as she sat with paintbrush in hand.

"It's going to be the first pink sky-ship in Lontown, Dora!"

"Vi, you can't paint it pink!" Eudora found herself giggling along with Violetta, who swiped pink paint confidently along the side.

"Can so, and just did!"

"Father's not going to like it."

"Father's not going to sail in it. It's ours."

She lifted the small sky-ship above her head and began running through the grass with it. "Let's go to Creal!"

"But Creal's already been discovered!"

"I don't care; it's got spooky caves and bats. Pink bats, Dora!"

And she chased after her, so happy and laughing . . .

No, not laughing . . .

Screaming . . .

* * *

Smethwyck cried out, utterly petrified, as the dark-whisper whipped its head around to him.

Eudora snapped out of her momentary daze and bolted below deck.

The *Aurora* was tilting and swaying in the air, threatening to shift into a spin.

"Hold the wheel!" Eudora bellowed from below.

Arthur knew she was right; if Smethwyck let go of the wheel now, he'd lose all control and they'd crash, but did they have a choice? There was one certainty; if he went down, they all went down. Smethwyck had ducked back and was clutching the wheel, white-knuckled, as the creatures spiraled in.

There was a *thud* as the darkwhisper took a step toward the terrified henchman.

Smethwyck needed protection.

He needed the weather canopy.

Arthur peered through the gap and willed Smethwyck to see the lever, but of course Smethwyck wouldn't know what it was for. He'd become suddenly statuestill, as though mesmerized by the creature. Arthur followed the chain link from above and started yanking it down manually. There was a *clonk* and a *whirr*, and the weather canopy began to rise. Smethwyck snapped out of his trance and looked around in amazement.

The wheeze of wind and the creature's shrieks were deafening, and Arthur thought he caught sight of reptilian eyes, thick and milky and impenetrable, just before the canopy closed around Smethwyck.

There was a cry and the scrape of claws as the creature took flight.

The ship lurched from side to side for a while, throwing Arthur and Parthena about in the small hiding cavity. He could hear Smethwyck grunting with the effort to regain control before the ship finally leveled. Arthur clung on to Parthena and trembled until eventually the cries of the circling creatures faded, and the clouds cleared.

Peace was restored and Arthur slumped into unbidden sleep.

Several chimes later he was woken by a shout from above.

"Land ho!"

PART TWO

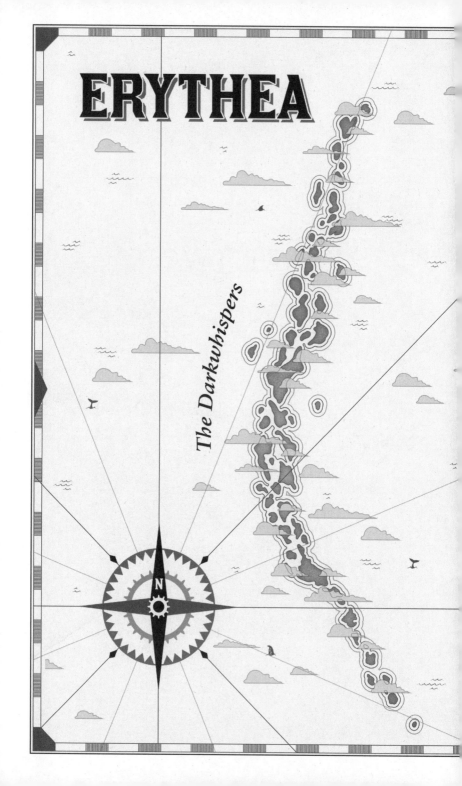

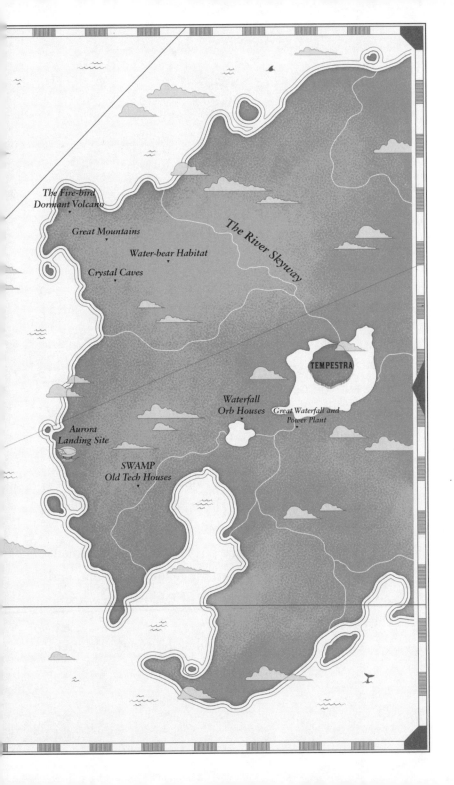

The Fire-bird
Dormant Volcano

Great Mountains

Water-bear Habitat

Crystal Caves

The River Skyway

TEMPESTRA

Waterfall
Orb Houses

Great Waterfall and
Power Plant

Aurora
Landing Site

SWAMP
Old Tech Houses

CHAPTER 13

CULPEPPER, ACTUALLY

A SEGMENT OF CRYSTAL-BLUE SKY cast a stripe of light across Parthena's feathers. Arthur had felt the descent and knew from the snatches of discussions and commands being relayed that they had landed on high ground and were preparing for an initial expedition. The Votary of Four *had* been right! What would Octavie say if she could see him now? There *was* more land to the east—possibly a whole new undiscovered continent.

Arthur could hear the busy sounds as equipment was gathered and preparations made to explore, and he became furious at the idea of Eudora's crew using the *Aurora*'s kit.

He needed a plan for what he would do next.

Eudora was issuing meticulous instructions, and Arthur gleaned that the whole crew was heading out.

The bustle continued for a chime or so as they got ready to leave, then suddenly several of the crew cried out in alarm.

Next he heard other voices, different from the crew's, speaking in another language. There was a flurry of footsteps toward the edge of the ship, and Arthur saw through the gap that the crew were hurrying to the gangplank. He pushed the hatch up just a little to peek.

He caught a flash of someone dressed in tight green trousers. A woman's voice said something that Arthur couldn't understand.

"Who are you?" Eudora demanded.

There was a slight pause, then the woman spoke again, this time in Lontonian. "This is our home. Who are *you*?"

The crowd of crew gathered together, and Arthur could now see only the feet of the woman and her companions.

Then came more hurried talk in the different language.

"The swallow on your sky-boat . . . Are you . . . Culpiper?"

"Culpiper?" said Eudora curiously.

"Are you of the Culpiper family of Lontown? Are you the captain of this sky-ship . . . Harriet?"

"Yes, yes, I am," Eudora said.

Below deck, Arthur's mouth dropped open. There was a pause and some hushed talking.

"Do you have the ring, Captain Culpiper?"

"Er, yes, back in Lontown. Please, do call me Harriet."

Liar, Arthur thought, alongside the hundred other questions now buzzing around in his head. How in the clanking cogs did they know about Harriet? Could they possibly mean Octavie's ring, the ring with the bird on it?

"Captain Culpiper, we welcome you home."

"Oh! Do you indeed . . . Thank you."

"Although we would not permit outsiders usually, in your crew. Did the ring-bearer not tell you?"

"I'm very sorry, but I wouldn't have made it here without them and they are the soul of discretion. But I must say the ring-bearer told me very little about my, er . . . heritage, so perhaps you could fill in the gaps for me?"

"Please follow us, Captain Culpiper."

"It's Culpepper, actually; the name was adapted a little."

As Arthur crouched in the darkness listening hard, he rolled his eyes at the nerve of Eudora. Not only was she taking on Harriet's name, but she was also correcting them on it!

"We will take you straight to the Professus Excelsis. The water-wings are not far. You won't need anything—we have plenty for you all."

"Plenty? How marvelous."

"Come, you must be hungry after your travels."

Arthur's stomach threatened to growl.

"Oh, yes, thank you."

The deck boards creaked above as the crew began leaving the ship.

Arthur counted to thirty from when the last footstep left the sky-ship; he didn't want to leave it after too long or too short a time, so thirty seemed like a good bet. He eased up the hatch, peered outward at the empty deck, then climbed out. It was bright and green all around. His eyes ached from being in the dark for so long. He whispered to Parthena and told her not to take flight. "I'm sorry, girl, they would see you—it's not safe."

He needed a plan, and quick. Stay and reclaim the *Aurora* and fly back to the Stella Oceanus? But he couldn't sail a sky-ship on his own, and there was no way he would go near those darkwhisper creatures again! He couldn't stay here and wait—for what? Following them was the only option. But did he have time to grab food and drink? He didn't want to lose them, and by the look of the dense green tropical forest all around, losing them wouldn't be difficult.

Parthena hopped out of the hatch, the waterskin in her mouth. Arthur smiled. "Yes, water's most important. Come on." She flew up and landed on his shoulder, and they hurried down the gangplank.

He wished he'd had more time to gather supplies, but if he kept up with them it would be all right. Perhaps he could declare himself as one of the crew? Eudora wouldn't be able to say anything because he knew her bigger secret. He shook his head as though to dislodge some truth or sense from the situation, but it still made no sense to him. How did they know Harriet Culpepper? Harriet couldn't have known about this place. Could she?

Their path was easy to follow, the vegetation having been trampled down by the crew ahead. He stayed back far enough to not be seen but close enough to not lose them. They were traveling uphill slightly; the *Aurora* had landed on a craterlike hilltop area, the vast ocean behind and a bank of lush green leafy plants ahead. As Arthur reached the ridge, he suddenly went still, paralyzed, such was the beauty of the scene before him.

The land was vast: a swathe of emerald forest as far as his eyes could see, with glimpses of silvery rivers and lakes among enormous trees, their tops taller than any he had ever seen, and in the east were colossal mountains also cloaked in green. He breathed in the humid air and felt the brilliant warmth of the sun on his cheeks. Birds chittered and insects trilled and buzzed all around. Parthena's claws tightened a little on his shoulder.

"I know. It'll be safe enough to fly soon, I promise."

The path ahead seemed to go in several directions downhill. He strained to hear the voices, but suddenly there was nothing. *Don't dither, make a decision*, he told himself, and took the path west.

Still he couldn't hear any voices and the path disappeared.

Arthur was lost.

He could've sent Parthena up to look, but despite his increasing worry, he didn't want to risk Eudora realizing he was there. He trudged on through a field of ferns; some of the fronds were now taller than him and it was difficult to see where he was heading.

There was one thing that he knew, that he

remembered Dad saying: if you have no idea what to do, make the best educated decision you can and stick to it with total commitment. Ahead was where he was going, and so what if there was an enormous swathe of jungle in between? He would just keep moving—they couldn't have gone far.

"Eyes on the goal," he said, and strode forward, smiling.

But after three steps, the ground seemed to disappear beneath him and he fell clumsily down, arm flying upward as the earth swallowed him.

CHAPTER 14

SEA GODDESS II

NONE OF THE Culpepper crew slept that night again.

Maudie felt as though her soul had been over-stretched like taut elastic, threatening to break at any moment. It had been four days. She'd never been separated from Arthur for this long, and she had no idea if he was even alive. If the Vane crew had been shooting at them, what would they have done to Arthur? She blocked out the hideousness of the thought and focused on the Acquafreeda ship as it sailed toward them.

The grave had indeed been empty, but Gallus said that they'd found Ermitage Wrigglesworth's shipwreck, not the body, so the grave was merely a mark of respect. It had proved impossible to get anything more out of the villagers. Maudie had told Harriet about the ring around Gallus's neck, but he no longer wore one and denied ever having done so.

When the Acquafreedas arrived, Evelyn Acquafreeda sailed a dinghy to shore to speak with the *Aurora* crew. She was dressed in an iridescent turquoise all-in-one suit, her hair braided like a fish tail over her shoulder. Maudie thought that the petite woman had an air of fierce capability.

Harriet spoke hurriedly with Evelyn then regrouped the crew. "The Acquafreedas' main ship carries a smaller vessel, and they've agreed we can use it to chase the *Aurora*. It's faster, so it suits our cause better. But I don't want to risk everyone going. Gilly, Meriwether, Barnes, Forbes, Cranken, Forsythe, Keene, Wordle, Hurley, and Dr. Quirke, I want you all to stay on Nova until we return. Evelyn has agreed to remain close by so that, should the worst happen and we don't make it back, you can sail to Lontown with them."

Queenie gave a sorrowful meow. Harriet picked her up and stroked her. "I'm sorry, dearest, you must stay here. Keep an eye on the island and watch over the crew for me." She passed Queenie to Gilly. "And can you look out for Queenie, please. She likes you, but she might be a bit resistant to staying on the *Victorious*."

Gilly nodded.

"Felicity and Welby will come on the sea-ship with me. Maudie, I presume you also want to come?"

Maudie nodded emphatically.

"Good. Then we set off immediately. We're already several days behind."

Harriet pulled Maudie to one side and looked directly into her eyes with absolute seriousness. "I'm taking the people I trust most in the Wide. But I want you to know that there is no shame if you do want to stay behind. We don't know what we're heading into. The people on this island still know more than they are letting on about what lies out there."

"I'm going."

Harriet nodded.

"Should we bring the sky-ak?" Maudie asked. It was still on the beach from when they'd arrived.

"Yes, good idea. Now let's get going."

After loading supplies into the dinghy, Harriet, Maudie, Felicity, and Welby sailed from the beach to where the *Sea Goddess*, the Acquafreedas' towering sea-ship, was anchored, Harriet and Felicity in the boat with Evelyn Acquafreeda, and Maudie and Welby in the sky-ak. The *Sea Goddess* had a great wooden hull, painted a deep midnight blue, three sturdy masts, and numerous sails of different sizes and direction. Tethered behind it was a smaller ship in the same blue with *Sea Goddess II* painted in gold on the side. It had two sails and a streamlined shape, which made Maudie hopeful of the speed it could travel.

They tied the sky-ak to the *Sea Goddess* and climbed the ladder aboard.

"We'll hoist your small sky-ship aboard the *Goddess II*," said Evelyn, "and load your supplies, although we have left what we can for you."

"Thank you, Evelyn."

"I'm glad to help you, Harriet. Your parents never looked down on me for sticking to my family tradition of the old ways, especially when others tried to revoke my family's status at the Geographical Society." Maudie didn't have to guess who that would be. "The *Goddess II* has dual sails; did you say you were familiar with such a vessel?"

"It's been a while, but we'll be fine."

"There is the pitch engine, of course, but we only use that for backup, if the winds drop." She put her hand on Harriet's shoulder. "Good luck."

Then she smiled at Maudie. "I hear you have quite the head for heights. Let's see how you fare at sea."

Harriet, Maudie, Welby, and Felicity climbed aboard the *Sea Goddess II* and set off.

The remaining crew waved from the beach, and Maudie's heart wrenched with the knowledge that they were now on different paths. She looked to the other three—Harriet at the wheel, Welby wrestling with the sails, and Felicity busily stowing equipment—and knew that she had to cling to them with everything she had. Her family. Except Arthur wasn't here, and the separation was a physical pain in her heart. The only way to get through was to do what she did best, and that was to be practical and focus on solving what she could. "I'm going to check over the engine," she called to Harriet. "I'll make sure all the valves are clean and clear, in case we need it."

"Excellent idea."

By the time she was back on deck, the island of Nova was a small dot in the west, but Maudie couldn't help but feel that if they'd been in a sky-ship they would have been much quicker. The waves were choppy, and already Maudie hated the rolling and lurching rhythm.

Felicity passed her a cup of sweet tea and a marsh cake.

"I don't think I'm well," Maudie said, looking at the marsh cake and feeling the same color.

"You'll get used to it. Here, I have some peppermint pastels. They might help."

"Welby's very quiet," Maudie said, looking across at where he sat, holding on to a sail rope and staring blankly ahead.

Felicity put an arm around Maudie and pulled her into a hug. "I think he's a bit lost without the certainty of his maps and charts, to be honest, and . . . well, I think he feels bad, you know . . . about Arthur. He said he was quite hard on him in the navigation lessons."

Maudie looked up into Felicity's dark eyes. "None of us wanted to listen to Arthur. He told me we should trust our instinct, but I thought he was just being his usual *act first, think later* self and that I needed to be the one to remind him to be practical, but . . ." She swallowed. "Do you think he's all right?"

Felicity looked down at her feet and wiggled her toes. "I'm certain he is, deary."

CHAPTER 15

ARTHUR ALONE

ARTHUR FELL THROUGH ferns, then vines and rock and mud and skittering debris, branches snapping and snatching at him. His clothes were torn and his skin clawed. Flailing, he tried to grab anything to slow him, and he nearly managed it, but then came the running water, and he slipped and tumbled.

When he could fall no farther, he eventually came to a stop.

He groaned and grimaced at the pain in his backside, his shoulder, his ankle. Everywhere.

The jungle seemed to fall silent around him for a moment, but within seconds a bird chirruped, then another, and the full soundscape was back. He felt as though he'd become an invisible speck, absorbed into the belly of a great leafy monster.

He might have lain there and let himself sink away into the squelchy foliage, when he suddenly realized . . .

"Parthena!" But his voice merely croaked.

Had she been on his shoulder? Maybe she was injured too.

He peered up into the yawning green gloom. It was hard to believe he'd been in blistering sunlight moments ago. He grabbed a nearby plant to pull himself up and spines bit into his palm. "Argh!" He pulled the spines out with his teeth as best he could, then yelled, "Parthena!"

But there was no sign of her. A waterfall drenched the rock face not far away, seemingly disappearing into nowhere. His trousers were ripped, and he examined his ankle. It didn't look broken, but it throbbed horribly. Something black was on his calf. He peered at it. It seemed attached. Realizing it was a living creature, he yelled, pulled it off, and threw it away from him.

Suddenly a rasping coughlike sound came from nearby.

"Who's there?" Arthur called. Could it be the Vane crew?

A strange, bent shadow moved through the trees. Arthur's heart was still racing from the fall and it began to thrum in his ears. The figure was getting closer.

The creature was taller than him, with green fur and a large head. *Please be good, like the thought-wolves*, he wished, *not like the darkwhispers*, but fear ran up his back and beads of sweat trickled down his face. The ground squelched as the animal came closer, until it loomed above him. His heart pounded like churning pistons; darkness and fear suffocated him. Then it stroked its great whiskers and said, "My dear old thing, what the clanking cogs are you doing?"

Arthur was agog, his mouth dropping open. Relief was instant, as though the knot in his stomach had been magically untwined, because it wasn't a creature, it was a man! He spoke with an undeniable Uptown accent, and the great head was in fact just a rather out-of-proportion hat, and the coat looked to be made of moss.

"Who are you?"

"It is you who dropped on my doorstep, so etiquette would say perhaps you should tell me first. You're not from Erythea, are you?"

Arthur couldn't believe it. He'd said that word, Erythea! He shook his head. "I'm from Lontown. My name's Arthur Brightstorm."

"Lontown?" The man's face erupted with a wide smile and he clapped his hands together excitedly. "Well, well, well, dear old Lontown, you say! I thought I heard a sky-ship, so I thought I'd venture out to see, but I convinced myself I'd imagined it. Arthur Brightstorm? Goodness, this is quite marvelous." He spoke quickly, his words galloping from his lips. "How did you . . . ? Where . . . ? What in all the . . . ?" He stopped himself and shook his head. "Plenty of time for questions. First things first; let me help you up." He held out a hand and Arthur immediately saw the four triangles tattooed on his arm and the realization hit as the man said, "I'm Ermitage, Ermitage Wrigglesworth."

Again, Arthur's jaw dropped. "You're alive!"

Ermitage Wrigglesworth looked down at his body. "Why yes, so I am, how perceptive of you!" He grinned cheekily and pulled Arthur to his feet.

Arthur couldn't believe what he was hearing and seeing. For a moment he wondered if he had bumped his head too hard on the way down and it was all some sort of dream, but the man's grasp was real.

"Dear me, you took quite a fall there. I'd say you're lucky to be alive, let alone to have gotten away without a broken bone. Looks like a twist to me." He indicated Arthur's ankle, then searched around and

snapped a branch from a tree close
by. "There, a temporary crutch for
you. Hurry now, I've been out long
enough, and we don't want to
get caught in a deluge. These
parts are particularly suscep-
tible and there was a storm out at
sea not long ago."

"But my friend is still up there.
She's a sapient hawk, and I've lost
her."

Ermitage looked up. "She'll
find it impossible to fly down
here. She'll be fine, I'm sure—
anything with wings or fins is safe here. It's the legs
that are a problem, so you're at a clear disadvantage
now. Come along, old thing. We need to follow the
streams; it'd take forever through the trees and we'd
get quite lost. But you'll have to take care not to slip,
so pop the stick under your armpit and I'll take your
other arm, ah, I see . . . Well, never mind, I'm sure
we'll do just fine."

They began navigating through the ferns, then
the first stream.

"Halt there, old thing!" he suddenly shouted.
"Leeches!"

He was staring at Arthur's arm. Arthur looked down to see another of the black shiny creatures on his wrist in the most unreachable place.

"They'll suck you dry, these things; lucky it's a small one."

"Small? It's two inches wide!"

"Ah, a baby. Some are the size of North Craggies seal pups!"

Arthur gave a quiver of laughter, hoping Mr. Wrigglesworth was joking.

"Allow me." Wrigglesworth plucked the leech off and tossed it away.

They continued slowly upstream, Arthur looking down at his arm and legs every few seconds, checking for the slimy, black bloodsuckers.

"We thought you were dead," Arthur said.

"Really? But I've barely been gone more than a few moon cycles."

"More like twelve."

"What? Really? Time flies when you're in Erythea!"

"There's a whole armada looking for you. That was, until we discovered you were dead, then they all turned back."

"Dead? What nonsense. But not quite all turned

back, eh?" He looked Arthur up and down. "A whole armada? Who'd have thought anyone would be interested in an old fuddy-duddy explorer like me when we have all you new-bloods coming up? Well, well. I thought I could slip away quietly and come back with the biggest surprise of all. Did you come with your father? Ernest, isn't it?"

The words were like a thump to Arthur's chest, but he didn't show it. "No, I came with Harriet Culpepper and her crew."

"Jolly decent family, the Culpeppers. Octavie Culpepper was a dear friend of mine, although we drifted apart." Ermitage stared at an invisible point in the distance for a moment, a glazed look in his eyes. "Is your father letting you branch out on your own? The best way to learn the ropes is to stand on one's own feet, you know."

Arthur was getting the feeling that Ermitage Wrigglesworth didn't ask questions with a view to getting answers, necessarily.

"Respectable chap, I always thought, despite the way some looked down on him. Don't get me wrong, I'm all for having a go. I mean, we can't all be heritage families of Vornatania. "How's the ankle?"

"Sore."

"Ah, look!" He grabbed a plant close by and tore off a piece of bark. "Chew that—it'll help."

It tasted bitter and was like trying to chew the sole of a boot.

After navigating the streams for a while longer and having awkward conversations about the weather back in Lontown, they appeared to be in a swamp. A humid haze drifted between thin trees with drooping branches. Frogs croaked in a raucous loop of noise.

"Here we are!"

"Are we?" Arthur said, feeling less impressed than he'd hoped. From what he'd seen before he fell, this land was a jewel box, so this dark, dank spot seemed like a strange place to reside. He slapped mosquitoes away from his face.

"Come along."

A structure came into view a little way ahead, something man-made.

It was a house on stilts, an old, shacklike structure at the top with a crooked chimney and arched windows. As they neared, it became apparent that the house wasn't on stilts exactly, but there were cranks of a sort.

"Impressive, isn't it?"

"It's certainly curious."

"The whole structure can move from ground level to fifty feet high. All based on cranks and cogs—but these are historic now in this continent, a relic of past times."

Arthur imagined how Maudie would've run straight over to examine the mechanisms. He missed her so much. At least he wasn't alone now, but he felt as though he'd been split in two and left half of himself back on Nova.

"Most of these are falling into disrepair with many preferring the bubble houses—very popular in the south, I hear. Standard treehouses are for traditionalists, or there are the modern waterfall homes, and of course, most choose to live in the city of Tempestra."

"I think that's where the rest of my crew were on their way to—before I fell, that is." Arthur considered telling Ermitage about the Vane situation, but he was still a little unsure of him.

"Perhaps we can get you there, after you've rested that ankle of yours. I'll wind the house down, save you climbing stairs."

Ermitage began turning a large crank. It creaked and groaned, and chains rattled. The whole house tilted forward and chunks of moss slopped into the swamp. Then, as he continued turning the crank, the building swung backward and began edging down.

"This technology dates back several hundred years. Fascinating, don't you think? It's the reason I stayed here—so much to document!"

The house reached just above swamp-water level, and Ermitage ushered Arthur inside. It was full of crooked shelves with papers, books, pots and jars, a bundle of blankets on the floor on a makeshift mattress, a few cushions, a rustic table and chair, and a stove. On the table was a huge barometer, but it was unlike the one Meriwether used, which stated very dry, fair, change, rain, and stormy. This one read fair, rain, rainy, rainier, torrential rain, storm, DELUGE. At the moment the arrow pointed to fair.

Ermitage tapped it, and it stayed on fair. "We'll stay level. I'll put the kettle on and see to your wounds. Do sit down. You take the chair and I'll prop your foot up."

Arthur dropped into the chair, relieved to take the weight off his ankle. "Deluge sounds pretty bad."

"The worst deluge we see around here is thirty feet, so we're quite safe."

"Thirty feet!" Arthur almost choked on his own words.

"Hmm, it tends to be less sudden here than on the northern side of the land." Ermitage pulled a tree stump from under the table and a cushion, then elevated Arthur's ankle. "Just under the mountains sees the most severe floods. The complex weather system here is caused by what I would surmise is a variation of factors, all combining to create, well, chaos."

"Chaos?"

"Chaos by our standards, but in this land they are perfectly used to it. Quite marvelous how the ecosystem and people have evolved here."

"Mr. Wrigglesworth? From what I've heard of the people here, they know all about us, yet we know nothing about them."

Ermitage squinted, his forehead becoming as wrinkled as tree bark. "Intriguing, isn't it? I made it my life's work to find a way here. Everyone said I was a blind fool."

"The Votary of Four," said Arthur, gesturing to Ermitage's arm with the four triangles.

"My, you *have* done your homework." He twisted the end of his gray beard around his finger and studied Arthur for a moment.

"I like books."

Ermitage smiled. "Me too."

"I read your original annotated copy of *Explorers in the Third Age.*"

"Did you now!" Ermitage puffed out his chest proudly.

"It was extremely . . . interesting in places."

"Just in places?" His shoulders sank a little.

Arthur leaned in. "In hidden places . . ."

A spark of light ignited in Ermitage's eyes. "My dear old thing, you didn't . . . ?"

Arthur nodded. "Words revealed by lemon was clever. As was the secret drawer on Mangrove Island."

"Well, I never! You *are* a bright chap. I shall have to work a little harder in the future!" Ermitage took a jug from the shelf and poured Arthur some water into a wooden cup, then shuffled to the door and opened it out to the rain forest.

There had been a constant backdrop of water trickling and frogs croaking. Every so often a bird would break out with its own signature trill or whistle. Everything smelled like being in an over-grown greenhouse. The combined scent of vegetation, moisture, and soil, wood, decaying plants. It wasn't a bad smell—it smelled of life.

"So, how is Captain Culpepper?" asked Ermitage. "I've watched her career with great interest."

Arthur gave a little cough. This couldn't go on.

"Mr. Wrigglesworth, I need to tell you something. I'm not actually here with the Culpepper crew."

Ermitage turned around and squinted curiously.

"I'm here with the Vanes, and not by choice," Arthur added quickly.

"What in all of the Wide is that woman doing here? How did she . . . ?"

"She broke into your house in Lontown and took some journals."

He banged the kettle on the stove. "I knew I should've burned them before I left! That woman has no honor. Thaddeus, her father, was the same. I'd sooner trust a mosquito who'd promised not to bite me." He slapped one away from his arm.

Arthur grimaced. "It gets worse. She's heading for the city, and she's pretending to be Harriet."

"Pretending to be Harriet Culpepper? Why would she do that?"

"I don't know. The people who came to the *Aurora* seemed to recognize the Culpepper symbol on the ship, the swallows."

"Did they, now?" Ermitage reared his head back and frowned.

Arthur nodded.

"Well, my dear old thing, I think we should head for the city and find out what she's up to. Just as soon as your ankle is a little better—it's quite a journey from this part of the land."

Ermitage went to the shelf and selected a bottle of brown liquid. He poured it into two coconut shells and handed one to Arthur. "While the kettle is heating we'll have some jungle vitamin soup. It's perfectly fine cold. I've been experimenting with various vitamins and minerals found in the locality."

Arthur held the shell and his stomach turned over at the marshy stench.

Mistaking his reaction for caution, Ermitage patted him on the back. "Nothing to worry about. All the ingredients are safe and checked out by the local population. Drink up, my dear old thing; this will put hairs on your chest and stop the insects coming after your blood at night: double benefits!" Ermitage leaned in toward him, wide-eyed and grinning.

Arthur smiled gawkily, pausing for a moment, certain that Mr. Wrigglesworth would tell him it was all a joke.

Instead, Ermitage said, "Come along now, do you call yourself an explorer, or not? Chin, chin!" Then Ermitage tapped his coconut shell to Arthur's and gulped his own murky liquid down.

Arthur pinched his nose, closed his eyes, and tried to imagine that it was Felicity's many-veg soup.

But it tasted vile, like rotten cheese and fermented grass. He retched.

Ermitage laughed. "That's my boy! How I've missed the true Lontowner spirit of adventure." While Ermitage looked longingly into the distance before turning back to fill up his own jungle soup, Arthur swiftly tipped his into a potted palm of red fruits beside him, muttering an apology to the plant.

"Now, it looks like we've time to pass while you heal that ankle of yours. I'd say about a week or so. I want to hear all the news of Lontown and all about what happened on your journey here."

Frustrating as it was to hear he would have to wait a week, Arthur accepted he couldn't get anywhere at the moment, so he nodded reluctantly. "But how did *you* find your way here, Mr. Wrigglesworth?"

"My sky-ship crashed, I ran out of fuel, and those blasted darkwhispers were swarming in."

"That's what you drew in your journals?"

"Yes. I'd not come across them in person when I drew them, but the people on Nova will tell rather a lot if you supply them with enough rum! Anyways, luckily one of Erythea's sea-ships was on the way back to the continent, being guided in by the fire-bird. They took pity and rescued me, then brought me to the city. When they asked if I intended to return, of course I said I didn't. I got the distinct impression it wasn't an option. So they let me stay, which suited me because I couldn't wait to explore this new world to uncover the history, the technology!"

"What exactly are the darkwhispers? We got past them, but more by luck."

"Curious things. They feed on energy, from what I know. Electrical energy, however they can find it, storms, memories . . . Why do you think no one has ever made it this far before? But I'm more of a historian than a zoologist." He shrugged.

"So they're a barrier to the outside world, keeping this land a secret?"

"Indeed."

"And the Erytheans let you stay here even though you're from the outside?"

"They keep a very close eye on me. There's always someone not far away. Of course, you'd never know it as an outsider—they blend into the forest as though they were chameleons—but I know they are there."

Arthur peered out of the window in suspicion. "Are they out there now?"

"Perhaps." Ermitage filled up Arthur's coconut shell and edged his chair in eagerly. "Now drink up and tell me about home."

Arthur grinned uncomfortably, his stomach

yearning for any of Felicity's dishes. He was happy to tell Ermitage about Lontown, but not so thrilled by a period of recovery, being confined to a hut drinking green sludge. He had the feeling it was going to be a long week.

CHAPTER 16

FIRE-BIRD

THE DAYS PASSED. Maudie hated the motion of the sea; it was harsher than the sky, like it had you in a gluey grip. In the sky you felt part of it, an equal with it, but the sea wanted to dominate. It took her in a sickly rhythm that made her swallow back for fear of retching.

She couldn't stop thinking about Arthur, so she busied herself with the sky-ak, cleaning the small water engine and working on the modifications in her diary.

A bank of ominous clouds waited on the horizon. What were they sailing toward? Storms were no fun in sky-ships, and Maudie imagined going through one in a sea-ship would be worse. Perhaps she should strengthen the rivets.

Harriet stared into the distance, her hands on the wheel, deadly focused and the quietest Maudie had ever seen her.

"Have this." Felicity passed Maudie a cup. "I'm trying a new mint tea to help with the queasiness."

The clouds had grown incredibly dark in no time at all.

"I wonder what Meriwether would make of that." Maudie indicated the looming gloom. She recalled the technical names of the clouds in her head: stratus, cumulus, cirrus, nimbus. But these clouds seemed unfathomably huge, like nothing she'd seen back home. Would it be possible to invent a machine to disperse them? She looked up at the sky; never had it felt more distant from her, apart, almost severed.

"Harriet will get us through it, don't you worry. It's likely just a bank of sea mist. It shouldn't be turbulent or anything to bother us."

But Maudie couldn't help but notice how Felicity wriggled her bare toes uncomfortably, and she didn't like the way the wind had dropped and the sails had wilted during the past chime. The waves became eerily smoother the closer they got to the mist. Dad had always said that silence comes before the storm, and she knew that to be true in the same way that quiet thought often preceded ideas, or the way that there was a moment of vacuum before an explosion.

Maudie stood beside Harriet as they approached the cloud. Welby and Felicity joined them. Had the *Aurora* flown through this? How far behind were they?

"Slow the engine, Welby. We'll need to be careful," said Harriet.

Welby disappeared below deck, and in a moment there was a *whirr* as the rumbling engines slowed to half power, then a quarter, then to almost nothing.

Harriet clutched her compass.

"Look at the water. Doesn't it seem eerily calm?" breathed Felicity.

Then they were swallowed by dense mist.

The only sound was the bow of the sea-ship cutting through the still water. All around was impenetrable gray.

Harriet looked down at Maudie and smiled reassuringly. "It's all right. Just because we can't see, it doesn't mean we can't navigate effectively."

They carried on into the gloom.

"Land ho!" Harriet called. "Steady . . . steady."

The mist had lifted a little so that they could see a hundred yards or so ahead. They were between tall, jagged islands—narrow land masses piercing through the sea.

"If we catch the hull on one of these, who knows what damage it'd do." Welby frowned.

Maudie said quietly, "We're . . . we're not going to turn back, are we?"

"No!" Harriet, Welby, and Felicity all said at the same time.

"We'll need to work together. Maudie, take the forward starboard side with Felicity. Welby, take the forward port. Watch like hawks."

They were in a labyrinth of great rock pillars, curiously barren of life and quite unlike the islands they'd left.

"We're edging close portside!" Welby called.

"Don't adjust too far, Harrie; there's not much left here," called Felicity.

Harriet glanced over her shoulder. "It's clearing. I think we're through the worst of it."

But no sooner had she said that than the ship began to sway. Waves were building ahead, and a breeze began to ruffle Harriet's hair. The clouds darkened even more, slowly at first, then more rapidly, as though the night were falling in triple time.

Maudie tugged Felicity's sleeve. "What are those

dark shapes on the rocks?" She noticed that Felicity was clutching her lucky spoon tightly.

"I don't know. Probably some foliage or . . . something . . ." Her voice trailed off.

Then a blaze lit up the sky in the distance, followed by the soft rumble of thunder a while after.

"The storm's coming in from the south; we'll veer northward," Harriet called.

Something caught Maudie's eye on the nearest island. "Did that move?" she asked breathlessly, her heart pounding. Whatever the "*it*" was, it seemed to span several yards, large enough to keep her eyes trained on it.

The ship veered northeasterly, but another flash lit up the sky not far away in front of them, followed by an enormous boom that made Maudie and Felicity yelp.

Then the dark shape on the crag twitched.

It *was* alive.

A huge tentacled head lifted away from the vertical slab of rock and looked to the sky. It clung on with enormous clawed feet.

"What is it?"

Harriet was watching. "Keep calm; hold your nerve."

They noticed another, and another. The creatures

were everywhere, clinging to the craggy rock. There was a curious whispering sound; was it coming from the creatures?

"I don't like this one bit," Felicity hissed.

"They're the creatures in Ermitage's journal," Harriet said very quietly. "The darkwhispers!"

"I thought Gilly said they were likely little bats!"

Lightning lit up the sky again, this time in a great jagged wire of blistering light. The sea-ship began rocking even more, and there was a strange noise, as though the air was being whipped as one of the creatures took flight, then another, then another.

"Maudie, Felicity, get below deck," Harriet called.

They both stared, paralyzed by what was unfolding around them.

"That's an order!"

Felicity grabbed Maudie's hand. "Come on."

The creatures flew in an undulating movement with claws dragging behind, black leathery skin glistening with moisture. There was the soft hissing of air, as though the wind had a voice.

Before Felicity and Maudie could reach the hatch to get below, one of the creatures landed right on top of it. Its great wings were folded inward, so its front claws rested on the deck. Feelers flowed from its head and down the length of its spine to its tail, which it flicked against the wooden boards. It observed them with smoky white eyes. As it took a step toward them, the strangest thing happened.

Someone was whispering to Maudie. It was Arthur. She was back with Arthur in Brightstorm House, just before Dad left for South Polaris. She could see him at the door, actually see him as though he was in front of her and . . .

As if from a great distance, Maudie heard Harriet call, "Full speed!"

The ship sped up and the creature stumbled backward, and Maudie and Felicity were thrown to the floor. As she hit the deck, Maudie saw hundreds of the creatures taking off from the rocks, spiraling up into the sky above. There was another flash of lightning, then another. Warm tropical rain pelted the deck like bullets.

The creature righted itself and observed them once more, fixing its eyes on Maudie.

She heard whispers. "It's all right, everything is all right."

Maudie saw herself and Arthur in the garden of Brightstorm House, with their father. They were laughing and running around, playing tag. It was a beautiful memory; she was three years old and she was hungry for the lemon biscuits Dad had just baked, but they were laughing so hard and the warm sunlight dappled the garden, and it smelled of roses and . . . something was brushing her cheek and—

Welby shoved her to the side.

"Get back!" he yelled, jabbing the creature with a huge stick. It retreated and took flight.

Felicity helped her up. "Oh my, oh my!"

"What happened?" Maudie groaned.

"You walked toward it; it had its feelers on your face for a moment. I tried to pull you back and you pushed me away."

"I don't . . . I don't remember."

Felicity pulled her to the back of the boat. Lightning flashed in swift succession, igniting the sky. The throng of dark creatures circled high above, their bodies sparked in the clouds as though, somehow, they were reacting to the storm, as though it was charging them.

The sea-ship rocked violently, almost toppling them over. Harriet gripped the wheel.

"Look out portside!" Welby yelled as a new island appeared from a patch of fog. Harriet spun the wheel hard, and the sea-ship lurched on the waves, creaking terribly.

Above, the darkwhispers were circling them, getting closer and closer. The ship began spinning.

One creature landed on the prow in front of Harriet. Again she ordered Felicity and Maudie below deck, but they couldn't even stand. Another landed starboard beside Felicity. "Maudie, get to the hatch. Save yourself!"

Maudie looked around frantically. Another was portside, close to Welby.

The rain was torrential now, drenching the deck, and as Maudie scrambled to help Felicity she slipped and fell.

Suddenly a bright red whoosh appeared above, as if from nowhere. Maudie looked up to see the muscular ruby chest of a bird with huge, fire-bright wings, at least three yards wide, beating in rhythmic swathes against the driving rain. Its tail swept like a scarlet cloak through the sky. It seemed to make a direct route toward where Harriet gripped the wheel. The enormous bird landed behind her on the deck, stretched out its wings around her in a strange, protective manner, then opened its crimson beak and screeched at the darkwhispers—a cry as shrill as a knife slicing the air.

The fire-bird.

Instantly, the darkwhispers began retreating.

Before relief could even set in, there was a colossal bang and an explosion of rock and wood. Everything

tumbled and rolled, and Maudie was thrown across the ship. She landed on her back, starboard side, as the ship tipped further . . . Then water . . . everywhere. She was half-buried by splintering wood and rising water engulfing her.

Maudie kicked for the surface, fighting against the weight of her tool belt. Above was chaos. Lightning, the darkwhispers fleeing, the fire-bird clutching the prow, the ship cracked and gaping, and no sign of Harriet, Felicity, or Welby anywhere. The waves were pulling her away from the ship. She yelled for Harriet.

Then she saw it, not far away—the sky-ak was floating in the water. It was her only chance. She kicked with everything she had and reached for the side. A great wall of mist enfolded her; all signs of the sinking sea-ship faded into gray as she was pulled and rolled by the waves. *Hold on*, she told herself. *Hold on!*

She found the rope, twisted her hand in it, and gripped for her life.

CHAPTER 17

DELUGE

IT WAS INCREDIBLE how quickly the barometer had changed from *fair* to *deluge*. This was Arthur's third deluge since arriving at Erythea. His ankle had swollen and bruised even more, and he'd been stuck in bed with Ermitage applying all sorts of leaves and ground concoctions to help it heal (however, Arthur had the distinct impression that Ermitage simply liked to experiment, as nothing seemed to help). Nonetheless, his ankle had started to feel better at last, so as soon as Arthur had seen that another deluge was on the way, he'd called to tell Ermitage, who was outside syphoning sap, and they both sprang into action.

Like a large, gray rabbit darting through the undergrowth, Ermitage gathered all the loose equipment from outside, hurling it through the open door.

By now Arthur knew to dampen the stove, close off the chimney hatch, secure the shutters, then grab the accumulating equipment being thrown his way and store it in its place. When the inside was secure, he went out onto the wooden decking and called to see if Ermitage needed help outside.

"It's all right, I'm almost done! Have you shut off the chimney?"

"Yes, and I've dampened the stove."

"Good job, my dear old thing. Too risky to have that going in a deluge."

All around, the jungle floor had come to life in a variety of ways: some leaves were folding in on themselves and retracting, insects and animals were scurrying up tree trunks, others were burrowing into the marshy soil, while some were emerging, like the dormant greebers. Ermitage had pointed out these strange, snapping water-lizards to Arthur during the last deluge, when one had tried to climb onto their wooden patio. They had razor-sharp teeth and thrived in the deluges by snapping up any creatures unlucky enough to be caught in the storm.

A drop of water landed on Arthur's nose as thunder growled somewhere in the west, and the soft patter of rain began, replacing the usual trill of insects and birdsong.

"I'm just going to help this little thing," Ermitage called out, picking up a snail so big that he had to use both hands. "Of course, this species is well adapted and can hunker down in their shell for over twenty chimes without air, but I do believe this dear old thing is sapient and rather fond of dry shelter, taking to human comforts during the odd deluge. I've called her Gert, after Gainsford back at the Geographical Society of Lontown. I did always have a soft spot for her."

Thunder rumbled once more, closer this time, and the forest darkened swiftly, as though time had sped up suddenly from day to evening. The rain quickened too.

"We'd better wind the legs up and get the house to safety," Arthur called, looking up with concern into the gray gloom of the incoming storm. It suddenly struck him how the cascading water droplets sounded curiously like a crackling fire as they splashed onto leaves and branches. *Strange how two polar opposites could sound so similar*, Arthur thought.

When he looked back, he saw that a large greeber had appeared several yards from Ermitage. "Hurry! There's a greeber about ten paces behind you!" he shouted above the tumultuous drumroll of falling rain.

Ermitage hopped swiftly through the already

ankle-deep water, his gangly legs flying about as the greeber swung its head in his direction, but the water wasn't yet deep enough for its signature razor-swift swimming, so it merely observed with gold-slatted eyes.

Ermitage hurried inside and placed the huge snail on a blanket. "Quick, light the lamp so that we can see to wind the crank."

Arthur sparked it with his strike-fire and set it in its holder, then they began winding the crank that drove the small rickety house upward. Lightning flashed and thunder boomed again, and once more almost simultaneously, and as the house rose, the clouds unleashed their watery fury and the rain streamed from the sky. Outside was now as black as deepest night, and there was no way to tell how high they were; they would just need to keep cranking until the mechanism locked into place. The handle was increasingly difficult to turn as the pressure from above increased, and sweat was beading all over Arthur's body from the humidity and the exertion. After several minutes, the crank would turn no further, and it locked into place.

"There. All done, old thing," Ermitage said loudly, to be heard above the downpour, and patted Arthur on the back. Flashes of lightning came in swift

succession, and the snarl of thunder made Arthur's chair vibrate.

"These things are built to last; nothing to worry about." Ermitage fanned himself with a journal. "One of the swiftest incoming deluges I've seen since I've been here. We must be hitting what Erytheans call *matarnya*—which I believe translates as 'even wetter.'"

"Great," Arthur said.

Ermitage chuckled to himself.

CHAPTER 18

MAUDIE ALONE

IT WAS AS though the storm had been a dream. Maudie lay motionless on the beach, her limbs like lead, letting the warmth of the sun drown her thoughts, because she knew the moment that she opened her eyes again, what had happened would be real. Beside her, she heard the sky-ak clunk softly in the steady whooshing of the waves that washed over her feet.

The sky-ak had saved her life. She could remember heaving it up the beach, retching and choking up salt water, before collapsing on the sand.

She squeezed the sand with her hands, soft and warm. Something hummed above. Her eyes fluttered heavily as she forced them open. The sky was so bright. How could it be so dazzling when it had been so fierce and stormy not long before?

A huge dragonfly with the wingspan of a dinner plate zipped above. Maudie sat up with a start, and it flew away; a few moments later it came back and hovered several yards away, as though curious about the strange creature on the beach. Maudie pushed herself up to stand. For a moment, she wondered if she was back on Nova. Perhaps the storm had driven her back? But when she looked up at the enormous mountains covered in dense, bright-green foliage, trees twice as tall as any she had seen—perhaps even three times—she knew that she was somewhere new, somewhere big.

Arthur had been right all along.

There *was* a fourth continent.

Even though it was futile, she called out Arthur's name, then Harriet's, Felicity's, and Welby's. Several birds took flight at the jungle edge and flew inland. She tried to control her breathing and looked around. The sandy cove was quite secluded, with almost pure-white sand, as though the sun had blanched all color from it. It was banked by the enormous forested mountains to the left, more jungle in front of her, and then the sea everywhere else. There was no sign of debris from the crashed sea-ship. Maudie squinted out over the water, the sun reflecting like diamond dust across the waves, but there was nothing. She suddenly felt very small, and it was as though someone had opened a great expanse around her heart and was whispering coldly in her ear—*you're alone.*

The tide looked to be coming in, so she heaved the sky-ak farther up the beach and searched for anything inside it that might be useful. She checked her tool belt: wrench, small folding knife, drivers, and a crushed compass. She tapped it.

Great. The thing that would be most useful was broken.

Suddenly she realized how incredibly thirsty she was, and there was still a horrible saltwater taste in her mouth. The sky was bleached with sun. She looked around and swallowed the urge to cry. It was easy to make decisions with Arthur and the rest of the crew around, but alone . . .

Think like Harriet, she told herself. *What would Harriet do? Stop, think, observe, and make a plan. Stay calm.*

The fin of the sky-ak had snapped and she didn't want to venture back to the sea, so she ruled that out. The mountains were unimaginably high and would give her a good vantage point to survey the region, but they would no doubt be too treacherous to climb and would take her far too long to get even a short way up. And without water she wouldn't last more than three days in this heat, perhaps less. If anyone else from the sea-ship had survived, they might have made it to another beach, maybe not far away, so she shouldn't go too far inland. Perhaps she should venture in just far enough to find drinking water. She would have to mark her route so that she could find her way back out again, and if Harriet and the others came upon this beach, they could track her. She bit down on her lip.

There was a patch of trees along the beach that appeared to be less dense. After heaving the sky-ak up the sand, she made her way toward it. From here, it seemed as though the land was going down farther still, so perhaps that would lead to water.

Before she left, she found a broken branch and wrote in the sand close to the tree line: *Maudie this way.* With her folding belt knife, she cut off a little of her sleeve and tied it to a nearby tree, then searched inside the sky-ak again in case she'd missed anything. There was a rope under the waterline. She dithered between taking it or using it to secure the sky-ak, so she decided to split it in two; if the waves came in too far and she lost her only possible mode of transport there would be no hope, but a rope might be useful in the forest. She would find water, collect dry wood, then come back to the beach and make a fire and shelter. Pulling up her sleeves, she made her way into the trees.

Maudie's feet squelched through the dark, humid forest floor. She realized that finding dry wood to start a fire would be nearly impossible here. Every so often she would stop and break branches so that she could trace her way back. The trees grew taller and denser, and a cacophony of chirps, caws, chitters, whistles, and trills filled the air. Above, she caught glimpses of light cutting through in white shafts, diminished by the hundreds of plants all fighting for their own piece of it until all that remained was murky gloom.

She tried to find the route of least resistance, but the going was slow because she only had the folding knife from her tool belt to clear a path. As she moved farther in, she recognized what she thought might be a cabbage palm, and it jogged her memory of something Harriet had told them about collecting wood in the jungle: up in the air is best, always look up in the air, not on the ground. She selected the highest palm she could reach and cut it close to the trunk. It was much bigger than those she'd seen in Stella Oceanus, but, sure enough, when she took the stem and pulled it apart, there were the thin stringy bits that would be good for getting a fire started. She stuffed it in her pocket and looped strands of palm around her neck in the hope that they'd dry out some more.

As she moved through the forest, she found tree ferns with fine hair on the side. She pulled some off and put it in her pocket, thinking it might make more good tinder. She remembered how Harriet had gathered resin from the trees in the Everlasting Forest to create a torch when they were on the Ice Continent, and so she collected some herself now. But there was still no sign of a water source.

How could somewhere so damp have no water to drink?

Then she heard what she thought was a slow drip of water. She followed the sound and saw a pool of water beside a bank of foliage. She cupped some of the liquid in her hand and tentatively put her tongue to it. It tasted fresh, but she resisted the urge to drink it, remembering how Felicity had always insisted on boiling water, even if it looked clean. But then Maudie realized she had nothing to boil or carry the water in. She absentmindedly tucked her ribbon behind her ear and looked around for a solution. There would certainly be nothing man-made or metal around here to use. She sighed, and Arthur's voice was in her mind telling her that there was always a way. She realized that although she was good at engineering

and making things, it was often Arthur's encourage-
ment that helped her solve challenges. All she needed
was something that didn't let the water seep through.
Some of the plants had immense, thick leaves, the
biggest she'd ever seen—perhaps she could shape one
to hold water, and she could use her ribbon to tie it?

After choosing a suitable leaf, Maudie looked
for the best place to make a fire. She pulled back the
curtain of vines and squinted into the dark. It was a
cave! She could build a fire there; perhaps it would be
a better place for a camp than the beach.

Soon she'd cleared the entrance and set about
making a fire. She was so relieved she'd attached the
strike-fire Harriet had given her to her belt. After
a few attempts the spark caught, and she carefully
arranged the twigs in a cone shape so as not to stifle
the flame. When she was confident it would keep
burning, she set about bending the leaf into a shape
that would hold water more effectively, creating two
holes on the rim which she joined with her ribbon to
make it into a bowl shape. The water boiled quickly,
then she submerged the leaf partway into the pool,
and when it had cooled enough to be bearable, she
tipped the whole lot into her mouth, gulping it back
as though it were the finest honey from Tarn.

The cave led enticingly inward, and Maudie

decided she'd investigate but with great caution. She didn't know what creatures lurked in this new land, but there were certainly many, and chances were that some wouldn't be the friendly sort.

As the cave turned and went uphill slightly, a faint light showed. She followed the light into another cave section, and her breath was taken away as the

hollow glittered with pink jewels embedded in the jagged walls. In the center above was a great opening where dappled sunlight streamed through. The floor was uneven here, so she decided to check out one more section in case it would be suitable for a base. Above, light crept in through several holes in the cave ceiling, and there was a large ledge that looked to be the perfect place to build a fire and rest a little.

Moving through the jungle had been exhausting and so was keeping all the thoughts about the others at bay.

She made another small fire, and soon there was nothing she could do to keep sleep away.

CHAPTER 19

SMEM

BY THE MORNING, the storm had well and truly passed. Arthur had never seen anything quite like the volume of rain that fell. Even though Ermitage kept telling him that it was nowhere near as bad here as it was in the northern mountains of Erythea, it had been little consolation as he listened to the creaks and felt the sway of the rickety old house above the flood-water. Ermitage saying that such things were built to last hadn't been exactly reassuring as Arthur bailed the water out that was pouring down the chimney and swept the flow from the windows back out through the door. Meanwhile Ermitage had seemed more worried about the water getting into his notebooks than making sure the water didn't kill them.

But Ermitage had been right. The risen house was still standing.

The first thing Arthur did that morning was to look at the barometer. It said *fair.* "Phew!" he said, looking out. It was extraordinary how swiftly the water had subsided overnight.

They cranked the handle and went down by a full ten yards.

"It's the root system. Some of the trees act as nature's drainage, sucking up the water and releasing it back into the air." Ermitage pulled Arthur to the door and pointed up to the tree canopy. "See the rising evaporation?"

All around, the leaves were giving off vapor in the morning sunshine and above it looked like a great steam bath.

"Of course, the cycle fuels itself—great deluges lead to enormous amounts of evaporation as the trees take it in and release it back, then the moist air heads up, gathers over the mountains, and down it comes again as rain. The Erytheans have installed much of their own drainage to assist, of course. Marvelous inventors, they are."

"In the city?"

"Oh, no, the city operates quite differently, it . . .

well . . . you'll see when you get there. Their inventions are all around us too. I've not pointed it out, as I was curious to see if you'd notice for yourself."

"Notice what?"

"Take a look out of the window and tell me what you see."

"Trees, trees, and more trees?"

"How about that tree over there?"

Arthur wrinkled his nose in a confused way. "Er . . . just another tree?"

"Wrong, wrong, wrong!" Ermitage did a funny stamp dance with his skinny little legs.

"What do you mean?" Arthur said.

"That tree is not a tree."

Ermitage was making as much sense as a marsh cake. "It *is* a tree," Arthur said, smiling and nodding as he would if a small child had spoken to him.

"No. It looks like a tree, but it isn't. It's a drain-tree! Made to look exactly like one of the surrounding trees, but this one has pipes inside that go into the ground, run through the marshes, and carry the water far away into the sea. Ingenious, isn't it?"

"What? But it looks completely real. It's even releasing steam back, like the others." Arthur was certain Ermitage was pulling his leg.

"They call it ecology-tech. Of course, in the

language of Erythean it's something different, but that's the closest translation in Lontonian. It works in utter harmony with the environment, draining just enough to give the local inhabitants time to seek safety when there's a deluge, while not altering the natural state of the habitat or damaging the climate in a way that would alter the natural ecosystems here."

"Really?" Arthur said doubtfully.

"Absolutely. I've got notebooks full here documenting it, and there's a whole library section dedicated to the technology in Tempestra."

"They have a library?" Arthur's eyes were bright with interest.

"The people here value knowledge above everything, and not just knowledge for the sake of it. Knowledge of their continent, knowledge of the plants, the creatures, the trees, and most of all, knowledge of their place within it all. Do you know they don't have kings or politicians or any of that nonsense? They have scholars."

"We have scholars too," said Arthur.

"Yes, but Erythea is *run* by the scholars. In fact, the highest position is Professus Excelsis!"

"A professor is in charge?" he said.

Ermitage nodded.

It sounded fascinating. Arthur couldn't wait to go

to the city, and he'd almost forgotten that the reason he needed to go there was to find Eudora, expose the truth of who she was to these people, and find a way back to Stella Oceanus, back to Maudie and the crew. Back to his family. He felt dizzy just thinking about everything he needed to do.

"My ankle feels better now," he said. "But I don't suppose we can head off until the water goes down a bit more; it still looks like it'll be up to our shoulders. Maybe later, or tomorrow?"

Ermitage grinned. "Come on, let's have some jungle breakfast and we'll leave after that. How does that sound?"

"But there must still be several feet of water down there?"

Ermitage simply smiled. "There is a way. Didn't I just tell you that the Erytheans are inventive? But first, breakfast. I have figs, pineapple, and this delicious purple fruit. I've no idea what it is, but it hasn't poisoned me yet." He shrugged.

After breakfast, Ermitage asked Arthur to help him move the table to the side. Then he rolled back a rug to reveal a door in the floor. Below, there was some sort of vehicle, like a miniature cart but with a glass roof; or more like a great iron shoe.

"I call this the sub-marshland-explore-mobile."

"That's a bit of a mouthful!"

"Or SMEM for short."

"What does it do?"

"It'll take us under the water and let us travel about."

"Wow, did you make it?" Arthur thought of the Acquafreedas and how they were mocked by some in Lontown for wanting to travel under the seas. He imagined Maudie would find the machine fascinating and would be straight down there, figuring out how it worked. He smiled to himself.

"Well, technically, the Erytheans made it. . . . It's very old tech, of course; they wouldn't use it these days. I've had to almost completely renovate it. It's powered by a wind-up mechanism, but I'd like to adapt it to use some of the ion plates they use in the city."

"And we're going to the city in it?" Arthur said doubtfully.

"It looks small and is built for one, really, but I'm sure we'll both fit at a squeeze."

"Is it reliable?"

"Yes . . . well, I predict it is."

"Predict?" Arthur didn't like the way this was going. Ermitage definitely lived on the rickety side of danger.

"Technically, it'll be its first run."

"Maybe we should wait for the water to subside some more." Arthur sat down resolutely.

"My dear old thing, after such a vicious deluge the bottom layer of water can often take several days to go into the marshlands . . . but if you'd prefer to wait?"

The past days with Ermitage had been interesting, but Arthur needed to make progress. "No, if you're sure."

"We're both here, aren't we, Arthur Brightstorm? Alive and well in a continent that up until a few days ago you didn't know was here. I'd say we have explorers' hearts and luck on our side."

Although Arthur wasn't sure how much was heart and how much was blind charging ahead, he couldn't knock Ermitage's positivity, which radiated in the same way that Harriet's did. Like his father's had done.

"Ready when you are!" Ermitage slapped him on the back so hard that Arthur was worried Ermitage had snapped his own thin, little arm. He nodded and climbed into the SMEM.

"That's the spirit, old thing!"

Inside, it was a tight space and smelled of stagnant ponds. As Ermitage wound the cog outside, Arthur listened to the curious tick of whatever powered the contraption. There was a *thud* as they dropped a little and Arthur clung to the seat.

"Nothing to worry about!" Ermitage said, climbing in clumsily beside him and stepping on Arthur's leg with a bony heel. Arthur stifled an *ouch*. Then Ermitage dropped into the seat, and they were wedged inside like two sardines in a can.

"Snug, isn't it?" Ermitage reached an arm up and pulled the glass canopy over their heads. "There we go."

Arthur stifled the panic rising in his stomach. The days in the weather canopy of the *Aurora* were not too distant a memory, and he was thinking about Harriet and how she disliked being in enclosed spaces. He was pretty sure he was starting to feel the same way.

As the platform descended, they began to see the marshlands around them. Vines drooped from the trees like mossy necklaces, and huge lily-pad leaves floated on the surface of the floodwaters. Patches of green leaf debris drifted in clumps, making it look almost like patches of grass. Then they began submerging in the water until it was up to the glass. Arthur crossed his fingers as they descended farther, and the water reached eye level, then farther down until it was over the tops of their heads. Then, after about two more feet, there was a *clonk* as the platform reached the bottom and they were completely submerged in a whole new world.

The water was murky, but they could see several yards in front of them, to the trunks and roots of trees. Branches swayed as though time had slowed; some leaves remained folded away, others danced slowly in the drift. A large golden frog swam past the window and paused to look before continuing on its way.

Arthur suddenly had a thought. "Er . . . how much air is in here?"

Ermitage tapped a gauge in front of him. "I should say there is enough."

"How much is enough?"

Ermitage gave an absent wave of his hand.

Arthur had to admit that at this very moment he was missing Welby's attention to detail.

"There's some sort of air generator thingy. I've not quite worked it out yet." Ermitage shrugged.

"Oh . . . very reassuring!"

"He who dares!" And with that he pulled back a large lever that led to a *clonk* and a *whirr*, which might have been a small propeller somewhere behind them, and they were off.

"I'll be captain and you can be navigator!" Ermitage said excitedly.

"But I've no idea where the city of Tempestra is!"

"Just direct me northeast-ish and cross your fingers! We can't go the whole way in this thing, that would take weeks, but there is a rather friendly bubble-house village half a day away and they might lend us a different transport."

It was clear that Ermitage Wrigglesworth had little regard for safety as he steered this way and that between the trees, with Arthur attempting to give directions from a roughly scrawled map he didn't understand.

After minutes of trundling through the submerged forest floor in white-knuckled tension, Arthur decided to try to enjoy this underwater experience. An entirely new world of animals had come to life, with fish, frogs, lizards, even water eels.

After a while, the water started to become clearer.

"Ah, this is it!" Ermitage declared.

"Are we near the village?"

"Of course not, not at the snail's pace this thing travels, but we're heading the right way. We're about to hit one of the main river causeways."

A huge shape swam past the window, but it was too quick for Arthur to see. Then it flashed past again. "Something's out there!"

"Just pink river dolphins, fascinating creatures. The only dolphin to live inland that I know of."

One swam alongside them on Arthur's side and peered at them with intelligent eyes. "Are they sapient?"

"Sapient is a wide term, Arthur. If there's one thing I'm sure of, the Wide is full of surprises and often we humans underestimate the possibilities. It's part of our nature, I'm afraid; we tend to put ourselves on a bit of a pedestal in Lontown. Well, some people, not all. Perhaps some feel threatened by others, that it somehow reduces their own standing?"

Arthur knew he was talking about the likes of Eudora and the Vanes.

"I suspect that's why it suits the Erytheans to keep themselves to themselves," said Arthur. "How's the air looking?"

Ermitage tapped the gauge. "We have a little longer."

They continued along the riverbed.

"I should have said, in the event of an emergency, break the glass and swim up. There's a hammer there."

"Oh, thanks," Arthur said, frowning.

After a while there was a *whirring* sound, and Arthur looked up to see something like a boat hull.

"We're nearly there."

"At the village?"

"Patience, my dear old thing. We're close, but not yet. This is where we leave the SMEM for now." He turned sharply and they began climbing up the riverbank. "The wheel tread should get us up here."

The light above grew brighter and they soon broke the surface. But with a jolt the SMEM seized and they slid back a little. Ermitage tried to drive them forward, but the SMEM just shuddered. "Ah, I do believe we're stuck in the silt. Not a problem. I'll drop the anchor and . . ." He looked at Arthur with his glistening, beady eyes and stroked his beard. "Did I ever ask you if you can swim?"

Arthur noticed Ermitage's eyes flick to his missing arm. "Yes, of course I can."

"Good, because we need to swim for the bank. Watch out for river snakes, greebers, and anything with lots of teeth."

Arthur must've turned pale as snow because Ermitage put a hand on his shoulder and said, "Only joking!" But he laughed a strange, nervous laugh that told Arthur the contrary.

As the canopy was released, they both popped

their heads out. The air across the lake was beautiful and fresh, and Arthur breathed in a huge lungful. Waterfalls cascaded from great rocky riverbanks that went on into the far distance.

"We're a little farther away than I'd hoped, but let's swim for the bank, there by that waterfall, and go from there."

Before Arthur knew it, Ermitage had launched himself from the SMEM and was swimming like a fish toward the bank. Arthur shot after him, doing his best to keep up and kicking his legs furiously, not only to propel himself forward but also in the hope that anything that might be viewing him as dinner would get a heavy kick to the jaw first.

Soon Arthur found he could stand, and they made their way up the rocky bank next to the waterfall.

Arthur put his hand on his knee and took gulps of breath.

"Don't forget to look up!" said Ermitage.

When Arthur looked up, he saw something glistening high among the trees: great glass orbs that appeared to be part of the rock face beside the cascading streams.

"Are those houses?" he asked breathlessly.

"Indeed. Aren't they something?"

Only then did Arthur notice that beside the waterfall, children with sun-blushed skin, tight brown leggings, and rubbery ankle boots were playing and climbing, and there were what appeared to be some elegant-looking boats moored.

They had already been spotted, and a woman was heading their way. She was dressed in the same tight green trousers that he'd seen the Erytheans back on the *Aurora* wearing, and a fitted matching jacket. Her long, braided hair hung over her shoulder.

"Ermitage, we haven't seen you in two weeks! We feared you'd got washed away in the old-tech!" she laughed, and looked pointedly at Arthur, waiting for Ermitage to explain who he was.

"Oh . . . yes, this is Arthur; he's lost. I expect you've heard news of the Vornatanian crew, the Culpeppers?"

She nodded. "Of course. It's quite the intertown talk."

"We're on our way to the city and wondered if we could borrow a water-wing?"

"No," she said bluntly. "If you look to the north, you will see great clouds are forming. Another deluge is coming. Please be our guests, and when the waters are safe you can travel on."

"We're staying in one of the orbs?" Arthur said nervously.

Ermitage patted him on the back. "Fear not. They're completely watertight, so when the lake level rises, they offer quite the view!"

THE FLOOD

I**T WAS THE COLD** that dragged Maudie from the dream she was having, where she had been back on the sky-ship with Arthur and the others.

It wasn't a debilitating cold like she'd experienced in South Polaris, more an annoying shift in temperature. Somewhere in the misty stairway between sleep and awareness, Maudie realized the fire must've gone out, and everything felt wet.

She forced her eyes open. There was barely any light coming in from above . . . because water was tumbling through! After a moment of disbelief, she sprang into action. The cave was already full of water up to the ledge, and there was no way to retreat down to the entrance.

❋ 223 ❋

She drew quick, heavy breaths of panic. The stream of water was torrential—she could hardly see.

Without thinking, she hurried along the rock base as far as she could, feeling the walls for any ridges, hoping that perhaps she could climb out. She found a ledge not too far from one of the holes above and pushed herself up, then reached for another. The rocks were horribly slippery, and her heart pounded like a great piston as she forced her fingers to cling with a determined grip. When she reached for the next lip of rock, her fingers slipped across the surface and she almost fell. The water tumbled and roared, but she could make it if she just hung on.

Below, something moved in the water, long and lizardlike. It surfaced and seemed to fix its eyes on her, pointed teeth poking from its jaw. It wasn't as big as a crocodile, perhaps just the length of her forearm, but she was certain it could do some serious damage, and where there was one there could be more. She had to get out.

After several breaths, she looked up into the grim light, water cascading all around. Suddenly she realized that a face was peering down at her from the hole in the ceiling of the cave. It belonged to a small, bearlike creature, and it was clinging on to the side and reaching toward her.

In her surprise, she lost her grip and fell back into the water, spinning over and over in the relentless flow, so that she lost track of which way was up. Her lungs were tight, fighting for air.

After several powerful kicks, one of which she felt hit something she hoped was the water-lizard, she broke the surface and gasped for air, but the cave was filling up fast. Her heart thudded. If she could make it back to the opening, perhaps she could let the cave fill and get out, but could she climb through the rush of water without falling back to certain death in the water-filled cavern? Something brushed past her leg, and she yelped and kicked with all her might, fighting to get to the opening again, but the push of the incoming water was so furious that she could barely get close.

Looking up frantically, she again saw the bear clinging to the rock at the opening, its eyes big and staring intensely at her. She wondered if she was only imagining it now in her panic.

Perhaps the rain would stop, and she could hold on to a ledge until the water level receded? But it seemed to be getting fiercer by the moment. Terror held her in an icy vise.

The jewels in the cave walls shone like crimson stars and she had a strange, unbidden thought that if this was the end for her, at least it was in a beautiful place.

Never give up. That's what her father had always said; it was what Harrie said. And Arty.

Arthur. She *had* to see him again; she couldn't let this happen.

She put every effort she had into getting as close to the opening as possible and found another small ledge. She gripped it as though she had the strength of a mountain and found a lip of rock for her foot under the water. Something brushed past her again, and with a mighty heave she pushed herself two thirds of the way out of the water.

The hole was about six feet away; she needed to get higher. There was one of the jewels she could use as a handhold, so she pushed in with her feet and reached for it.

She made it.

Above, the small, bearlike animal kept watching with its urgent eyes, but Maudie forced herself to ignore it; if it was dangerous and that intense look meant it was deciding if she was its next meal, there was nothing she could do about it. Perhaps it was simply waiting for her to drown. Whatever it was didn't matter; she had to get out of the cave top. It was her only option.

She scanned the wall for another ledge. There was nothing. A thousand thoughts flooded her brain with every moment. If only she'd not fallen asleep in the cave; if only they'd not crashed the sea-ship; if only Eudora hadn't stolen their sky-ship with Arthur on it.

It was Eudora's fault. Everything was. Maudie yelled in her frustration, but the sound was lost in the torrent of water.

The bear disappeared. She'd probably frightened it away. Now she really was alone and about to die. The water was flowing at such a rate that it was making it almost impossible to hang on.

Suddenly the bear reappeared, hanging down into the cave somehow, reaching a strange little webbed hand toward her. It was trying to help!

She gripped for her life with one hand and let go with the other, stretching up to her unlikely rescuer, grunting with the effort and frustration.

But she lost her grip.

Maudie splashed back into the water and was pulled down by the current. She managed to kick to the surface, but tears of frustration and impending disaster were raging in her eyes as the power of the surge prevented her from swimming back toward the hole. She gave one last flurry of kicks, but she was caught in the cascade falling from above and was pulled beneath, whirling around and around in the flow.

Something brushed her hand. And a strange thought flashed through her mind that she might not have a choice between death by enormous lizard or death by drowning; it would be whichever got to her first. And it was almost funny that she was even contemplating this as she was pulled by the torrent.

But the thing, whatever it was, hadn't just brushed her hand; it grabbed and held her, and it tugged. Its grip was incredibly strong. Maudie needed air and tried to kick to the surface, but she was being dragged down. Perhaps it was the first bite of the lizard? She would've screamed if it hadn't meant losing what little breath was left in her lungs, but they were moving away from the torrent now and she was able to turn to see in the eerie pink light that it was the bear creature that had hold of her. It yanked her fiercely and she went with it, knowing she had little choice, her lungs burning to breathe. They surfaced in another small section of the cave and she gasped a lungful of air.

The creature kept hold of her arm, its eyes full of concern, not aggression. Something like gills contracted around its jawline. What *was* this strange animal? Some sort of water-bear? Could it be the creature Arthur had claimed to see back in Nova?

But there was no time to think, as the water was still getting higher. The water-bear pulled on her arm gently as though to say, *We need to go again,* and Maudie nodded. She took several deep gulps of air and they submerged. The flow was less turbulent, and they seemed to be going up into another cave section. They surfaced once more and again she gulped in air. It was a larger cavern, and Maudie thought perhaps they could stay here and wait out the deluge, but she could see that even here the level was rising.

Her companion grasped both her arms with its funny webbed hands, and it looked intensely into her eyes. It was trying to tell her something, and Maudie realized at that moment with absolute certainty that this creature was sapient.

Its eyes were telling her to trust it.

And she did. She didn't know why or how, but she felt it in her heart.

So she breathed in several more deep breaths and nodded, but the creature continued staring at her, so she took several more breaths, in the certainty that the water-bear was telling her to prepare.

They submerged once more and the water-bear towed her along, this time through a long tunnel. She could barely see, but there seemed to be fewer pink jewels in the walls. *Don't let go, don't let go,* she repeated in her head, but her lungs were squeezing for air again. Dizziness and panic were gripping her, and the faded pink light blotted away as she verged on blacking out. Yet she kicked on, and the small water-bear pulled with all its strength.

Suddenly there was light! Not the pink glow of the cave jewels, but the gray light of the storm. There was an opening ahead!

They surfaced and Maudie gulped the fresh air. The water-bear, still clutching her hand, pulled her up a bank of rock and out of the opening. Around was dense forest, enormous trees with trunks that six people could link arms around. Water cascaded from the sky at a rate unlike anything she had ever seen before in her thirteen years. She was already drenched from the caves, but the rain plastered her hair to her face and her clothes felt twice as heavy as the unyielding rain pushed down. The water was above her calves, and the water-bear's furry little snout was only just above the surface. It hurried her forward. It was clear that they weren't safe yet, and the water was still rising. Soon it was up to her thighs, and the water-bear tried to pull her along and swim at the same time, but she was too slow, so it climbed up her body and sat on her shoulder, looping its tail around her neck and pointing its clawed webbed paw

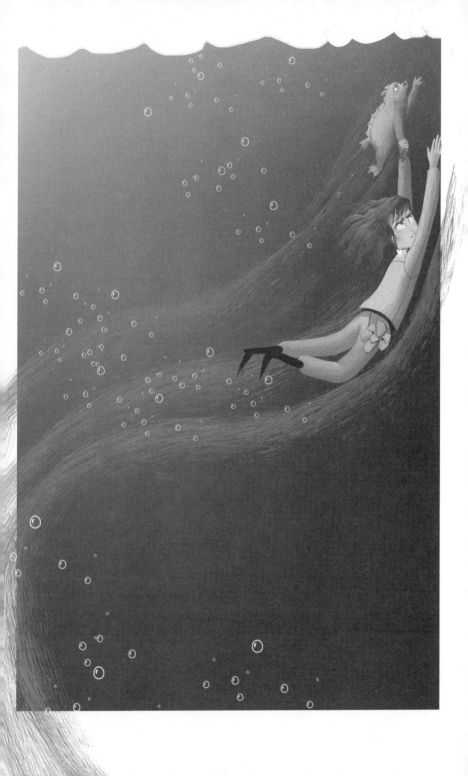

onward. The water was above Maudie's hips now and it was getting harder to move. Something moved close by—a fallen branch?

No, this had eyes.

Gold-slatted eyes fixed on them. A scaly, pointed tail flicked—it was the same kind of creature she'd seen in the cave: a giant lizard with a pointed snout, but this one was as large as her and it was coming for them with teeth bared.

The water-bear frantically pointed to a tree. She lunged for it and grabbed a branch, heaving them both up and finding a foothold. She yelped as she looked over her shoulder to see great jaws opening, a thousand knife-sharp teeth coming at her. With a mighty effort, fueled by a great rush of adrenaline, they were out of the water, the teeth snapping just inches from her, and she was climbing the tree. The water-bear jumped off and led the way from branch to branch. When Maudie looked down, she thought the water was catching up, but just when she thought there couldn't possibly be any more energy left in her body, she doubled her effort and reached for another branch, pushing down into her feet, up and up. And up.

They must've been higher than the rooftops and chime towers of Lontown, higher than the Geographical Society tower.

The water-bear had slowed a little, and Maudie took it as a sign that they were reaching a safe point. They must've been about two thirds of the way up these colossal trees. She paused with her feet on a great branch and clung to another, gasping for breath. Maudie risked a peek down to check the water, but it was now far below. Breathing out in relief, she looked around and gasped in surprise. There were hundreds of water-bears in the trees around her, hanging by their tails from branches, hugging the tree trunks and peeking over the top of what appeared to be something like huge birds' nests.

The water-bear that had saved her now wore an expression that looked incredibly like a smile and reached for her hand from above. She took its little webbed paw in hers and followed it up through the tree and into one of the nests. A canopy of leaves above sheltered them from the still-falling rain. Perhaps it had eased a little; Maudie couldn't be sure. She sank back into the nest and counted ten breaths, each one getting progressively calmer. The water-bear passed her a pawful of nuts and berries. She examined them, wary that they might be poisonous, but as though to show her there was nothing to fear, the water-bear ate a few.

The foods were sweet and wholesome, and with

each tiny bite, she could feel herself revive. The other water-bears had mostly disappeared back into various nests, but she noticed two water-bears in a nest looking down, slightly bigger water-bears than the one that had saved her. They didn't strike Maudie as being sapient like this one, but they did look a little concerned.

"Are they your parents?" Maudie asked.

For a moment Maudie wondered if the water-bear might answer, in the way the thought-wolves did through thoughts, but it didn't. Instead it took her hand and brushed the back of its own across it. It was furry, unlike its webbed areas and palms. Could that small action mean "yes"?

"So, they are your parents?" she said. Again, the water-bear brushed her palm with the back of its hand. "I think you are saying yes!" She smiled to herself; despite all the horrors of the past day, she felt safe for the first time. She lay back. The nest was lined with leaves and moss, and there were some of the glowing, pink jewels embedded in the sides. Her eyes suddenly felt uncontrollably heavy. The storm was passing, the rain slowing, and night was falling. The water-bear lay down close by. Maudie didn't want to sleep until the rain had completely stopped, but in this new land, who knew what was possible, or if it would ever end. However, the water-bear seemed relaxed, the rain finally petered out, and the clouds passed, leaving space for stars to soothe the sky. Only then did she allow herself to fall into a long, deep, healing sleep.

CHAPTER 21

WATERFALLS

ARTHUR AND ERMITAGE had been given their own orb house for the night. It was completely different from the old-tech houses, and as the water had risen in the deluge, the lights came on, which Ermitage said were driven by ion batteries charged by the waterfall, and it felt as though they were in a magical underwater kingdom. The orbs were perfectly watertight but had side escape pods as standard, which could detach and float until the waters subsided. Inside, the pods had special compartments to store food and keep it cool and fresh, and indoor gardens and even bathrooms. Arthur had snoozed lightly through the night, looking out at the underwater creatures swimming past, illuminated by the glittering lights of the pods, until the water levels dropped, and it was almost day again.

By the time Arthur awoke, many of the elegant-looking boats were out in the lake fishing.

"Ah, the water-wings," said Ermitage.

"Is that what Erytheans call their boats?" asked Arthur.

Ermitage nodded. "Well, this particular boat, which is their most common mode of transport. The rain and flood bring in nutrients from the canopy and it causes a feeding frenzy in the fish," Ermitage explained. "The Erytheans make good use of the post-deluge abundance."

They climbed down from the orb using ladders that crisscrossed the rock face.

Arthur called to Ermitage. "We can't just take a boat. Won't the people who live here be a bit, well, furious?"

"My dear, you're in Erythea now. Here things tend to be shared: houses, vehicles, food. Water-wings aren't possessions; they're part of life. If it's moored in a certain direction, it's a sign that it's free for whoever should find themselves with a need next."

"Wow! Imagine if Lontown was like that and full of sky-ships! You could just take one to get you wherever you like."

"There's lots we could learn from these people. If they'd let us."

"They're letting you stay here and learn, aren't they?"

Ermitage went very quiet for several moments. He looked at the ground, then sighed and said, "As I've said, that's because I've promised them that I'll never return to Lontown."

Arthur felt panic flood his veins. What if they made him stay here too? What if they didn't let him go back to Maudie and the others?

Ermitage patted him on the shoulder. "Don't worry about what hasn't happened yet. The Erytheans will already know you are here, so there is nothing you can do. Let's cross each bridge, or fallen log, as we go, shall we?"

Arthur nodded.

They had to walk a little upstream to find a free water-wing. They saw one tethered over on the other side of a small gorge.

"How do we get over? How about this?" Arthur indicated a fallen tree that spanned the gap. It was perfect. He put his foot on it but Ermitage grabbed his arm and pulled him back.

"Not so fast, old thing. I know you seem to have a particular liking for falling, but take a closer look. The only living things there are the vines growing around it; that tree looks rotten to me." He tore off a small chunk and it crumbled away.

"Oh, that was close! What do we do?"

Ermitage tugged on a nearby vine hanging from one of the great trees. "This seems quite secure."

There was a sudden squawk from above.

Arthur looked up. "Parthena! You're all right! You found me!" She landed in front of him and hopped into his arms.

"Ah, your sapient bird," said Ermitage, impressed. "She's a beauty indeed, and what an impressive wingspan." Then he took a run up and swung to the opposite side, shouting "Woohoo!" all the way.

Arthur shook his head. "I wish I could fly like you, Parthena." He stroked her head and set her on the ground. "Here goes nothing." He found a vine, made sure he gave it a great yank, then took a run up and . . . "Wahoooo!" He couldn't help himself.

He landed with a great crash on the other side.

Ermitage pulled him to his feet. "Up you get. Nothing damaged this time, I hope. Good."

Parthena flew over with just one flap of her wings.

The water-wing was more of a narrow platform than a boat. "You pull up the steering column like so . . ." Ermitage pulled up a thin metal rod with a handle on the end. "It's customary for the driver to stand, but passengers can sit. They have small, efficient engines underneath as part of the fin, or 'wing' as it's referred to—hence the name 'water-wing.' When you start to move, the momentum lifts the platform and it hovers a little above the surface of the water. The lack of friction means they are extremely fast. The propeller uses ion batteries powered by the falls. They stay charged for weeks!"

It struck Arthur that the water-wing was similar to Maudie's sky-ak, although this wouldn't be able to take off and fly away from the surface of the water for short bursts like hers could.

"Hop on," said Ermitage.

Arthur sat behind Ermitage and held on to the narrow lip of the water-wing. "Have you done this before?" he asked.

"Absolutely! Well, once or twice on my own."

Arthur gulped. "Parthena, perhaps it's safer if you fly above."

Ermitage twisted the handle at the top of the steering column and the engine started. As he pulled the column back, they were off, rising just a foot or so out of the water and speeding along the river with Parthena flying happily above.

"I think we should try to stay hidden from Eudora when we get there," Arthur called. "We'll say I was separated from the crew, that way we can observe what she's up to from afar."

Ermitage nodded. "If you think that's best."

Soon the river fed into an enormous estuary. Waterfalls cascaded into it all around, and at the far end was an unimaginably enormous waterfall that looked as though it could be as wide as the Uptown area of Lontown. As they neared it, Arthur saw that an enormous structure ran from top to bottom, part of the falls.

"Impressive, eh?" Ermitage called.

"What is it? Do people live there too?"

"It's not a habitation as such, more a great engine."

"Engine? Does it use pitch?"

"Great Wide, no! Erytheans wouldn't touch pitch. They see it as quite an affront to nature to dig huge chasms in the ground to find a fuel. They only use what they can, and what doesn't harm their land."

"How does it work?"

"Turbines turn in the water flow and make power."

"What's it making power for?"

Ermitage gave another wry smile. "Come on. Time to go up!"

CHAPTER 22

VALIANT

MAUDIE WOKE to bright sunlight. The water-bear was gone. Tentatively, she peered over the edge of the nest and into the forest below. The water had subsided, although she couldn't be sure if it had gone completely; it looked as though nothing much had happened. The leaves below were different shapes than when it was raining, now full and flat, lapping up any splash of sun they could reach. She could see other water-bears in the treetops, some just swinging happily by their tails, others climbing up and down, but there was no sign of her water-bear, the one that had saved her life.

There was a pile of berries and nuts beside her. The creature must've left them for her. She ate them, leaving half because she didn't want to presume it had left them all for her. In the daylight the pink jewels in the nest lost their glow and looked like ordinary gems—not that any gem was ordinary, but they'd lost the brilliant luminescence they'd held in the dark.

She heard rustling below and her water-bear climbed inside the nest. It held out a bell-shaped flower to her.

"Well, that's very pretty, and kind of you." She took it, smiled, and tucked it behind her ear.

The water-bear frowned curiously at her. Then it took another of the flowers and put it to its mouth, drinking the contents.

"Oh!" Maudie said, feeling embarrassed. "I was meant to drink it!" She retrieved the flower and sucked from the end of the bell, just as the water-bear had. Nothing happened, so the water-bear took it gently and demonstrated where to squeeze so that the bell opened. Sweet nectar water ran down her throat. It was utterly delicious and felt almost more thirst-quenching than water. For somewhere with so much water, it struck Maudie that thirst still seemed ever present. She examined the flower and made a note that she could use it as inspiration for a valve in her sky-ak engine, to keep it in the air longer.

The water-bear climbed on her shoulder again.

"Have you got a name?" she asked.

It didn't answer, of course. The water-bears didn't seem to make much noise at all. It took her hand and brushed the back of its hand across it.

"Does that mean yes?" But then she realized this time he had brushed in a horizontal rather than a vertical direction. The water-bear did it again.

"So this way is *no*," she said, gently taking his paw and sweeping it horizontally across her palm. "And this way is *yes*?" she moved it vertically.

The water-bear made the motion for *yes*.

She put a hand to her chest. "My name is Maudie."

It looked at her.

"Maudie," she repeated more slowly.

It seemed to smile.

"I think you need a name. Someone as brave as you deserves a good name, a name fitting of what you are." She thought for a while.

Then it came to her. "Valiant, I shall call you Valiant. Is that all right?"

After a moment, it took her hand and motioned *yes*.

"So, Valiant, the bravest water-bear in . . . wherever we are, how the clanking cogs am I going to find my family?" she said sadly. Her body ached terribly from being tossed around in the water and from fighting so hard to swim. Plus, she had no idea where she was in relation to the beach she'd washed up on. And she wasn't sure if she wanted to head down just yet, in case the great razor-toothed water-lizard was still lurking. She was safe for the moment, and again she imagined what Harriet would do or say; she would probably tell her to take a step back and analyze the situation. Look at what you have, where you are, the environment. Look for things that will help on the next part of the journey.

Maudie checked her tool belt and sighed heavily at the broken compass. At least she'd fallen asleep with her tool belt on in the cave, so she still had her strike-fire and her knife. Perhaps the water-bears would let her stay here for one more day, and she could watch the pattern of the sun from east to west; that would give her some sense of direction. She could eat, drink some more of the flower water, and rest her aching muscles, then move on with strength. She peered over the edge of the nest house once more. It was a long way down—she'd no idea how she'd managed to get this high—and she didn't feel quite ready to attempt the climb back to the forest floor. So that was decided.

* * *

There was no escaping the fact that rolled through Maudie's mind all day: the only way to truly get her bearings was to climb higher into the canopy so that she could see what was out there. She'd roughly figured out the compass points by tracking the sun, but that would be difficult to follow down below in the deep undergrowth, and she wasn't entirely sure how accurate she was, being in a completely different part of the Wide. Plus, if she was going to set off in the morning, she needed an idea of the shape of the land. She had decided to check on any incoming weather; the last thing she wanted was to get caught in another one of those awful deluges. Heights had never bothered her in the sky-ship or on rooftops, but she wasn't used to treetops, so she'd spent the morning creating a safety hitch with the few items she had on her tool belt—she was certainly glad now that she'd divided the rope. She could clip the hitch around a medium-sized branch that would comfortably take her weight.

Valiant disappeared for a while, along with most of the other water-bears, but when he returned, he carried fresh fruit in a stomach pouch that Maudie hadn't even spotted earlier.

"That's clever! I could do with one to keep my tools in," she smiled.

Then Valiant took out one of the pink jewels from the pouch and handed it to Maudie.

"Thank you, it's lovely." Maudie noticed many of

the other returning water-bears were carrying fruit and pink jewels.

Valiant took another gem from his pouch and pushed it into the side of the nest, then looked at Maudie. She found a space that looked fitting and pushed hers in too. "Well, that's going to look mighty pretty this evening!"

What curious creatures they were. So happy in their life: they could breathe in water, climb, build homes in the treetops, and then make them an even more magical place to be.

"Wait until I tell my brother Arty about you. When I find him, I'll bring him here, if that's all right?" Valiant took her hand and brushed her palm with a *yes*.

"Do you have a brother? They're your parents in the house above, aren't they?"

Valiant motioned *no*, then *yes*. Then he handed Maudie some fruit. She peeled it apart and shared it with him. It was refreshing and sweet, and she felt contented, but this couldn't last forever.

"I need to go higher into the canopy so that I can work out what to do next." She had no idea how much Valiant really understood, but his eyes seemed to tell her that, somehow, he understood quite a lot. He also looked slightly concerned.

"I've made a safety hitch, so I'll be fine. You probably don't trust my track record, but usually I don't get into too much danger . . . apart from when we crashed in the Ice Continent, and the time Arty and I sneaked on to Eudora's sky-ship and Tuyok almost died . . . and then there was when Arty fell in the frozen lake . . . and then at South Polaris when Eudora Vane was going to kill us . . . but apart from that."

Valiant gave a small whimper.

"You can climb with me, if you like?"

Up she went, extremely slowly, being careful of the branches she chose, clipping her safety harness methodically from one to the next. With every movement up, the light was getting brighter, until eventually she was almost at the top.

"One more branch," she whispered to herself as she clipped on her harness and took a step onto the branch. Carefully, she stood up.

Maudie wanted to call out to the wonder around her, but she had to control her breathing and stay focused. She was partway up the great jungle mountain range she'd seen from the beach. The treetops were a sea of emerald all around. In front of her was what she thought had been the tallest mountain when she was on the beach, but from here she could see that it had the shape of a volcano, although it was covered in foliage and looked totally dormant, thankfully; the last thing she needed was something else to worry about. The light was blindingly brilliant. There was a majestic view of turquoise sea to what she guessed was the west and she speculated that the beach she'd landed on was somewhere in that direction. In the distance she could just see a hazy mist and some jagged shapes that she surmised must be the islands of the darkwhispers.

She paused and gulped back the emotion that wanted to bring tears. Where were Harriet, Felicity, and Welby? Were they even alive? But there had been that strange scarlet bird: the actual fire-bird. She paused as the thought struck her. Of course she'd not really had time to think about it, what with being washed up on shore, almost drowned, attacked by a water-lizard, and rescued by an amphibian bear, but ... the ruby bird with wings and tail as red as fire, it had been real, she was certain, and it looked exactly like the bird on Octavie's ring. She put her hand to the pouch on her tool belt where she'd put the ring when she'd argued with Arthur.

It was the same!

She steadied herself. So why did the fire-bird come, then, and why had it gone straight to protect

Harriet? These were questions that she knew she had no hope of answering, but it didn't stop them rolling through her mind.

"Concentrate," she told herself, then she turned a little to take in more of the view. Beach and mountains, higher ground, low-lying areas, thick jungle as far as she could see—and silvery streaks not far away.

Carefully, she detached her binoscope from her belt. "Rivers!"

If you're ever stuck, follow the river. Rivers lead to people, her father had once said. If Arthur was here somewhere, she should follow the rivers. But she had to try to find Harriet and the others too. She drew her gaze back to the beaches and focused in as far as she could. Nothing looked irregular, but if Harriet and the crew had made it to shore this would probably be where they would have come in. Either that or they were stuck on the jagged rocks at the mercy of those vile creatures, and she doubted the fire-bird could have kept them at bay for long, and . . .

She shook the thought away.

She decided that if the weather looked fine she could try to head back to the beaches, then follow what looked like a gap in the trees farther south. A break in the trees would likely mean a river, although it was difficult to tell for sure from here. She looked back at the silver streams of light in the green far away. They were like great veins across the land.

Then she panned around and saw something that made her lose all concentration and footing—she slipped and fell!

In that moment she was certain that she would keep falling, but the harness bit and she wrenched to a stop, left swinging just beneath the leaf canopy. Her binoscope shot through the leaves and clattered horribly downward.

The water-bear had let out a squeal and jumped to the nearest branch, as Maudie swiftly put her feet on the branch below and righted herself. "Clanking cogs, that was close."

She took several very long breaths because what she'd seen through the trees had seemed so clear. There had been a boy in the canopy, and he had been watching her.

CHAPTER 23

TEMPESTRA

THE SOUNDS of the jungle were drowned out by the roar of the huge waterfall. As the water-wing neared, the true enormity of it was clear to Arthur and he was having a job shutting his mouth, which had dropped open in awe. High above, a colossal tower teetered on the precipice and down over the edge into the constant stream, so that the stone was at one with the falling water. It was a thing of beauty, with curved angles, pillared archways, and what looked to be enormous wheels turning steadily with the flow. Arthur couldn't imagine how such a thing would have been engineered.

"Impressive, isn't it?" Ermitage called to him.

All Arthur could do was nod. After a few more moments of standing and staring he shouted, "I never imagined a building could look like this. I mean the Citadel of Nadvaaryn is amazing, but this equals it. The city must be close. Where is it?"

Ermitage simply pointed. "Up."

"How are we supposed to get there?"

"See just beyond the veil of water, there's movement up and down in places?"

Arthur nodded.

"That's how. Come on, we need to get behind first."

They steered the water-wing to the side of the falls and tied it to a jetty.

"Careful, it can get slippery." Ermitage led him along the edge, close to where the waterfall hit the lake in a great tumultuous rush. "Of course, the Erytheans have highly adapted clothing for the environment. Microtechnology boots that grip the rock with hundreds of tiny suction pads. I must remember to ask for some while in the city; I lost my last pair in a deluge."

Arthur cried out as he almost slipped.

"See? Take it slow, old thing."

They edged along until they were in the space behind the falls. The noise was incredible; even with Ermitage shouting, Arthur wasn't entirely sure what he'd said. Ermitage pointed to a doorway, and Arthur followed him inside.

Arthur found himself in an empty white room with a few doors leading off. "Where is everyone?"

"The power supply technology is quite self-sufficient, so you usually only get a few people up top, and there should be someone by . . ."

They passed into another room, where they found a lady standing, as if waiting. She was dressed in smart green trousers and jacket. The material looked light and airy, and it had an iridescent quality. She said something to them in a different language. Ermitage tried to reply, but the lady just smiled and shook her head. "You are the Vornatanian. They said you were heading this way."

Ermitage glanced at Arthur. "I told you they keep a close eye on me."

"Who is your companion?"

"He's part of the Culpepper crew who landed several days ago. He got separated."

Her eyes narrowed, then she gave a nod and gestured for them to go into what appeared to be a glass elevator. They stepped inside, and after the woman pulled a lever, the elevator began to rise. They were just behind the flow of water, making it look as though a shimmery filter had been placed on the world, but as they rose, the elevator pod occasionally broke through the downward stream and they got brief glimpses of the great lake sparkling below. Arthur thought he could see beyond the jungle and the glistening of the sea. Eventually they reached the dizzying heights at the top and stepped out into a stone hallway. A man in similar green clothes nodded to them and took them forward.

"Will you be resting here, or will you go straight to the city? The rest of your crew are guests of the Professus Excelsis; I expect you are keen to be reunited." He observed Arthur curiously. "We can send word to them, so that they know you are safe."

"No need, we will take ourselves over directly," said Ermitage. "Let's surprise them, shall we, my dear old thing?"

They followed the woman through more stone hallways, until they came to the last door. Just when Arthur had thought it would be nearly impossible to surprise and shock him more, he saw the city.

Some distance away, in the middle of the vast, watery plateau in front of him, Tempestra rose like a great jewel that had been carved in ivory stone. There were domes not unlike those in Lontown, but more decorative, as the lines and curves imitated the twists and shapes of nature. Tall, majestic archways rose at different heights and bridges arced gracefully between structures. In the center was the tallest cupola, the highest point in the land, aside from the mountains that embraced the plateau to the north and east.

Arthur couldn't wait to take a closer look. A long jetty extended from the back of the power-falls into the lake plateau.

"We have to walk far out as the water-wings can't go too near the edge, at least not for us novice Erytheans!" Ermitage led the way along the wooden platform, his spindly legs half-skipping with excitement, and Arthur couldn't help but smile at him and this incredible place.

"Do they not have any sky-ships?" Arthur asked.

"My impression has been that they generally dislike the things. They call them thunder-clouds!"

Soon they were racing in another water-wing across the lake toward the city. Spray spattered Arthur's skin, cool and refreshing in the blistering heat, and Parthena joined them with a great squawk. She flew alongside them, tilting so that her wing tips brushed the surface of the water. As they neared the city, Arthur was reminded of the Citadel, but while the Citadel rose from the rock, Tempestra rose from the water.

Now that he was closer, Arthur could see that some of the rooftops were green, and the walls looked to be made of stone and glass. The city even continued beneath the water level!

"The water level ebbs and flows, just as it does in the rest of the land. It's not as extreme as in the western areas, but it still happens."

Ermitage steered them to the closest jetty and tied the water-wing to a post. It was clear they had been expected. A delegation was grouped at the far end. A tall, elegant-looking lady approached them, with shiny black hair and perfectly smooth brown skin. She wore a high-necked jacket, which looked to be made of the same light silky material as the previous woman's uniform, but it was intricately embroidered with bronze thread so that it looked as though vines wound in beautiful patterns around her torso and sleeves. She observed them with forest-green eyes.

"Welcome to Tempestra. My name is Tauria Verada, I am Professus Excelsis of Erythea."

Arthur wasn't sure whether he should bow or shake hands, but as she didn't move, he nodded his head respectfully and said, "I'm Arthur Brightstorm. I'm with the Culpepper crew."

She frowned. "Miss Culpepper hasn't mentioned a missing crew member?"

"I was separated from the group, but luckily I ran, or rather, fell, into Mr. Wrigglesworth."

"I will have someone inform Miss Culpepper that you have been found."

"No need," Ermitage chimed in. "We will surprise her. Where can we find her?"

"She has quarters in the visitors' sector. I'll ensure you both have rooms made up there as well." Tauria beckoned to a man waiting a short distance away.

He wore similar clothes and carried the same calm demeanor, almost as though he'd mastered the art of keeping the rest of his body absolutely steady while walking. His skin was pale, but his hair was dark and long like Tauria's. "I am Cassea. I will show you to your rooms." They followed him through a gabled entrance into a building and along beautiful corridors filled with lush plants and drinking fountains, so it felt as though a piece of the forest was inside the city, or vice versa. Every part of the stone walls and ceiling was carved with vines, leaves, and other natural forms. It had both an ancient and a modern feel at the same time, and there was a calmness in the white stone and greenery. Every so often they would pass an opening to a courtyard filled with an orange grove, or with palms, and seats where people sat reading, writing, and drawing. The place filled him with awe.

Arthur's room was just as impressive, and Ermitage was put in the room next door. "You are free to come and go as you please here," said the man. "I can take you to the rest of your crew now, or perhaps you would like a tour, or some refreshments?"

Arthur wasn't yet sure what to do if he saw Eudora. He needed time to think and speak to Ermitage. "I think I'll rest for now, thank you."

It felt good to have his own space again, but also

to know that he at least had Ermitage close by. But what was he going to do next?

"Your crew will be dining this evening with Tauria; you will be most welcome to join them after you have rested. Call for me if you need anything." Cassea dipped his head and walked toward the door.

"Excuse me," Arthur called after him. "How do I do that?"

Cassea smiled and put out his hand flat. A white butterfly flew from the wall and landed on his hand. He spoke quietly to it, then the butterfly flew to Arthur. He instinctively put out his own hand for the butterfly to land on.

"Simply hold out your hand, and a sapient butterfly will come. Tell it your news, who you wish the news to reach, and it will relay it."

Arthur couldn't believe it! The tiny voice had come from the butterfly!

Cassea left and Arthur lay on the huge bed in the middle of the room. Through the window he could see Parthena happily circling above the lake plateau.

"What an incredible place," he said to himself. But he couldn't relax for long; he had to make a plan and expose Eudora.

He sat up, an idea forming in his mind.

CHAPTER 24

FLORIAN

AFTER ANOTHER NIGHT sleeping in the water-bear's nest, Maudie decided she'd been seeing things and that the boy had been a figment of her imagination; she'd probably been thinking of Arthur, so her brain had conjured it up. It had rained during the evening, not a patch on the previous day, but it had still set her heart hammering. She couldn't sleep until it stopped, which thankfully wasn't too long. Today the weather was fine and there wasn't a single cloud in the sky. Below, the ground layer appeared to be fairly well drained. Valiant's parents had come to sit close by.

"I have to go now," she said to Valiant. "Thank you for saving me. I'll always be grateful, and part of me wishes I could stay in this place forever, but . . ." She sighed, not relishing the thought of returning to the dangers below. "I need to find my own family." She stroked them all goodbye, then she gave one last look at Valiant and began the climb down the tree. Valiant tried to follow her for a little way and kept jumping on her shoulder, but she eventually took his webbed paw in hers and made the motion for *no*. "You have parents, and take it from me, that's a lucky place to be. You belong here in your beautiful treetop haven."

Valiant took her hand and signed *no*, three times in succession, then kept his paw there.

"I really must go." Maudie smiled sadly and brushed her eye with her free hand, then she placed Valiant on a branch and peeled her hand away. The water-bear gave a sad exhale, then put a hand in his pouch and passed her one of the pink gemstones.

"To keep?" she smiled.

Valiant signed *yes*.

At least having the stone would be like taking part of this place and Valiant with her on her journey forward. She looked into his bright, intelligent eyes and said, "Thank you again for saving me. I'll never forget you." Then she continued down, focusing on her route and trying to contain the horrible lump in her throat. She took one last look back to see Valiant's face, then carried on into the jungle. Now she was, yet again, utterly alone.

* * *

Maudie had forgotten just how stifling the forest floor was. She felt as if every tiny insect wanted a nibble of her. Worse still, she couldn't see any of the water flowers Valiant had given her and she was starting to feel thirsty. She'd passed the caves, and for one chime she was certain she was heading for the other beaches, and by the next chime she'd lost all confidence. She was gathering more cabbage palms and looping them around her neck to dry—when something caught her eye.

Her heart leaped to her mouth.

Someone—or something—was there. She was *certain* she'd just seen a face through the trees, but now there was nothing. She carried on with the distinct feeling she was being followed. Perhaps it was Valiant? She would catch a glimpse, and then as quick as a blink it would be gone.

After a while, she decided she needed to try to climb and get her bearings again, and it would also give her a chance to scan the surrounding forest for whatever it was that was shadowing her.

She was about to unclip her harness from her belt when something launched at her. She threw her hands up defensively and kicked out, but she tumbled to the ground.

Looking down at her was the face of a boy.

"Get off me!" she yelled.

The boy frowned and blinked huge, bottle-green eyes at her. He shook his head as though to dislodge an incorrect thought.

"I . . . I thought you were from the city. . . . But you speak Lontonian to me. Are you practicing?"

"Practicing what?"

"Lontonian."

"Of course I'm not!" she said indignantly.

"Wait, why *are* you speaking Lontonian?" He peered into her face. "Where are you from?"

"Where are *you* from?"

"I'm from here. You're . . . *not*."

She pushed him off. "It's very rude to jump out on someone. You were fortunate I didn't have my knife in my hand—I might have stabbed you."

"No, you wouldn't have."

"How do you know?"

"Because I saw no knife in your hand before I jumped." He reached out and touched her clothes. "Such strange items."

She stiffened and tilted her head back a little. "Well, yours are very . . . green."

"Do you live in the west? Are you Vornatanian?"

"I am, and what of it? Do you live here?"

"Of course I do. Yet you speak to me as though this is *your* home! How did you get here?"

". . . Well, that bit's complicated. Is there a town close by?" she asked hopefully. If there were more people, she might find Harriet and the others.

He looked at her curiously. "There's a treetop town in the east. You won't find any Erytheans living around here. It's too volatile."

"Then what are you doing out here?" she said suspiciously.

"Again, you talk to me as though I am the intruder! What's all that on your belt?"

She slapped his hand away. "My tools."

"Let me see."

"No."

"This looks broken," he said, reaching for the compass.

"Well, there's nothing I can do about that at the moment without my other tools and I'm pretty certain that you can't help me mend it either." She flashed a slightly sarcastic smile, then found herself scowling as she remembered how she'd almost fallen out of the tree. "So it was you that I saw in the canopy?"

He grinned.

"You made me fall."

"Was I anywhere near you?"

"Well . . . no, but—"

"Then how could I make you fall?"

"You scared me."

He squinted. "I'm not sure you are the scared sort. Clumsy, yes, and so noisy in the jungle." He shook his head and tutted.

She huffed. "You can speak the same language as me." It suddenly struck Maudie that she was in a continent unknown to those of Vornatania, yet he was able to speak their language, so it must be that the people here knew of them. Was it because of Ermitage Wrigglesworth, she wondered?

"We speak many languages." He shrugged. "The languages of the many islands, the language of the southernmost reaches of Erythea, the language of the ancients, the language of the forest." The boy turned his face to the sky, formed his mouth into a large O shape, and called out, a strange, hooting howl that was so loud it made Maudie jump.

Moments later, a returning howl sounded from somewhere in the distance.

"That's . . . er . . . impressive," Maudie said.

"What are you doing here? How did you get past the angariis?"

"Angariis?"

He narrowed his eyes, and she could see that he was weighing up whether she was just a lost girl in the jungle or a potential threat. His frown told her he still hadn't decided.

"We weren't looking for your land. We crashed." She felt content that she wasn't lying to him; after all, they had been looking for Arthur, technically.

"And you were separated? Are the others alive?"

"I hope so."

"I need to take you to the city. It's the way of the book."

Maudie's heart sank. "The way of the book? Do you mean law?"

He nodded.

"What if I don't want to?"

He shrugged. "If you're sure you can survive a day without being eaten—or another deluge."

Her skin quivered.

"But you can suit yourself. I thought you might want to look for your people." And without giving her a chance to respond, he shrugged, turned, and jumped up into another tree.

"Hey!"

"Good luck, foreign girl."

The branch the boy had jumped to looked impossibly far for her to reach. She braced, gritted her teeth, pulled back, then leaped.

He went higher up the tree, so she followed. Then across to another tree, and higher still. She was now high enough to get hurt badly if she fell. "Come on," she willed herself.

Vines trailed all around her; perhaps she could tie one to herself? She caught a glimpse of the boy several trees away now. "Wait!"

He glanced back and she thought she saw a smirk.

Under her breath she hissed, "Clanking cogs!" then grabbed the closest vine and leaped.

She landed clumsily on the next branch and for a terrifying moment of indecision her hands wavered between hanging on to the vine for dear life and letting go to grab any part of the tree she'd landed on. She yelped and lunged for the branch, stumbling and falling, legs on either side so that she ended up hugging it.

"I'm OK!" she shouted—not that the boy had shown any concern whatsoever. But the boy might be her only chance, so she had to keep up with him. Branches rustled and cracked a few trees ahead. She steadied and stood, looking for another vine. This time she managed to land closer to the trunk and at least didn't fall.

The boy peeped his head from around the other side of the tree, making her cry out.

"Stop scaring me!" she snapped.

"I didn't think you'd actually follow me up! I was going to come back for you." He was looking at her as though she was quite deranged. "You understand that you need to come with me to the city?"

She nodded.

"But I need to go to the treetop town first. I think you'd be better off a little lower to the ground."

"I'm fine, but if you insist."

"You move through the trees with the grace of an oversized water-lizard. Come." He held out his hand, but she ignored it and looked for the best route down.

"I'll have you know, I'm very good on the rooftops of Lontown. I'm just not quite used to these trees yet, but it won't take long."

"So, you *are* all as directional in your thinking as we've heard."

"What do you mean?"

He didn't answer and swung down to a lower branch.

She hurried after him, taking a similar route but trying to do it a little differently.

"Stubborn. Thinking you know best."

She put her hands on her hips, but felt unbalanced, so she leaned one hip on the tree. "Not at all."

"You are clumsy with nature."

"No, I'm not. *We're* not."

He continued on until they were at ground level. All his movements were precise and perfectly balanced.

"You have dug great chunks from your hills to make your sky-boats fly."

His look was bemusement rather than disgust.

"Not *everyone* does that."

"And your main city is more brick than trees."

"Well . . ." But again, he was right.

"You think you are forward, but really you are behind."

"What's that supposed to mean?" She slipped and almost fell again. "I'll have you know we have a great universitas and inventors who are revolutionizing sky-ship exploration."

He was moving faster, darting through the

undergrowth. "In Tempestra you will see what real progress is."

She wished she had her sky-ak right now. That would shut him up. Maudie decided to keep quiet, for fear she'd yell at him again, although she didn't have a choice in it: the boy was moving at such a pace she could barely draw breath.

"I hear you call the great lands First, Second, and Third. Yes, you Lontowners like to think you are at the top of the mountain."

The boy might be her best chance for survival right now, but he was rapidly becoming her least favorite person. "Now wait just a chime!" She sprinted after him and reached for his arm, but in her urgency she slipped and went tumbling over, bashing her elbow badly. It might have made her cry if she hadn't been so cross. She gritted her teeth. "We've made mistakes and are learning and improving all the time."

The leaves around them stirred in the breeze.

"I'm sorry. I was teasing too much. Are you hurt?"

She shook her head and pressed her lips together tightly. Crouching down beside her, he gently examined her arm. "Bruised but not broken. What's your name?"

"Maudie. I'm a Brightstorm," she said proudly.

"I'm Florian." He observed her. "Rest here a moment."

In a flash he was scurrying up a nearby tree.

"What are you doing?" she called after him.

"Getting you something for the pain."

He pulled off a piece of bark. "Here, chew this, it will help."

She looked at him strangely, then decided to give it a go. It was horribly bitter.

"Where are your family?" he asked.

The words brought a lump to her chest. She pulled her shoulders back.

"Did you come past the angariis on your *own*?"

"Not quite, we crashed and . . ." Again she quelled the explosion of worry in her stomach. "And I don't know what happened to the others yet. We don't want any trouble. We're just looking for a missing explorer. He was coming this way and, well, we thought he was dead, but we found out he wasn't. Well, I didn't, my brother . . ." She paused for a long breath. "At least he was certain there was more to it, and I, well, I didn't listen, and we left him, and then this awful woman," she stared into the large green eyes of the boy, "I mean, *really awful* woman, well, she stole our sky-ship and Arthur was still on board and they were coming here, and I don't know what happened to him and—"

The boy moved a bit closer. He half smiled in a way that indicated he felt bad for her. "I'm sorry." He thought for a moment. "I need to take you to the city. I'll be going against the rules if I don't, and perhaps they can help."

Maudie nodded. Presuming that Eudora Vane and Arthur had made it through the darkwhispers, they would likely head for the city, or would have been found and taken there.

"We can search as we travel."

"Will we be in awful trouble for being here?"

He shrugged. "We've only had one other come from your lands recently."

She frowned. "Not Ermitage Wrigglesworth?"

"Yes, that's him."

She couldn't believe he was alive, and in this land after all!

"We head east. The treetop town will be safe if the rains come and a good place to stay for the night."

They walked through the forest for many chimes until it was late in the afternoon and then reached a place where Florian stopped and declared simply, "Here we are."

Maudie looked around. There was nothing apart from the usual forest tree trunks. "I don't see a town," she said dubiously.

"Look harder," he said.

CHAPTER 25

EVIDENCE

THE WARDROBE in Arthur's room contained some of the green trousers and tops he'd seen many Erytheans wearing. They looked too tight for him, too hot to wear perhaps, but he decided to give them a try as his own clothes were tired and ripped. After a bath in the most enormous tub he'd ever seen, it was time to explore the city and see what Eudora was up to, and blending in would be the best way.

When Arthur put the trousers on, he was amazed to find that the fabric was strangely cooling as it touched his skin. He rolled up the right sleeve of a green smock top and put it on. Again, it was incredibly refreshing to wear and comfortable to move in. He ran his fingertips over the intricate leafy pattern. He wondered what Lontowners would make of this new fashion!

He knocked for Ermitage next door, but when he answered, Arthur barely recognized him. His beard was trimmed, his mossy coat had gone, and he wore a smart, green, embroidered smock and trousers.

"My dear old thing, you're like a new pin!" Ermitage said, slapping Arthur on the arm.

"Er . . . you too! I'm going to look around and see if I can find Eudora. You've been here before, so I thought you might help me look around? Cassea offered, but I don't want him to suspect anything yet."

Ermitage nodded. "I don't know the city well, but they gave me a good tour when I arrived, so I'm sure I can get us about."

They moved through walkways of intricate latticework between buildings, and along corridors where small rivers twisted the length.

"The library sector is down here."

Arthur wondered what sorts of books they would have here. Stories of their history, of the plants, the storms, the darkwhispers . . .

"I should say libraries," Ermitage corrected. "They span five levels."

"Five levels of libraries?" said Arthur in amazement.

"Their whole society values learning above everything. They believe that the only true wisdom is in knowing you know only a little and striving to learn more, so yes, libraries are an important feature of the city."

It would be the place that Arthur would love to explore first, but possibly not the most likely place to find Eudora Vane.

They took an ivory spiral staircase upward; it opened out above the lake before going back inside again. Now that they blended in with their new clothes, the city people that they passed smiled at them as they did at other Erytheans.

"This is the intelligence arena, where people come to share advancements and knowledge from around Erythea and further afield."

It was a large space with a fountain in the center, with views through pillared archways to the mountains and forests all around. Groups of Erytheans sat on benches or stood chatting in groups.

Ermitage paused and leaned in toward Arthur. "I know this because I was quite the talk of this room for some time, and the agents tend to congregate here when they return."

"Agents?"

"Erytheans who go out into the Wide. Agents make it their business to blend in and integrate, and they report back all the time."

There were white butterflies resting on the walls of the intelligence room. He wondered what messages and secrets they had heard.

"Let's go to the market area," Ermitage tapped his stomach. "It's just through here. There's a huge sector devoted to schooling on the east side, and . . ."

Arthur pulled Ermitage to a stop. He'd heard a voice. A voice that chilled him, the honeyed tone masking so many heartless intentions.

Eudora Vane.

". . . Wonderful, yes, that's almost the correct shade. It needs to come down a tone."

Slowly, Arthur crept to the door where the voice was coming from and paused outside.

"I believe that these are the fabric technology rooms," whispered Ermitage.

Arthur cautiously peeked through a crack in the door. The room was busy with people stitching and working.

"But, Miss Culpepper, the traditional color is green for a reason; it not only acts as camouflage in some of the more dangerous areas of the forest, but it also symbolizes our unity with—"

"Malarina, that is your name, isn't it?" said Eudora sweetly.

"Marinya," the woman corrected.

"You must remember that things are different in the Wide, and that it is time to embrace something new. What harm can it do to try it, Malarina?" said Eudora.

The woman smiled awkwardly.

"I'm sure there must be something you can do to enhance the color. Perhaps a plant of the forest with the correct pigment? Or a beetle?"

Arthur rolled his eyes. He couldn't bear the thought of the Erytheans thinking this was Harriet Culpepper. The real Harriet wouldn't care about the precise shade of what she wore, let alone crush beetles for it.

"Now, would you point me in the direction of the Erythean map archives? I should very much like to acquaint myself further with the geology of the land. It's an absolute passion of mine."

"Of course, Miss Culpepper. It is in the library sector, in the geology rooms."

"Wonderful. Now where is my assistant, Mr. Smethwyck?"

Quickly, Arthur retreated from the doorway as Eudora turned his way. He pulled Ermitage down the corridor just as Smethwyck's smarmy tones sounded from around the corner.

"In here," Arthur said, pulling Ermitage into the

closest room. It had high arched ceilings and the walls were filled with stone shelves.

Inside, a young man approached and spoke in Erythean to them. Arthur smiled and nodded.

The man frowned and said something else in Erythean, then pointed to Arthur's feet.

When Arthur looked blankly, Ermitage said, "*Methia, etia.*"

"What did you say?" Arthur whispered, as the young man crouched and studied Arthur's feet.

"I've picked up a few words in my time here and I believe that means *shoes, please.*"

Ermitage nodded toward the shelves where numerous pairs of different green and brown shoes were neatly stacked.

"Oh . . . right."

As they made their way to the library sector, Arthur couldn't help but feel rather thrilled at his new footwear. "They feel like a second skin!" he said. "And so grippy. As though I could climb a horizontal wall. They'd be great for Lontown roofs!"

"Here, I believe this is the geology room."

The room was huge, with rows of stone shelves holding large books, some as tall as Arthur.

There were people studying at various tables. They caught sight of Eudora sitting at one of the large tables with Smethwyck, so Arthur hurried down an aisle close by. Carefully, he parted some books so he could spy on them.

Eudora flicked absently through the pages of an old green book. "There must be gold here. We know that the agents have gold rings, and if we could find the source and retrieve as much as possible before we return, it would both be worth a fortune and give the people an appetite for what is possible here."

"I've tried to investigate the source, but no one here seems to understand our word for gold, Eudora."

She tutted. "You're not trying hard enough. Find ways of persuading them. Pay them if you have to."

"I've tried. Sovereigns hold no value for them. That's not how it works here."

"Everybody has their price. And if they won't be persuaded, then we'll return with enforcements. They won't know what's hit them."

Smethwyck hushed his voice. "We'll need to get back through those creatures. It's not going to be easy."

"It will be in the *Aurora*. We got past on the way here."

"Barely." A bead of sweat trickled down Smethwyck's forehead.

Eudora narrowed her eyes. "If you're too scared,

then I'll leave you here and promote someone who isn't."

Miptera took flight from Eudora's shoulder and gnashed her mandibles at Smethwyck.

"Oh, wipe that distressed look from your face." She lowered her voice a little. "I've been asking questions. The Erytheans are very obliging to one of their own; the long-lost relative has returned, and they'll bring me anything I ask for. All I have to say is how wonderful it is here, and how I'd like to stay forever, and they answer all my questions. It turns out that there is a creature here that protects Erytheans from the darkwhispers. A fire-bird."

"From the myth?"

"It's the largest bird in the world, and no one knows how old it is. We'll need the right equipment to catch it, of course . . . and a suitable cage. Put it on the list for when we return."

Smethwyck began scribbling in the pages of a journal.

"We could use it to help protect us on the way back, perhaps. We could take an Erythean with us as back-up—that seam-master, perhaps. She could at least be useful to me in Lontown."

One of the books on the shelf clunked forward.

Eudora whipped her head up, but Arthur was swift to duck.

"Let's get out of here!" Arthur whispered, pushing Ermitage ahead. They hurtled up the shelf aisle.

"This way," Ermitage said in an urgent hiss, pulling Arthur to a different door and into the adjoining language library.

From there, they hurried back to Ermitage's room.

"We need to expose her. You heard what she's planning. And if they catch on to her, they'll believe it's Harriet responsible."

"But we have no proof that she's not Harriet. It'll be our word against hers and her crew's."

"We do have proof!" Seeing Miptera was just what Arthur had needed. "Her tattoo. Did you notice how she keeps her sleeves long?"

Ermitage thought for a moment. "Yes . . . I daresay that could work."

"Cassea said they'll all be dining with Tauria Verada this evening—that's when we'll do it."

* * *

Arthur and Ermitage left early for dinner and made their way up rounded stairways to the large, open hall where arched windows let in a welcome breeze.

Arthur styled his hair differently to remain as

inconspicuous as possible, and he wore both sleeves of his shirt long to try to disguise the fact that he had one arm; if Eudora's crew saw that, it could be an instant giveaway. Ermitage wore a green, brimmed hat.

"It'll draw attention to you, Mr. Wrigglesworth."

"Nonsense. It keeps my face in shadow," Ermitage said, tipping it to a rakish angle and admiring himself in a window's reflection.

There were already some professors in the dining area chatting in groups, but there was no sign of Eudora Vane yet.

"Come on, let's sit here." Arthur smelled Eudora's sickly sweet perfume before he saw her.

"Harriet, won't you sit beside me?" said Tauria as she walked into the room, closely followed by Eudora. "I'd like to tell you some more about our secrecy pact and perhaps a little more about your heritage."

"That would be an honor," Eudora said brightly.

The numerous professors and crew began taking seats. Arthur had persuaded Ermitage to remove his hat and store it under the table, but they tried to stay locked in conversation so that their faces were hidden.

Soon, dishes of food were brought into the room: coconut rice, fragrant vegetables, and an array of colorful fruit. The room became a thrum of eating and discussion, but the sound of Arthur's heart beating echoed in his ears. When would be the moment? It had all seemed like a great plan, but now that they were here, it seemed too big, too much to do on his own. . . . He had Ermitage beside him, but usually Maudie was there. He thought back to Nova and what Eudora had planned to do to them, her cruelty overwhelming him. Before he knew it, he was on his feet, pointing.

Soon everyone in the room had stopped what they were doing and were looking at him.

Eudora's eyes widened.

Before he could question himself, the words tumbled from him. "This woman isn't Harriet Culpepper. She's an imposter!"

"I'm sorry?" said Tauria. "Did you just say that this isn't Harriet Culpepper?"

Eudora laughed breezily. "How ridiculous."

"That's exactly what I said."

Tauria looked at Eudora then back to Arthur. "But you're a member of Captain Culpepper's crew?"

"Yes."

"And you flew in on the Culpepper sky-ship."

"Yes, but they didn't know I was there."

"So you are a stowaway?" Tauria said, narrowing her eyes.

"No . . . it wasn't like that. Harriet Culpepper,

that is, the *real* Harriet, is back on Nova. Her sky-ship was stolen by the woman you believe to be Harriet. That woman."

Tauria's frown deepened and she looked back at Eudora. "Do you know this boy?"

Eudora nodded. "I do. But you mustn't blame him for his confusion. The boy lost his father last year and he has never been the same. He doesn't know what he's saying."

Arthur suddenly realized that Ermitage hadn't said a word. "Tell them who she really is, Mr. Wrigglesworth."

Eudora's mouth parted widely at the realization that Ermitage was also in the room.

"Well, er, yes . . . the boy came on the ship," he stuttered, "and . . . I helped him get here, and he's right, she's—"

"She's not Harriet Culpepper!" Arthur said fiercely. "The Culpepper symbol is two swallows in flight. This woman doesn't have it—she's Eudora Vane of the Vane family! Show them your tattoo, Eudora."

"This is quite ridiculous. I shouldn't have to prove who I am in such a humiliating way. And on the accusation of a stowaway boy." Eudora stood up.

"See, she won't show you!" Arthur said, starting to feel triumphant.

Tauria put a gentle hand on Eudora's arm. "Captain Culpepper. Surely it would be a swift way to quash this accusation so that we can all carry on with our meal?"

The beginning of a grin spread on Arthur's lips. His heart raced.

"Very well," Eudora said, thin-lipped, not taking her eyes from Arthur's. She rolled up her sleeve, and . . .

There was the tattoo—two swallows in flight.

CHAPTER 26

TREETOP TOWN

MAUDIE'S ATTENTION was caught by unusual shapes around the trees, spiraling upward.

"Is that a staircase?" she breathed.

Florian smiled. "In the forest you must always remember to look up."

The stairways twisted above as high as she could see, disappearing into the canopy. Florian pulled her over to one and hopped onto the first step. "Come on, we can rest here for the night, and there is someone I'd like you to meet."

"What is this place?"

"Althuria, or some call it the treetop town."

They ascended the spiral stairs, formed from intricately entwined branches, into the understory and up through archways of vines.

"It's incredible. Like natural engineering," Maudie said dreamily.

Soon light began piercing in larger spears through the canopy, and structures became visible in the upper layer of the trees. Her father had made a tree house in the garden of Brightstorm House back in Lontown when she was young. Her skin still prickled when she remembered him letting her use the tools from her mother's tool belt that had been left to her, how their hands had sawn and hammered and crafted the small house in the garden tree. She laughed to herself; how that tree would look like a miniature sapling compared to these great trees. The whole grand parlor of Brightstorm House would fit inside one of these trunks!

Now she could see that there were numerous buildings in the canopy layer. They enclosed the branches yet at the same time looked to be part of the trees, as though they had naturally grown that way: nature and construction working in unity.

"They're so beautifully crafted," Maudie said, staring in wonder at the pointed archways for the windows and doors, marveling at how the connecting bridgeways crisscrossed.

"It's simply incredible."

There were people in the treetops, crossing the bridges, moving through the archways. Maudie's frame stiffened; what if they didn't want her here?

"You're with me." Florian smiled, reading her thoughts. "You have nothing to fear. Come."

He led her up and across a bridge. He smiled and greeted the people he passed, exchanging words in a language Maudie didn't understand, but it had a beautiful ring to it.

They stopped before one of the treetop houses. "My sister lives here." Florian looked at Maudie. He bit his lip.

"What is it?"

"I need to let you know that she might not know who I am. . . . She has problems remembering."

Maudie frowned and nodded. Tentatively, she followed Florian inside.

"This is Herminia." He gestured to a young woman who was sitting at a table screwing together what looked to be some sort of light. Her dark brown hair was intricately braided down both sides, and she had high cheekbones and wide green eyes. "*Herminia, pre dada istea, Maudie Brightstorm.*"

Herminia frowned and looked between them, the look of someone trying to work something out.

It was similar to how Arthur appeared when he was grappling with something from Welby's lessons, but it was as though she was trying to work out not only Maudie but Florian too.

"*Istea manina, Florian*," he said slowly, and Maudie saw a sadness in his eyes that she recognized. It was the sadness she'd carried since she'd been separated from Arthur.

Florian took some fruit from inside his bag and held it out to her, his hand trembling. Herminia stared at the fruit, then at Florian.

"*Istea manina*," he said softly.

Like the unfurling of a new bud, a smile of realization grew on her lips and in her eyes. "Florian?"

"Yes," he said, grinning broadly at her.

Herminia cut the fruit and shared it, and they sat on the floor eating. Maudie was quiet while the siblings continued speaking. Mostly it was Florian talking while Herminia listened like a child enraptured by a story, even though she was clearly several years older than him.

Florian glanced across. "I'm sorry, Herminia doesn't speak Lontonian. She used to, but . . . well." He smiled sadly. "I've just asked her if any strangers have been here in the last few days, but she says they haven't, although I'm afraid she may have forgotten. I'll ask at some of the other houses too."

Outside, dusk had fallen. Florian put something that looked like a power cell into a receptacle and a beautiful golden light filled the room.

"Wow, what is that?"

Florian thought for a moment. "We don't have a word in your language, something like water-energy-keeper?"

"Well, whatever it is, it's fascinating! Quite different from our pitch lights back home. I'd very much like a closer look . . ." but her voice faded as she noticed numerous other lights igniting in the treetops. She went to the arched opening and stared out in astonishment. There were hundreds of treetop houses and the stairways and bridges all glimmered with lights. It was utterly breathtaking.

Florian held out his hand to her and smiled. "Come."

He led her up a staircase that went even higher, until they emerged above the leaves onto a platform. Stars glimmered in the indigo sky, and, despite her anxiety about Arthur and the others, Maudie couldn't help but feel reconnected with them in this moment, wherever they were. She could almost feel that she was on the deck of the *Aurora*, flying into the night.

After a while, Florian said, "Is it a big world out there?"

Maudie looked across at him, and in the golden light of the platform she could see so much in his face: sadness and yearning. It reminded her of Arthur. She nodded. After a while she said, "Is your sister . . . all right?"

He turned to face her. "You flew through the darkwhispers to get here."

"Yes."

"My sister wanted to be an agent."

"What's that?"

"Erythean agents keep watch on the outside world and report back to the city."

"Oh," she said, thinking of the people on Nova.

"She was refused. The city professors sensed that her intentions were driven by her own wants rather than the interests of Erythea."

"But she only wanted to see the Wide?"

He shrugged. "One night, she decided she would go."

"Your sister was caught by the darkwhispers, wasn't she?"

He nodded. "She was sailing toward them, and she knew the fire-bird would protect her, but she'd been followed by a group of agents who had seen her leave.

The fire-bird can only protect so many of us, and it will always protect the group with the most Erytheans. My sister was separated from them in the cliffs."

He was quiet for a while.

"By the time they found her, she had no memories at all . . . she didn't even . . . she didn't even know my face. I'm helping her build the memories. I come here when I can and tell her stories of when we were growing up, how she taught me to climb and find the pampa fruits close to the water-bear habitat."

"You were gathering fruit when I saw you?"

He nodded. "The stories help her remember. She sees and tastes the fruit and it helps bring things back. Sometimes she will remember a small detail, adjusting the water-wing with me or something. We always liked to adapt them and make them faster, adding sails and things. Some days she remembers nothing at all. I try to visit when I can, but the professors think my language skills are best nurtured if I am based in the city."

"I'm sorry this has happened to her. To you." Maudie thought about all the memories she shared with Arthur, experiences that only they could recall, things that united them in joy, discovery, sadness, loss. The memories breathed a past, the past that built them. "It's a bit strange to stay hidden away like this. The Erytheans have got so much to share, so much we could learn from you, things you could learn from us."

Florian shrugged and looked away. "It's the way it is. It's not for me to question."

But the look in his eyes told her that he did question it.

"If you could see Lontown, go to the Citadel and meet the kings, and see . . ." She stopped herself, sensing it was making him feel worse.

They sat in silence for a while longer until Maudie said, "What's a *water-wing*? You said you liked adapting the water-wings?"

Florian grinned widely and stood up. "I'll show you tomorrow."

They went back below, where Herminia greeted them with smiles and gave them sweet red berry juice.

After breathing in the air deeply, Florian said, "I think it will stay dry tonight."

They climbed into leafy netted hammocks on the deck.

"Goodnight, Maudie Brightstorm."

"Goodnight, Florian."

Maudie took her broken compass and the pink gemstone from her pocket and held them tight. She fell asleep listening to the orchestra of competing calls and croaks that the night brought, a world away from the fox barks, cat fights, and rumbling pitch carts of the streets of Lontown.

✶ ✶ ✶

In the morning, Maudie found her compass in the hammock beside her. It had been mended.

She looked around for Florian, then saw him inside the treetop house talking with Herminia.

It hadn't all been a dream. She looked around at the incredible bridges and buildings in the trees and began to analyze the structures, making a note of how they fitted together.

Florian appeared, bottle-green eyes shining and a broad smile. "Today is a good day. Herminia remembers yesterday."

"How long have you been awake?"

He shrugged. "Long enough to make a few things."

"Oh, yes, thank you," she said, holding up the compass.

"And I made this, because it will be easily lost if you have it loose in your pocket or hold it in your hand. It fell during the night but luckily didn't fall off the edge." He passed her a necklace made from cleverly braided twine with the pink gemstone that Valiant had given her attached. He looked away.

"Oh! I guess it's . . . double thank you," she said, and put the necklace over her head.

"The clouds are coming in from the east. We should head for the city now. I'm sorry we haven't found your friends yet, but we can look on the way. A neighbor said they saw smoke in the south this morning, perhaps a campfire."

Hope flooded her chest.

"It might just be another Erythean," he said. "But we will go and find out."

They said goodbye to Herminia and made their way down the great spiral stairs.

"The report of smoke was not far from here, so we'll go on foot, then come back for a water-wing."

After trekking through the forest for a while, Florian suddenly stopped dead still and sniffed. He said something in his own language. His eyes looked wide and alert.

"What is it?" asked Maudie.

"Pantheras."

"What's that?"

"Quick." Florian took a handful of mud and gave it to her.

"Yuck, what are you doing?"

He started smothering his body in mud. "Hurry!"

For a moment she thought he was joking with her,

but his face was deadly serious. She began doing the same with the mud.

"Your face, too. Quick, put it everywhere; it will mask our scent, if it hasn't already caught it."

Then he pushed her forward into the ferns. He put a finger to his lips. They waited. After a few minutes, he pointed ahead. At first, she didn't see anything. Then she saw a shape moving through the trees not far away. They stayed motionless until it had passed.

"They don't often come to this area. They aren't the best swimmers, and they wouldn't want to get caught in a deluge, but the clouds are away. It has likely come in from the west, so it may not have caught our scent, or perhaps it sensed some others . . ."

Maudie was filled half with elation, half with panic—could it be? "Do you think the pantheras may be tracking others?"

"Possibly. Come on, we'll follow it. But shadow my moves."

They stealthily pursued it downhill.

Then Maudie caught a glimpse through the trees of a large clearing that made her almost cry out in happiness. Maudie clamped her hand over her mouth. It was Felicity, standing by a campfire! Her clothes looked bedraggled and her hair was flowing messily over her shoulders, but she was alive!

The pantheras stalked inside the tree line, looking like a huge version of Queenie, but sleeker and with *much* bigger teeth.

"What do we do? It could attack at any moment," she whispered urgently.

Florian looked at her. "Then we will have to draw it away."

"You're joking!" she hissed.

"Again, I'm not. We make ourselves known; it will be intimidated because there are two of us, but if it charges, we must make our bodies as large and fierce as possible."

She gave a shaky nod and then together they stepped from the foliage. It worked, and the pantheras turned to look at them.

"Don't look at its eyes, or it will see challenge."

"You could have mentioned that!"

Then the pantheras took a pace forward in their direction.

Felicity must have caught sight of the pantheras because she cried out, but Maudie was focused on the creature as it prepared to pounce, and suddenly Florian had his arms above his head, and he was shouting fiercely, with a strength that made Maudie jump. She sprang into action and did the same as Florian.

The animal faltered, so they shouted louder.

It backed up a few steps, then hurtled away into the jungle.

Maudie turned and ran for Felicity, who yelped in surprise at the sight of her, and then Welby and Harriet rushed from the jungle beyond, brandishing branches aggressively. Maudie stopped, realizing she was totally covered in mud. "It's me!" she cried, over and over, and in a moment, Felicity had enveloped her in a bone-crushing hug, and she was swarmed by Harriet and Welby.

"I told you! I felt it in my toes, Harrie—today is a good day!"

Harriet smoothed Maudie's hair back from her face. "What happened? We've been worried sick! I lost sight of you; I feared you'd drowned, but Felicity wouldn't let me believe it. She said she knew you were all right."

"The sky-ak saved my life. I somehow made it here—well, to a beach just north of here and then . . ." Maudie took a breath. Too much had happened. She shook her head.

"There's plenty of time for that later. Now, tell us, who is your friend in the tree there?"

Florian had climbed a little way up a tree and was observing them cautiously.

Maudie beckoned to him. "This is Florian. He's

been looking out for me. He can take us to the city—we think Arthur and the Vane crew may be there, and he has to kind of *report us* because no one here wants Lontowners to know about this place."

"Oh, I see, really?" said Harriet, tilting her head curiously. "So he speaks Lontonian?" She exchanged a quizzical look with Welby. "Is it far, Florian?"

"It is not far if we are traveling on the channels by water-wing," said Florian.

They gathered their belongings and hiked through the jungle in the direction of the treetop town. Welby, who was the best at recalling stories in his sagacious, deep tones, told them about the dark-whisper attack and how the great red bird with the fire tail had saved them. How their ship had been dashed against the rocks and how they had just made it on a large piece of the wrecked hull. The fire-bird had guided them to shore.

Florian stayed silent as he walked, listening intently to their stories.

"Can you tell us more about the fire-bird, Florian?" Harriet asked after a while.

He thought for a moment. "We call the bird Aeterna, for it is as old as the land and is neither he nor she; it just is. Aeterna lives in the highest mountain and watches over the Erytheans."

Maudie thought Aeterna was a beautiful name. The more she saw of the Wide, the more it amazed her.

"What do you mean by 'watches over'?" asked Felicity.

"It protects us from the darkwhispers, if we want to travel west."

"Don't talk to me about those darkwhispers!" said Felicity, waving her spoon. "Although there are parts of it I can't remember. Like fragments were stolen by them."

"It's what they do," said Florian. "If you don't get away, then gradually everything, all your memories, disappear."

They walked from the trees to a brook below the treetop town. The water was crystal clear, and a group of narrow vessels were tethered to a stand of trees nearby.

"This is quite something," said Harriet, spinning around in awe and looking up at the spiral staircases.

"We'll fit better on two water-wings. I need to teach one of you," said Florian. "Maudie?"

She nodded eagerly.

Harriet, Welby, and Felicity looked around the immediate area of the glade, pointing and discussing the amazing structures above, while Maudie and Florian rinsed their mud off.

Maudie sidled up to him, retying her hair with the spare ribbon Felicity carried in their supplies. "I'm sorry I thought you wouldn't be any good with mending my compass."

"I'm sorry I thought you wouldn't be any good at . . . anything."

"Hey!" She flicked water at him. They laughed, and Maudie thought how different Florian seemed, now that she knew him better.

Florian untied two water-wings from the trees and patiently explained how they worked, answering Maudie's numerous questions about the tiny engine, propeller, and power cell. She marveled at how similar so much of it was to her sky-ak. Then he demonstrated how to hook your feet in and steer with the handle and rod. Maudie took to it instinctively and was soon flying around the glade to the applause of the others. Some of the treetop inhabitants had even come out to watch.

She skidded to a stop beside Florian's water-wing. "What's that on the back of yours?"

"Ah, this is my adaptation." He pulled a small sail up at the back of the water-wing. "I steer with this hand and adjust the sail with the other. It doesn't work down here, but on the sky-way it practically flies!"

"The sky-way?" Maudie said, mesmerized.

Felicity and Harriet rode with Florian, and Welby with Maudie. They started the small engines and were soon speeding along the river eastward.

After several chimes, the forest opened up and they were on high ground. The river they'd been traveling along led to an elevated waterway, something like a natural aqueduct, although parts looked to be constructed. In the distance was what appeared to be a great shimmering lake with a small mountain in the middle.

Florian led the way. He was using the sail now, deftly catching the wind, and even though there were more people on his water-wing it shot ahead at almost twice the speed. Maudie's water-wing sped along the water, and Florian slowed to let her catch up.

"Impressive," she called, and he smiled broadly.

As they progressed, they saw there were many more waterways, all leading to a great plateau, and other water-wings busied along them.

"There's still no sign of the *Aurora*," Welby said.

Maudie could tell he was missing Arthur, and the concentrated furrows in his forehead told her how concerned he was. "Maybe they didn't make it here?" she said. "Perhaps they turned back before they got to the darkwhispers. At least we didn't see any sign of them there." She wondered if the fire-bird had helped them through too. Either that or they'd been . . .

It didn't bear thinking about. In her heart, she felt that Arthur was all right. Or was that simply false hope she was clinging to?

They all stopped talking as they approached the lake plateau because they'd realized that it wasn't a small mountain, it was a great city.

"Well, just when you think you've seen it all!" Felicity called. "Welby, you've traveled a fair bit, but I bet even you've not seen anything quite like this!"

"Miss Wiggety, I have not."

The structure was amazing; the archways and pillars were mathematically precise and symmetrical, and it looked like part of it was below water! Maudie marveled at the incredible engineering involved in keeping it watertight.

Something caught Maudie's eye in the sky above: a V shape flying over the lake. Her heart filled with elation and relief. The water-wing wobbled as she lost focus for a moment, but she regained it and squeezed the handle even tighter in the joy of what she was seeing.

"Parthena!" she shouted. Then she called to the others, "Arthur must be here!"

CHAPTER 27

TRUTH, LIES, AND TATTOOS

O N THE JETTY they were greeted by a lady dressed in elaborate green robes. She said something in her own language to Florian, and he replied at length.

"Can you work out what they're saying?" Maudie whispered to Welby, who was standing beside her.

"This language is different from any other I have heard. I'm afraid I have no idea."

Florian turned from the woman and said to them, "We need to wait here."

"But Arthur's here!" said Maudie, trying to get past, but the woman barred their way.

Maudie sighed and resigned herself to waiting, her attention caught by the elaborate structure in front of her with its sweeping curves and twists, elegant archways and domes. In addition, there were elements of technology cleverly concealed, like tracks in the wall made to look like decorative carving, but she could tell they were guides for the jetties to rise and fall with the water level, connecting them to different archways.

After a while an elegant woman and man walked up the jetty toward them.

"I am Tauria Verada, Professus Excelsis of Erythea. This is Cassea Sigart, my assistant," the woman said, and introduced the man next to her.

Harriet stepped forward. "I'm Harriet Culpepper, and this is Felicity Wiggety, William Welby, and Maudie Brightstorm, all of Lontown, Vornatania."

The woman looked taken aback for a moment. She began whispering to Cassea.

Maudie looked at Welby, also taken aback. She had no idea his first name was William! To them he had always simply been Welby. She couldn't believe they'd never thought to ask!

When Tauria finished whispering, Cassea nodded, and Tauria turned to them again. "We are peaceful people. We don't look for trouble; in fact, we actively protect ourselves from it."

Harriet held her hands up. "We don't bring any

trouble. We have no weapons, and we mean no harm to you. We are simply here looking for someone. A boy, Arthur Brightstorm."

Tauria Verada's mouth was clamped shut in thought for a while. Then she said, "We are honest in Erythea, honest with our land, honest with each other, so I will be honest with you. We already have a Harriet Culpepper in the city."

"Pardon?" Harriet said, quite in shock.

The four of them exchanged glances of disbelief.

All of a sudden Eudora Vane appeared, striding as though she owned the jetty, pink scarf blowing in the breeze. "Did you call for me, Tauria? I thought we could go over the—" She stopped dead at the sight of Harriet.

Maudie rushed forward, but Harriet pushed past Tauria first and stormed toward Eudora.

Felicity grabbed Maudie's hand. "Let Harriet deal with it."

"Where's Arthur?" Harriet demanded. "What have you done to him? If you've harmed so much as a hair on his head, I'll—" She shoved Eudora in the shoulders, making her totter backward.

"Miss . . . er . . . other Culpepper, we are peaceful here," said Cassea, pulling her back.

"There is only one Harriet Culpepper," Harriet said calmly but firmly. "And I can assure you that it's not this woman."

"We can all vouch that this is the real Harriet," Welby called.

"And the other Harriet has a crew who will vouch for her," said Tauria. "Can you show me your family mark?"

"Of course," said Harriet, wrenching up her sleeve.

"Exactly the same as the other," said Tauria, shaking her head.

Two of the Erytheans pulled Harriet back forcefully.

"That's impossible!" said Welby.

"Too right it is," Maudie muttered, as she charged up the jetty and launched herself at Eudora. Eudora screamed as the two of them hurtled into the water.

Eudora kicked away from Maudie, swimming back to the jetty. Cassea hoisted her out of the water, spluttering, while Florian put his hand out to Maudie. "You certainly have spirit."

Welby grabbed Eudora's arm and Felicity pulled up her wet sleeve. Ink smeared as the fake tattoo dripped away to reveal Eudora's real symbol.

Tauria stood openmouthed. "Arthur Brightstorm was right."

"Please, he's my brother. I need to see him!" Maudie said, tears welling in her eyes.

Felicity put an arm around her.

"Cassea, ensure that this woman—" Tauria gestured at a soaking and fuming Eudora before looking to Harriet. "What is her name?"

"Eudora Vane," Harriet said flatly.

"Cassea, ensure that this Eudora Vane and every member of her crew are accounted for and locked away."

✳ ✳ ✳

The lock turned.

"About time, too!" Arthur said, jumping up from his bed. "You can't keep me prisoner here. I thought you were meant to be peaceful people. Holding me hostage in a room is . . ." He whipped the door open.

Arthur's heart exploded with surprise and a joy so huge he couldn't believe it was happening.

"Maudie!"

They jumped into a tight hug, and clung to each other, neither wanting to be the first to let go in case it

broke the spell, in case it made it not real. Eventually they stood back and looked at each other, their eyes wet with tears.

"You look like you've brought half the jungle with you!" Arthur said. "New ribbon?"

She felt her hair, her fingers touching the dark blue fabric.

"Oh, I forgot. I used the old one to boil water."

"What? Another invention?"

"More improvisation. *You* look rather at home here." Maudie looked him up and down.

"Er . . . yeah, after several days in the swamps my own clothes were ruined, and these are rather nifty, don't you think?"

She laughed. The tension in her heart had lifted; the awful tight feeling since they'd been separated was gone.

"What's that pink stone around your neck?" he asked. "It kind of glows!"

"A water-bear gave it to me. Long story."

"Like the creature I saw in Nova?" he said.

"Yes, I think so. And the one I met was sapient!"

"No way!"

Cassea, who had been standing back in the hallway, coughed. "I'll leave you to update each other.

Tauria Verada would like to see all of you soon." He turned and walked away.

Arthur stared at Maudie. "*All* of you? Wait, how the clanking cogs did you actually get here? Who's here, Maud?"

"Harrie, Felicity, and Welby. They're waiting to see you. They let me be first."

"Harriet's here? That means . . ."

"Arthur, the strangest thing happened when we arrived; this Professor woman—"

"Tauria Verada—I've met her too."

"Yes, her. Well, she said Harriet Culpepper was already here! You should have seen Harriet's face when Eudora appeared!"

"She's been in the city pretending to be Harriet."

"Why would she do that?"

"It started when we landed the *Aurora* here . . ."

"So the *Aurora*'s here?"

"Well, not here in the city—it's back in the jungle near the coast somewhere."

"And it's in one piece?"

"Yes. Stop interrupting, Maud, or I'll lose my thread."

"Sorry."

"We landed, and the Erytheans found us, and

they saw the swallow painted on the *Aurora* and they said Culpiper, and their attitude suddenly changed from hostile to friendly, so she—Eudora, that is—she said, yes, that's me, I'm Harriet Culpepper!"

"Wait a minute. How the clanking cogs do they know Harriet?"

Arthur dropped into a chair. "Exactly! That's what I've been wondering."

"But Harriet said she knew nothing about this continent."

"Do you think she was telling the truth?"

"Harriet would have told us if she knew more. Wouldn't she?"

"Have you still got the ring?"

Maudie took it from her pouch and passed it to him.

"It's something to do with this, I just know it."

"Harriet is the most truthful person we know, Arty."

"Ermitage says the fire-bird is real."

"It is! I've seen it. The Erytheans call it the Aeterna."

His mouth gaped like a guppy.

"I saw it when we were attacked by the darkwhispers."

"No way! You saw them too? Those creatures are terrifying!"

"Florian said if they catch you, they take every last memory you have."

"Who's Florian? Wait, never mind, just tell me about the fire-bird and the darkwhispers."

She told him about the storm, about the darkwhispers' attack; how the fire-bird arrived and protected Harriet; how Maudie herself had been thrown into the sea and the sky-ak had saved her.

"Could Harriet be . . . one of them? An Erythean?"

"If she is, I'm certain she knew nothing of it."

"There's more to this ring than we've figured out."

"Do you know where Harriet is now?"

"I told you, they're waiting to see you!"

He grabbed her hand. "Let's go and find them!"

Maudie pulled him to a stop. "Hold on; you mentioned Ermitage?"

"Oh, yes! He was here all along, and I kind of fell into his path."

"Fell?" Maudie tilted her head and put her hand up. "What did you do? You clearly weren't looking where you were going, *again*."

"Maybe, just a little," he laughed. "Come on."

"Hold on, one last thing before we go."

"What?"

"Did you know that Welby's full name is William? William Welby!"

Arthur's heart pinged a little. He couldn't believe how much he'd missed Welby, for all his nagging and annoying corrections and eyebrow judging.

"Will Welby," he said. "Just when you think you know someone, eh?" They looked at each other and there was a moment of total contentment. Both felt back home even though they were thousands of miles from Lontown.

Then they heard an unmistakable voice: "Now listen here, I can't wait a moment longer. If you don't take me to Arthur Brightstorm this instant, I shall take my spoon and—"

"Felicity!" Arthur called.

She suddenly appeared at the door and stared, her eyes swollen with tears. "Oh, my blessed bunions, I knew that tingle in my toes wasn't for nothing!" She ran to Arthur and scooped him into her arms, then pulled Maudie in. "Together again," she sobbed.

Harriet came in next, and Arthur called out in happiness, and she joined their huge embrace, and a cacophony of chatter ensued in which no one could hear what anyone was saying because everyone was speaking at once. Eventually they all had to pause for breath and were interrupted by a gentle cough behind them.

"Welby!" Arthur smiled. And Welby's eyes were wet with tears too, and they all hugged again.

CHAPTER 28

REVELATIONS

THAT EVENING, the Culpepper crew were invited to dine with the professors. Ermitage joined them.

"My dear old thing, it's a delight to meet you!" Ermitage said to Maudie. "And my, you are one and the same, aren't you, with your matching freckles and your russet hair. And who'd have thought two people could carry that same determined fire in their eyes!" He explained to Arthur that Eudora and her crew had managed to convince the Erytheans that Arthur had poisoned his mind with fanciful stories, until Harriet and the others turned up. "I may be getting on in my years, but I'm not *that* impressionable!"

Tauria Verada directed them to chairs around the rectangular table in the large domed room. Harriet sat beside Tauria, Ermitage opposite, then Welby and Felicity, with Arthur and Maudie at the end beside Cassea and a spare place.

"Well, Ermitage Wrigglesworth lives after all," Welby said dryly.

"Thank you for inviting us to eat with you," Harriet said respectfully.

Tauria nodded. "I am sorry about what has happened. The imposter, this Eudora Vane, has been taken with her crew to a secure zone."

"A secure zone?" Arthur said, wondering if any place with Eudora near it could be classed in that way.

Tauria smiled. "We rarely have to use it. As I have told you, our people are peaceful. We live a fortunate life, away from the difficulties of the Wide. The dark-whispers see to that."

"Do you not feel you are missing being part of the Wide, though?" Harriet asked.

"It is the way it has always been," Tauria said.

There was the soft *thud* of footsteps, then Florian entered. He took the spare seat beside Maudie.

She grinned at him.

"We owe you thanks for helping these people, Florian," said Tauria. "Florian is one of our brightest young scholars. He shows an incredible aptitude for languages. I suspect he may become Professus Linguis one day."

He smiled shyly and glanced at Maudie.

Arthur observed him suspiciously, then whispered to Maudie, "How do you know him?"

"He helped me, I mean, us, in the jungle."

"He keeps smiling at you."

"What a crime," she teased.

"As I was saying about the secure zone," Tauria continued, "we have never had reason to use it, but as proven by the arrival of Mr. Wrigglesworth and two more crews in succession, it was justified."

"Please tell me how you recognized the Culpepper symbol," said Harriet.

"Our agents are mostly within the Stella Oceanus, keeping watch for any who would try to go farther. Of course, we'd prefer that they didn't make it to the darkwhispers—it's not something we would wish on people, even those from Lontown."

"But I don't understand why you welcomed Eudora when she pretended to be me?"

"We thought perhaps it was time."

"Time for what?" Harriet looked more confused than ever, and Arthur and Maudie exchanged a look that told each other they were convinced she knew no more than them.

"That you had brought back the ring."

Arthur took the ring from his pocket and put it on the table. "This one?"

"Why, yes!" said Tauria, surprised.

"Is that . . . ?" asked Harriet.

"We have an agent in Lontown," said Tauria.

"Octavie!" Harriet, Arthur, and Maudie all said at once.

"The Erythean Culpiper—I mean, Culpepper— heritage goes back generations. Usually our agents prefer to stay close, but many decades ago when Lontown exploration was reaching new heights, we sent an agent named Argentia Culpiper. She is very famous here. She met a young explorer and had two children, Octavie and Leviah."

"It appears that you know more about my family than I do," Harriet said quietly. "I have Erythean heritage?" she added in disbelief.

Tauria nodded. "It was decided that the ring of the guardian, the Aeterna, would be passed on to the next generation, along with the knowledge of our lands. As Octavie had no children of her own, she would pass it to her brother Leviah's bloodline."

"My grandfather?"

"As the youngest generation of the Culpepper line, the knowledge and the ring would pass to you.

Octavie must have decided it was time, just as Argentia decided it was time when Octavie and her friends had nearly discovered us." Tauria looked pointedly at Ermitage, who looked dumbfounded. "It's why the Aeterna protected you at the darkwhispers. We don't understand how it knows, but it will always bring true Erytheans safe passage home. Argentia decided on the swallow as a symbol that she could always find her way home, back to Erythea, if she needed to. The swallow migrates from here to Vornatania every year, so it seemed fitting."

"And when the people here saw the swallow on the sky-ship, they knew it meant a Culpepper had returned home," Arthur said.

"Then why didn't Octavie tell my grandfather, Leviah? Or my mother? Why didn't I know?" Harriet sounded doubtful.

"Because secrets can be hard to keep; they are a great burden to place on someone, and Argentia knew her decision to stay and settle in Lontown was the hardest she would have to make. She wanted to protect Erythea by binding the knowledge to just one person at a time."

"Pardon me for butting in," said Felicity, "but protect you from what?"

Several moments passed as Tauria carefully

formulated her words. "We didn't go out of our way to keep our land a secret. At first, many years ago, when our sea-ships reached the many islands of the west, we observed and learned, but the farther we went the more wary we became of some of the dangers. Your sky-ships and their polluting pitch, for example. And some of the people, obsessed by title and possession, apparently like this Eudora Vane."

"We're not all like that," Maudie said.

"The darkwhispers became a natural barrier for us, as though meant to be there to protect us. At first, only sea-ships ventured our way, and they would encounter the darkwhispers and disappear, or crash—if any survived, they had no memory of what had come to pass."

"That's why everything became mythical," said Harriet. "The Bestwick-Fords were sure they'd seen the fire-bird, but in their journals they described it as a dream and even dismissed it themselves. But it was real! They had seen it and forgotten."

"It makes sense, Harrie," said Maudie. "Look at the water-technology here: the skills you've learned from your parents and them from theirs, all leading to you designing your amazing sky-ship with a water engine."

"Your sky-ship is powered by water?" Tauria said,

impressed. "I had wondered how your sky-ship had reached this far using pitch."

Harriet nodded. "This young lady is a talented young engineer too. She's designed a smaller version, a sky-ak, also powered by a miniature water-engine. It's very similar to your water-wing."

"Fascinating. Are you sure you're not Erythean too?" Tauria smiled. "We must show you our engineering libraries."

"What will you do with Madame Vane?" asked Ermitage curiously.

"It's still to be decided. But when we discovered her true identity, we found the journals she had made during her time here in the city. There are extensive notes on materials she wished to take back to Lontown. Of course, we could never allow such a thing. The School of Professors will meet tomorrow to decide the best course of action."

∗ ∗ ∗

Later, Arthur headed for the geographical library with Maudie, even though he could tell she was itching to go to the engineering library. They walked into the great space filled with books, globes, and maps. There were numerous volumes documenting the different areas of Erythea, which Arthur piled on a table.

"Maudie, this is just the tip of this continent. There's so much more south of here, and so many islands even farther east. I wonder if you kept sailing, would you reach the Isles of Carrickmurgus on the other side?"

"Maybe!"

"It's pretty cool that all the people in charge are professors," said Maudie. "Where do you think they've put Eudora and her crew?"

Arthur shrugged. "In a deep dungeon beneath the water, hopefully."

"That sounds horrible."

"A horrible punishment for a horrible woman."

"I wonder what they'll decide to do."

"Lock her up forever."

"I meant with us. We know about them now, and so we're a danger to them."

"We won't tell anybody back home. I mean, it'll be hard, but—"

"Dad always said your word is your bond."

Arthur nodded.

"*We* know that we won't say anything, but how do they? They didn't trust Mr. Wrigglesworth enough to let him go back. They might trust Harriet because of her heritage, but they might not trust us, or Felicity, or Welby."

"Will Welby—I still can't get over that . . ." A cough from a nearby table halted Arthur.

A map rustled and Welby peered out from behind it.

"Oh, sorry, I didn't see you there," Arthur said, his face reddening.

Welby raised his eyebrows, then smiled. "I like to keep a few surprises for you."

The door opened and Florian walked in. He glanced over and smiled.

Maudie beckoned him over.

Florian sat down, and Maudie leaned in and whispered, "Do you know where Eudora is?"

He nodded. "Over at the power-falls."

"Where's that?"

"That's the way I came into the city," Arthur said.

"And she can't escape?"

"It's very secure, with locked rooms. If you did get out, you're stuck anyway, if you don't know how to run the elevators. And someone would see you if you tried to get across the lake."

"And the professors will decide what happens to her tomorrow?"

Florian nodded.

"What usually happens to people who do wrong here?" asked Maudie.

Florian shrugged. "They would give back to the city—help more."

"Ooh, maybe they'll have Eudora scrubbing the bathrooms!"

Arthur laughed. "Now that I'd love to see!"

CHAPTER 29

CONFESSION

THE FOLLOWING MORNING, they were all summoned by butterflies to meet in the central dome room. From there they were led through an archway at the back, up another set of twisting stairs, until they emerged into a small, open pavilion with alabaster columns and a curved roof. A tropical breeze drifted through and, in the distance, clouds hugged the surrounding mountains. They were in the uppermost point of the city.

Twelve professors of Erythea sat on a semicircle of stone benches in the center. They were dressed in official-looking robes in an array of the natural colors of trees, mountains, stones, and waters from the rain forest: olive, umber, cinnamon, sage, lime, chartreuse, turquoise, graphite, gold, silver, bronze, and emerald.

The robes had long, open sleeves, high collars, wide trousers—all intricately embroidered with twisting patterns and forest creatures.

"I feel suddenly underdressed," Arthur whispered to Maudie.

"Please sit down," said Tauria.

Harriet, Arthur, Maudie, Felicity, and Welby sat opposite the professors.

Tauria, dressed in her signature emerald, stood. "The professors have spoken at length with Harriet and have gathered the facts about Eudora Vane and her crew. If we were unsure before, the disclosure of what happened at South Polaris, what she did to your family . . ." She looked at Arthur and Maudie. "We have come to a unanimous decision."

The crew leaned in eagerly.

"This woman cannot be trusted to stay in Erythea as she is. We allowed it with Ermitage Wrigglesworth because we observed him to be a good, peaceful man, but this woman is clearly a danger to our people. Tomorrow morning, Eudora Vane and her crew will be taken to the darkwhispers, where they will be left until their memories of Erythea—indeed, all their living memories—have gone."

"I wasn't expecting that," Arthur whispered.

"Harsh," Maudie said under her breath.

Tauria threw them a glance.

Harriet stood up. "Will you leave them there?"

"We will return them to work within Erythea. They will have no memory of a life before, and we will rehabilitate them with a new perspective."

"What about me and my crew?" Harriet asked, with her hands on her hips and legs slightly apart.

"This was debated somewhat at length."

Arthur swallowed.

"We trust you, Harriet. And on your word, we are prepared to trust all five of you. We will let you return to Lontown on the condition that you do not disclose anything of your journey past Nova. If we have your promise on this, then you may return."

They looked between each other and Arthur knew they were thinking the same thing. That exploration widened horizons, and not just theirs but those of the people back in Lontown too. There was so much Vornatanians could learn from these people, and things the Erytheans could learn from them in return. But what choice did they have, really?

"You have our word," Harriet said solemnly.

"And how about Wrigglesworth?" asked Welby.

Tauria shook her head. "He must stay here for the rest of his days. Too many of your people think he is dead, and if he arrived back alive, even if he swore not to release any information . . . well, it would cause too many problems. We have spoken with Mr. Wrigglesworth and he understands."

"You are free to remain here as long as you wish, of course," continued Tauria. "But be mindful of the stories you will need to make up in order to cover your tracks."

"Can't you just lock Eudora away?" said Felicity.

"Our judgment is final. I'm afraid it's not up for discussion."

"Eudora will never let you do this to her. She'll find a way to escape," said Arthur.

"She will believe she is being banished and taken back safely to the west. She won't realize her fate until the last minute. Until it is too late. Neither will her crew."

* * *

Back in Arthur's room, the twins sat at the window overlooking the plateau.

"I don't like it, Maud. As much as I hate Eudora Vane, this doesn't feel right. She's technically our aunt, and I know she's done nothing to earn that title, but she was our mum's sister."

"We shouldn't feel bad about their decision with Eudora, not after what she did."

Arthur thought for a moment. Parthena squawked. "There's something else."

"What?"

"If Eudora loses all her memories to the darkwhispers, then the truth, and the proof of what she did, is lost too. How will we ever get true justice for Dad?"

Maudie stared. He was right. Her shoulders sagged.

A knock sounded on the door. It was Florian.

"Some of us are going on the plateau in water-shoes, and I thought you might like to come."

Maudie smiled broadly and glanced in Arthur's direction.

"Both of you," Florian added quickly.

"What are water-shoes?" asked Arthur.

"You'll see—come on!"

The plateau shimmered in the afternoon sun. It felt as though they were at the top of the Wide, in its best-kept secret.

The water-shoes were like miniature boats for their feet. They stood in them and floated on the top of the water, making it possible to skate across the surface, with a paddle to control momentum. Arthur decided that on this occasion his iron arm would've been useful. Paddling with one arm was not going to be easy.

He pushed the paddle across his body into the water and nearly toppled over. He looked across at Florian, who was holding his paddle lower and just flicking it in the top of the water rather than scooping. Arthur adjusted his grip and tried again. After a while he got the hang of it. He paddled up alongside Maudie.

"You got the hang of this quickly!" he said.

"It's easy once you work out the physics of what's going on and trust your instinct. It's amazing."

"We won't be able to tell anyone about this."

"The water-shoes?"

"Not just that, this whole thing—*Erythea*. We won't be able to tell the Geographical Society, or the *Lontown Chronicle* or . . ." Arthur paused.

Maudie looked at him. "I know."

"I can't get what they are going to do to Eudora and her crew out of my thoughts. After tomorrow it will be as though what happened to Dad in South Polaris has been erased, along with all Eudora's memories of Mum, and it just doesn't feel right. Imagine if the darkwhispers had gotten us? Imagine if we lost all our memories of Dad? We lost Brightstorm House, all of our things were sold off. The memories are all we have."

Maudie shivered despite the heat of the afternoon. "It would be terrible. When the darkwhispers attacked our boat on the way here, for a moment one had me. I relived a memory about Dad. It was something about . . . I don't know. I can't quite remember, of course. If the fire-bird hadn't arrived, I could have lost it all. It happened to Florian's sister. It's so sad to see someone like that, as though a great part of them has evaporated."

They fell silent and swooshed a little farther into the lake together.

Arthur glanced across. "I've been thinking."

Maudie threw him her *what bonkers plan have you come up with now* look. "Go on then," she said slowly.

"We get her to confess in writing before tomorrow."

She laughed, then realized he was totally serious.

"You're going to have to say that again because I thought you said you were going to ask Eudora Vane to confess, which would be the daftest plan since the invention of daft plans!"

"I've been thinking about it. We sneak over and ask her."

"So we just turn up, break in to wherever she's being held, and say, 'Hi, Eudora, you know you poisoned our dad's crew, so we think it's time for a written confession!' "

"Not exactly."

"Or perhaps, 'Eudora, your conscience must be

burdened by the weight of what you did in South Polaris. Here's a pen and pencil; that's it, get it all off your chest.'" She shook her head. "Eudora won't freely do anything for anyone. She only understands currency—currency of power, resources, and keeping the Vane name on some pedestal of explorers in Lontown."

"We have currency."

She frowned at him.

"We have the knowledge of what is going to happen. What they are going to do to her. What if we agree to help her back west without getting her memory taken?"

"And how are we going to do that?"

"That bit I've no idea about; I mean, we don't actually have to keep our side of the deal."

She stared at him. "That would make us the same as her."

"Then we ask Harriet to help."

They continued farther into the lake, both in deep thought.

Soon Arthur noticed that Maudie was motionless, staring into the northeast. "What is it?"

Dark clouds were on the horizon. Lightning sparked in the far distance. Another deluge was coming.

Florian paddled to join them. "Do not worry. We'll be quite safe in the city. It will pass swiftly. But we must go inside now."

By the time they reached the jetty, the gray bank of cloud had reached them, and spots of rain dappled the plateau, forming thousands of rings in an ever-changing, dancing pattern.

"Will the water rise above here? We're fairly high, aren't we?"

"It will, but we are used to this. Come and see."

They followed him downstairs to where the water came halfway up the windows. "The whole city is watertight. And the three levels above us are too, although it rarely goes above this floor."

Arthur had a thought. "Florian?"

"Yes?"

"You know where Eudora Vane and her crew are in the power-falls, right?"

He nodded.

"We need to go and speak to her tonight. There's something really important that we need to do before she's taken to the darkwhispers tomorrow."

Florian frowned. "And you want me to take you to her?"

"Yes."

He looked to Maudie. "Is this your wish too?"

She felt her freckles blush brightly with the dilemma. Then she nodded.

He thought for a moment. "If Tauria found out . . ."

"She won't. We'll be in and out quickly."

"Then we should go now, before the storm gets too bad."

∗ ∗ ∗

The sky was an ethereal gray, and warm rain fell in heavy splashes across the plateau as the water-wing sped soundlessly toward the power-fall building.

"How will we distract the guard?" asked Maudie.

"Leave that to me," said Florian.

They floated up to the jetty, but when they reached the building, Florian led them straight past.

"What are you doing?" Maudie said, alarmed.

"The windows to where she is being held are here. The guards will never know."

Arthur had to admit it was a simple yet clever idea. "But won't we be too near the falls?"

Florian steered them to a small window and held the water-wing steady. "We will be all right as long as the rain doesn't get too heavy."

"Too heavy?" Maudie pushed her sodden hair away from her face and glanced at Arthur with wide eyes.

"Let's get this done," Arthur said. He peered inside.

Eudora was in the room, which had various pipes running across the walls and a makeshift bed that had been placed in the middle. Eudora wasn't her usual neat self; her shirt was creased, her hair looked dull and untidy, and her cheeks were drawn and pale.

"Hey, you!" Arthur said in a hushed whisper.

Eudora looked up, clearly bemused. She put on a bright voice and said, "What a pleasant surprise."

Maudie looked in too.

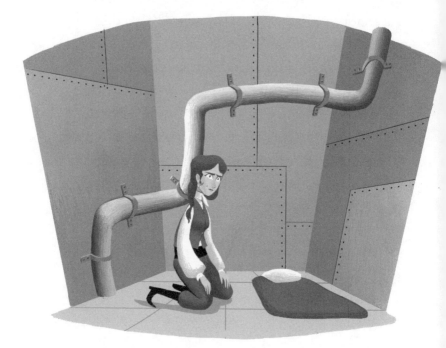

"Well, now, both my nephew and niece come to visit me!"

"Don't call us that," Maudie hissed.

"What did she say?" Florian called, looking suddenly panicked.

Maudie looked back at him. "Don't worry, I'll explain later—it's not what it seems."

Arthur decided the best approach was to get it over with. "They are taking you to the darkwhispers tomorrow. They will leave you there until all your memory is taken, so that you can never be a threat to them."

Florian shuffled his feet uncomfortably on the boards. "Should we be telling her this?" he whispered to Maudie.

She put a hand on his arm.

For a moment there was a barely perceptible waver in Eudora's composure.

"You're going to lose all knowledge of everything," Arthur iterated. "It's what the darkwhispers do. Feed off your memories until there's nothing left—you won't remember your expeditions, Lontown, your crew, your parents, your—"

And that was the moment Arthur saw a glint of terror pass over Eudora's face.

"—sister."

She wouldn't remember Violetta. Their mother and the sister she had loved so dearly, who had chosen a different path, a path that had driven Eudora to do terrible things. It was the one thing that she cared deeply about, and for a moment he saw it in her eyes.

"We want a confession about what you really did at South Polaris," said Maudie.

Eudora was uncharacteristically silent for a while. Then she said plainly, "I don't know what you mean."

"You know exactly what we mean." He shoved a notebook and pencil through the window at her. "If you help us, we'll pick you up and take you back to Lontown. You won't have your memories, but you'll have our word that we'll take you back."

She observed them for several moments. "A confession for my life. An interesting proposition, Brightstorms. But not one I mean to entertain."

"But they're going to let the darkwhispers take every memory you have!"

She smiled. "Perhaps. And if they do, what difference does it make to me whether I confess? If I confess, my reputation is lost; if I don't, then my reputation remains."

"But you won't even know who you are!"

"When confronted by an offer, I always ask myself one question: what's in it for me? You've brought me a proposal that offers me absolutely nothing." She walked toward the small window. "Quite the worst negotiation in history. No wonder your father was usele—"

"Don't you dare—"

Maudie put a hand on Arthur's arm. They looked at each other and knew they needed to offer more.

"Then we'll plea to the Erytheans to lessen your sentence. We'll talk to Harriet, she'll persuade them," said Maudie.

Eudora observed them, and for a moment her facial muscles lost their hardness and she looked exposed, almost vulnerable. Then she smiled as sweet as sugar. "Thank you for your offer, but I decline. I guess my final victory will be taking the truth to the grave with me."

"We need to go," Florian urged. "The rain is getting heavier."

Eudora's eyes suddenly lit up. "Come closer! What's that around your neck, child?"

A pink glow was coming from Maudie's neck. She cursed herself for forgetting about the gemstone.

"Where is it from? I should very much like it; as

I am fated to lose all my memories, could you not at least gift me one thing that you know I will love when I am no more than a shell of myself?"

Maudie drew back. "You're having nothing, and tomorrow you'll be nothing. Let's get out of here. She's not worth another breath."

CHAPTER 30

PURSUIT

"**I** KNEW IT WAS A STUPID IDEA!" Maudie hurried back along the jetty to Tempestra. "I don't know why I let you talk me into these things, Arty."

The rain bombarded the jetty with thunderous force.

"At least we didn't get caught, and no one needs to know," she said, huffing and glancing sideways at Arthur.

"But it was all for nothing!" Arthur said, kicking a post.

She stopped walking and pursed her lips. "We have to accept that there's nothing we can do, and let the Erytheans take her tomorrow. Then we go home and get on with our lives."

"I want justice," Arthur snapped.

"Well, you can't always get what you want!"

Florian was slowly distancing himself from them. "Where are you going?" Maudie said forcefully.

He shrugged awkwardly. "I thought I would just leave you two to argue it out."

She sighed. "Come on, at least show us where we can get some more of that delicious pampa fruit before we go."

Florian led them through the ivory corridors. "Look! The water is up to another level now; it must be falling in great volumes in the northern mountains," he said.

They all went to the window where the water was halfway up.

Lightning sparked in the distance, one bolt every few seconds.

"It's fierce here," Maudie said. "Fierce, but beautiful."

Florian looked at her and smiled.

As Arthur watched the lightning crack across the sky, a flash of silver flew past the window. An insect. "What was that? It looked like Miptera!"

Another flash came.

"There, did you see?"

"I saw something," said Florian.

"Maybe it *was* Miptera, Arty. They were hardly

going to imprison an insect along with Eudora, were they? If they even know about her!"

"I suppose not, but the thought of her being free makes me uneasy."

"I know what you mean. Perhaps she's feeling lost without Eudora and is trying to find shelter from the storm." Maudie was thinking about Valiant.

"Careful, Maud, sounds like you feel sorry for that mandible-gnashing monster."

"Not likely!"

The children continued on through the hallways toward one of the kitchens. They turned a corner and Arthur yelped as he almost collided with Ermitage, his arms full of food.

"Sorry, my dear old thing! I was just . . ."

"Raiding the kitchen? That's what we're about to do."

"Yes! Famished!" He chuckled and hurried past.

They found Felicity in the kitchen with one of the cooks of Tempestra. She was furiously scribbling down notes.

"Twinnies!" she cried, then added, "and friend!" She tapped her lucky spoon excitedly on the table. "Look at these recipes! I'll have to improvise with some of the ingredients, but there are some similar things I can pick up on our way back to Lontown.

I shall collate it in a book, just for our personal use, of course, because I can't spill the beans, so to speak. We'll call it Delights of Erythea . . . no. Eats of Erythea . . . hmm, perhaps a bit obvious if it got into the wrong hands . . ."

"Secret Feasts?" suggested Maudie.

"Perfect!"

Lightning flashes were now happening every ten seconds or so. There was a rumble as shutters rose from beneath the windows to cover them.

"What's happening?" asked Maudie.

"Looks as though we are in for a full deluge tonight," answered Florian. "When the water reaches a certain level, the second layer of protection goes up, because the weight of the additional water puts more pressure on our buildings. It takes longer to flood here than the far west, but when the deluge is particularly fierce over the mountains it can get deep. We'll likely not be able to go out until it has receded enough to be safe."

After gathering a feast of spiced yam tarts, chocolate coconut sweets, pineapple and pecan cake, and mango juice, Arthur, Maudie, and Florian went back to Arthur's room, which was one floor up and still free of the shutters.

They went to the window and watched the lightning crack the night sky with splinters of white heat in the northwest.

"I imagine the darkwhispers would love that," said Arthur.

"Maybe the storm will pass over them and they'll get so much energy tonight that they won't want the memories of the Vane crew." Maudie sighed. "Did you see Eudora's face when you mentioned losing her memories of Mum?"

Arthur nodded. "I don't think I've ever seen her look scared before, but that thought really got to her."

"I wish *we* had memories of Mum."

"I'm sorry that you never got to know her," said Florian.

Maudie sat on the window ledge. "I know what Eudora did was unforgivable, but it isn't right to take someone's memories away as a punishment."

"Imagine if we lost all our memories of Dad, of each other," said Arthur.

Maudie coughed loudly.

"Oh, sorry, Florian, I forgot that . . . er . . . Maudie told me what happened to your sister."

Florian gave a nod as though to say it was fine.

They watched the lightning spark three times in succession, and fell silent for a while until Arthur said, "Perhaps . . ."

Maudie looked at him. "What?"

"What if we helped Eudora anyway, even if she won't confess. Because it's the right thing to do? Can we live with knowing we should have done something to stop this? She's a horrible person—the worst—but even she has a right to her memories."

Arthur and Maudie's eyes locked.

"Arty, we have to help her, don't we?"

He nodded. "Yes, because everything about this feels wrong, and Dad always said—"

"Trust your instincts."

Arthur thought for a moment. "We should find Tauria Verada first thing and persuade her to reduce the sentence. I know we won't get a confession from Eudora, but at least we've done the right thing."

"What do you think, Florian?" asked Maudie.

"It may be difficult to sway them, but if you can suggest a way to keep her here safely, perhaps."

"We'll have to all think overnight. At the worst they can keep her locked up in that building," said Maudie.

The water was almost up to the window. The second-layer shutters began rising.

Arthur watched as the flashes of lightning slowly disappeared. "Looks like all we can do until morning is work out what to say and try to get some sleep."

✳ ✳ ✳

Arthur, Maudie, and Florian stayed together in Arthur's room talking through different ideas of how they could try to lighten Eudora's sentence, then drifting in and out of sleep until the shutters opened to reveal the hazy peaches, muted grays, and shadowed greens of a rain-forest dawn.

They rushed to the central dome to look for Tauria Verada or one of the other high professors, but just as they reached the doorway, they saw the Professus Excelsis already talking with a man who spoke angrily in Erythean, making sweeping gestures with his arms.

They hid just beyond the doorway and listened.

"What's he saying?" whispered Arthur.

A frown deepened on Florian's forehead. "He's a guard over at the power-falls. The Vane crew escaped."

It felt as though someone had punched Arthur in the rib cage.

"He was bringing them some food this morning, not long ago, and when he opened the door, they were gone. He says there are many water-wings missing." Florian paused and strained to listen some more. "They say they must have escaped in the early hours or late last night, before the deluge took hold on the plateau. The storm was heaviest in the north, so they may have taken refuge in the south in the orb houses, or they may have made it across the sky-way to Althuria."

Florian paused to listen again, then pulled them back toward the stairs. "Hurry, she's instructed him to assemble Cassea, Harriet, and her crew on the jetty."

They hurried away. "But how did they escape?" Maudie whispered.

Arthur remembered the flash of Miptera flying past when they'd arrived back the previous evening. "They had help."

"Who?" said Maudie.

Arthur shrugged helplessly. "I don't know, but I'd bet that when we saw Miptera last night she was carrying a message."

They walked the long way to the jetty to give time for the others to assemble, then joined Tauria, Cassea, Harriet, Welby, and Felicity.

"Have you heard what happened?" asked Harriet wide-eyed.

They nodded.

"Where's Ermitage?" Arthur asked, but as he spoke the words he remembered running into Wrigglesworth rushing out of the kitchen with all that food and supplies. The realization hit—he was the one who had helped Eudora!

"He must have broken them out!" Arthur shouted.

Tauria and Harriet began talking quickly and quietly together. Arthur heard Ermitage's name mentioned.

After a moment, Harriet turned to the others. "We think they may be heading for the *Aurora*; perhaps Eudora realized what they were planning. Tauria is sending a search party straight there."

Arthur looked to the jetty, guilt like a heavy weight around his neck. It was wrong to take Eudora's memories, but it was wrong to let her escape with the *Aurora*. If they hadn't told Eudora about the Erytheans' plan for her, would she still be locked up?

The Erythean water-wings were already setting off.

"They don't know her strategy for making it past the darkwhispers, but they want to catch her first," said Harriet.

"I know what she'll do; she'll use the weather canopy to get through. It's how she made it here," said Arthur. "Perhaps we can try to cut them off if they've not gone too far. Parthena could fly ahead to find them and tell us which way they're heading."

"Good thinking, Arthur."

He called to Parthena, who was waiting on the jetty. "Can you scan the area and see if you can find Eudora?"

She squawked, then took flight and zoomed away.

Arthur went in a water-wing with Welby and Cassea, Maudie with Florian, and Harriet with Tauria and Felicity. The vessels traveled like the wind across the sky-way. Florian's was the fastest with his adapted sail, and he had to slow down several times so that the others could catch up. Shortly, Parthena reappeared in the sky and landed in Arthur's water-wing. The group came to a stop and Welby spread out the map. Parthena pecked at an area in the mountains.

"Looks like they've gone via the caves, if your bird is right?" said Tauria.

"She's always right," said Arthur.

"Then I suggest we split up. Harriet and I will head for the *Aurora* and cut them off with the rest of the search party. Arthur, Felicity, and Cassea, you travel up the center just in case the Vane crew tries to double back. Florian and Maudie will take the northerly river, as a second boundary point. The sky-way splits into the river systems just ahead. Good luck."

The water-wings sped off in different directions.

✴ ✴ ✴

Maudie and Florian could go full speed now that they didn't have to wait for the others. It was strange to Maudie not to have been paired automatically with Arthur, but she supposed they had arrived separately and Tauria knew that Florian had traveled with her to the city.

As they rushed along, Maudie couldn't stop thinking about why Eudora would head toward the caves. She called out to Florian. "The pink gemstone—she saw it. She must've found out their location."

Florian glanced back at her.

"I didn't tell her. You were there. I wouldn't, but I know how her mind works, and that's why she's gone there."

Florian nodded. "We must hurry!"

They sped onward. Florian was navigating them the fastest way he knew: along the river north of the treetop town, cutting through rivulets to avoid rapids, through the tunnel of enormous trees, and into the dense forest. They stopped briefly to check their direction as they pushed on through the jungle, the midday heat bearing down on them.

When they were close, and the rivulets could get them no farther, they left the water-wing.

"Through here!" said Florian urgently.

Maudie thought she recognized the wide trunks of the water-bear trees and she glanced up, suddenly filled with hope that she might see Valiant. But everything was eerily still, not a breath of breeze. Even the usual croaks, thrums, and chirrups, the song of the jungle, had fallen mute.

"I don't like this," she breathed.

As they moved silently, the ground became rocky. A ball of lead formed in Maudie's stomach as they approached the cave she remembered from the flood. But it wasn't just the memory.

Something wasn't right. She could sense it.

Florian stopped to pick up a pink gemstone discarded on the floor.

And then she saw.

A suffocating wave of emotion came over her. Florian grabbed her hand. It was clear that he was feeling the same. Pink gemstones were scattered on the forest floor as though someone had left in a hurry, and among them were several dead water-bears.

Florian let out a wail and Maudie sank to her knees. These poor creatures. It was too awful, as though being trapped in a nightmare. And then she had the terrible thought that one of them could be Valiant.

A soft whimper sounded from behind one of

the trees that made her heart fill with both sorrow and joy.

"It's all right," Maudie said softly. "You can come out. No one here will harm you."

But the water-bear ran off and scampered up a tree.

"It's terrified of us!" Maudie said.

She glanced at Florian. "We were going to help Eudora, and now look what she's done. If we hadn't tried to help, she wouldn't have known about the punishment, she wouldn't . . ." The weight of responsibility pressed on her chest like she'd been gripped in an enormous vise.

Florian pulled her to look at him. "*You* did not do this."

"I know, but . . ." Her voice quivered.

"You can spend a lifetime asking what if things had been different, and it won't change a thing. What if the professors hadn't decided on such a harsh punishment? What if we had caught them escaping? What if my people didn't shut themselves away from the rest of the Wide, what if . . . ?" He sighed. "You can't live like that. You are good and you wanted to do the right thing. I know that."

Rustling sounded close by, then another water-bear emerged. Maudie recognized the markings on his face—it was Valiant. He whimpered again and let out a pining moan that made every inch of Maudie wish she could make it all go away, turn back time.

She scooped Valiant into her arms, and he climbed to her shoulder and wrapped his tail around her arm and buried his head in her neck. "Did a woman come here? Did she do this?"

He took her hand and brushed it with *yes*.

Valiant clung tightly to her.

"We need to go," said Florian. "I will come back later and bury them."

Maudie nodded and looked to Valiant. "I'm sorry, I have to go now." But Valiant wouldn't let go. She tried to pry his little webbed paws from her arm.

Florian put a hand to hers. "Take him with you."

"But . . ."

"I don't think you have a choice, Maudie."

CHAPTER 31

UP, UP, AND . . .

MAUDIE AND FLORIAN returned to their water-wing and continued on in the direction of the beach. Florian instinctively wove their way along the rivulets and gullies. After a while, two rivulets joined and they caught sight of Arthur, Welby, and Cassea, who had taken the central route. Their water-wings stopped side by side.

"They're on their way to the *Aurora*," said Arthur. "Parthena managed to fly ahead and keep us updated. It's not far from here. Wait . . . is that a water-bear around your neck, Maud?"

"Yes, the sapient one I told you about."

"It really is just like the one I saw on Nova! Incredible! How is it . . . Never mind, you can tell me later. Harriet and the others are trying to catch Eudora before they can take flight, but from Parthena's indication it seems we're closer, and it doesn't look good."

Maudie groaned in frustration, her blood coursing like a hot river. She'd never felt so cross, so furious, so helpless—except in South Polaris. "Not again," she hissed.

The soft chug of engines sounded as the *Aurora* rose in the sky in the south.

"What can we do?" Arthur looked to each of them.

Then an idea hit Maudie like a bolt to her chest. "The sky-ak! I left it on the beach . . . but the fin snapped in the storm."

"What's a sky-ak?" asked Cassea, confused.

"It's a small sky-ship. It's got a water engine, and skims the surface, but has a balloon, too, for height, so it actually flies . . . well, for about a minute at a time."

"Can we mend it?"

"What if we use the water-wing to fix it? It would fly across the sea then."

"But they've already taken off!" said Arthur hurriedly. "We don't have time; they'll be gone!"

Maudie shook her head. "Well, we don't have any other plans, and at least it's something."

They continued along the rivulet for a short while, until the tree line broke and white sand came into view.

"The *Aurora* hasn't gone as far as I thought," said Arthur, pointing to the sky.

"It's the jet stream above," said Cassea. "It flows into Erythea from the west. If you are flying west it is against you, so you'll be twice as slow. When it hits the mountains, it drops and creates a low, fast flow in the opposite direction. It's great if you're in a boat trying to sail west, but not if you are higher up in an air-ship."

"Why don't they just fly lower?" asked Arthur.

"Because they don't know that. They probably assume the winds shifted as they rose," said Welby.

Maudie jumped out of the water-wing and ran over to the tree where she'd left the sky-ak. She inspected the damage on the hull again. "I don't know if we can do this in time," she muttered. Florian came up beside her, and she looked at him. "What if you pull us in with the water-wing? You get us as far as you can, as fast as you can, then release us and we go up until we're above the *Aurora*."

Florian thought for a moment. "It's possible. But we would be far faster if you also had a sail like my water-wing."

"Then let's see what we've got to make one!" said Maudie.

Maudie, Florian, and Cassea set about rigging up a

makeshift sail from the fabric that covered the storage area on the sky-ak.

"What happens when we reach the *Aurora*?" asked Arthur. "There's more of them than us. And the sky-ak only fits what, two, three at a push?"

"Have you so readily forgotten my martial-arts expertise?" Welby said with a wink.

Arthur smiled. "But shouldn't we have, you know, a plan?" Arthur couldn't believe that Welby wasn't giving them a hundred reasons why not to do this.

"There is the odd occasion when plans must be thrown into the depths, and this is one of them, Arthur Brightstorm." Welby smiled at him and turned to the others, who were busy with the sail. "Florian will tow initially; I will go with you both in the sky-ak, and Cassea will tell the others when they get here."

They nodded in agreement.

Maudie finished tying off a rope.

"The sail will help us gain speed to get the lift we need," said Welby. "I'll go in the back and control it; I had plenty of practice on the way here. Cassea, when Harriet gets here, send her as close as you can in one of the water-wings, just in case." He clapped his hands together. "Right. What are we waiting for?"

Once Maudie had promised that she'd come back

for Valiant, the water-bear slowly let go and reluctantly stood on the beach, watching them intently. The remaining four carried the sky-ak and the water-wing to the shallows of the waves to tie them together. Arthur kept looking out over the water at the *Aurora*, which was making progress but was still slow. When the sky-ak was hitched to the back of Florian's water-wing, Maudie climbed in the front with Arthur in the middle and Welby in the back.

"Arthur, we'll need to time the balloon just right so that we hit the correct elevation at the perfect time. There's no way to calculate this exactly, so we'll have to guess. But guess well," said Maudie. She noticed sweat beading on his face from the unbridled sun and from the nerves of what they were about to do.

Arthur glanced over his shoulder at Welby. "Aren't you worried about the guessing part?"

Welby put a hand on Arthur's shoulder and said, "We made it back from South Polaris, didn't we?"

"Florian, we're ready!" Maudie called.

The water-wing sped off into the waves and there was a sharp wrench on the line, then with a lurch the sky-ak was being pulled into the sea.

Fine spray from the waves spattered them. At first the *Aurora* looked too far away to catch, but after a short while they were moving at such speed it was clear that they were catching up. Ahead, the water-wing rose from the sea like a great whale.

"There's one other thing I've just realized," Maudie called. "We need to reach them before they get to the darkwhispers. Remember, the fire-bird helps Erytheans. We won't be protected."

"We're gaining on them," Arthur called.

"They probably won't even see us coming," called Welby.

He looked younger with his gray hair waving in the wind, and once more he'd lost the stiffness that Lontown seemed to bring on him.

Maudie muttered under her breath, furiously trying to calculate the trajectory and the optimal time for the balloon and release. Florian kept glancing back at them to check.

They were getting closer and closer.

"Shall I do it yet?"

"Wait."

"It looks close!"

"Arty, I'll say when."

They kept getting closer. The waves were calm, and they were moving so fast that Parthena was having difficulty keeping up. Maudie put her hand briefly to the pink stone. Then after a moment she said, "Arty, release the balloon valve!"

The balloon swelled and they rose high into the air with the momentum. The wings and balloon, along with the stream of warm wind, took them up until they were level with the *Aurora*, then high above it. Fortunately, those on the deck of the *Aurora* were looking straight ahead and hadn't noticed them yet.

Something furry brushed Maudie's leg. She glanced down to see Valiant tucked under her seat. "What are you doing. . . ? Hey, who let Valiant sneak on the—"

"They've seen us!" Arthur called as he saw Miptera take flight. She flew straight for them. Parthena flew for her, talons outstretched, but Miptera swerved and Parthena shot past, disappearing below. The balloon thwacked as Miptera hit it, and her mandibles sank into the fabric. Valiant climbed the ropes, leaped up and grabbed Miptera from the balloon, then landed on the bow of the sky-ak and flung her back into the sky.

Welby stood up. "Take the sail, steer us in, Arthur. I'll jump out onto the deck."

"Are you out of your mind, Welby? What if you fall?!"

"Do it!"

But the balloon was deflating, and the sky-ak was faltering.

"I can't keep her up!" Maudie grunted.

"Get as close as you can!" Welby was bent-kneed, ready to spring.

"I can't hold control, but we might make the deck!" she yelled. "Brace yourself!"

On the *Aurora*, most of the crew had dashed over to the side. Smethwyck leaped out of the way as the sky-ak hurtled down toward the sky-ship's deck, and with a huge *bang* and yawning scrapes, the sky-ak crash-landed and came to a stop just beside Eudora Vane at the wheel. Arthur and Maudie tumbled out and, with the swiftest of glances to each other, they gave Eudora Vane a mighty shove so that she was thrust across the deck.

Welby lunged and, in a rapid series of moves, had Smethwyck lying on the ground groaning.

Arthur hurried to take control of the wheel while Maudie grabbed the sky-ak's sail post, yanked it out, and brandished it, ready for anyone who dared try to come near. Valiant was at her side growling and baring his small white teeth, while Parthena was diving in circles, threatening with ear-piercing squawks and bared talons.

Welby took over from Arthur and turned the wheel hard. The *Aurora* banked east, but suddenly everyone on the deck froze. Eerie wisps of water vapor were all around them. A hushed murmur flowed on the wind. Claws gripped the wooden rail of the ship's prow, talons rippled, cloudy white eyes scanned the deck.

A darkwhisper.

CHAPTER 32

MEMORY

MOST OF EUDORA'S CREW dived below deck, but Eudora was back on her feet, lurching toward Welby, who was trying to keep control of the sky-ship.

The *Aurora* was almost above the first darkwhisper island. Down below, Florian's water-wing was a short distance behind, circling warily.

The darkwhisper's gaze flitted between those left on deck.

Maudie blinked quickly as the darkwhisper fixed her with its smoky eyes.

Her father was passing her a package wrapped in brown paper, tied with a red ribbon. She was about three years old. She took it as though he'd passed her the most precious treasure in the Wide, and to her it was, because when she carefully pulled the ribbon off and opened it, inside was her mother's tool belt.

Maudie absently put her hand to her waist, and she felt a small paw tugging at her hand, trying to pull her away—Valiant. It was enough to snap her back into reality. She shook her head in an attempt to regain a grip on herself.

In the distance, Arthur could see two more water-wings heading out to sea, but they were mere specks. He cried out as something grabbed him around the throat and ice ran through his veins, then almost relief as he realized it wasn't a darkwhisper; it was Smethwyck. Suddenly, the cold tip of a blade was at his neck. But Arthur wasn't there at all.

He was on his first flight on the Violetta, *taking off from the docks of Lontown, the wind in his hair, Dad at the wheel. It was just a short trip to the northern marshlands, but bubbles of excitement fizzed in his stomach like word-leweed pop. Maudie sat on the deck not far away banging something, then screwing nails into the deck, and . . .*

The tip of the knife lifted from his skin slightly; it was as though Smethwyck were losing concentration—was he reliving a memory too? Arthur drew his arm back and elbowed him in the ribs. The knife clattered to the deck and Arthur slipped from Smethwyck's grip.

The darkwhisper jumped down. It had chosen.

Smethwyck dropped to the ground, and Arthur and Maudie dashed for the back of the sky-ship to get away. But Eudora saw her chance, and as Welby leaped to the side and the darkwhisper crawled menacingly toward Smethwyck, she grabbed the wheel and ran it through her hands in a furious turn.

There was a moment of nothing, then the *Aurora* tilted so suddenly that the port side lurched in the direction of the sea. They all skidded across the deck, and a barrel rolled and smashed over the side, sending gemstones over the edge in a glittering shower of pink rain. Eudora just managed to keep hold of the wheel and rapidly turned it the other way as fast as she could, and the tilting stopped just before it became heart-stoppingly difficult for them to stop sliding further. But the tilt revealed a view they'd not been prepared for: they were swinging close to one of the dangerously high crags. Numerous dark-whispers clung to the rock, watching and waiting. As the sky-ship began to right itself, it was clear that Eudora was totally unused to the subtle steering that the *Aurora* required, and as soon as the sky-ship had righted, it suddenly tilted in the opposite direction. They were all seized with horror as the back end swung toward the crag and clipped it with an ear-cracking splintering of wood. The *Aurora* was propelled out of control.

Maudie was thrown into the balustrade along the edge, with Valiant clinging to her, but just before the sky-ship tilted again, she managed to grab a safety rope and clip in.

Arthur wasn't so lucky. He flailed for a rope and just as his fingertips brushed one, the ship swung, and he rolled across the deck.

There was an enormous *bang* followed by a heart-juddering *scrape* as the *Aurora* slammed into the crag again, then began tilting toward the ground. They were barely a hundred yards from the rocky base.

Welby yelled with the force of thunder at Arthur to hold on.

As the sky-ship swayed, it began to roll into a deadly spin.

The darkwhisper still had Smethwyck pinned, having pierced the deck with its claws, and was clinging to him. Eudora gripped the wheel, and Welby and Arthur hurtled across the deck together.

The *Aurora* began tipping almost vertically. Welby and Arthur exchanged looks of utter terror. They were about to tumble over the edge to certain death on the rocks below. Arthur's brain reeled.

And at that moment, one of the safety ropes swung past on the other side of Welby.

Swift as a blink, Welby grabbed the harness.

Good—at least Welby is safe, Arthur thought.

With a superhuman twist and reach, Welby managed to clip the safety rope to Arthur's belt.

"Hold on to me!" Arthur screamed as he bashed into the railings. He reached out his hand. Welby found it, and for a moment they grasped each other, but then the sky-ship tipped too far and, like trying to hold on to water, his hand slipped from Arthur's.

An anguished yell filled the air and Arthur wasn't even aware it had come from himself as he watched, utterly helpless, as Welby fell overboard.

The sky-ship's hull was now grating down the side of the rock face, juddering until it came to a violent stop at the bottom.

Ringing silence fell, but only for a moment. The leathery wings of the darkwhispers circled in a spiral above, coming closer with every breath.

* * *

Maudie unclipped her safety rope and looked around frantically. Valiant, who was still clinging to her, gave a soft whimper as though to ask if she was all right. She stroked his head and tried to take in the scene. Eudora had her hands clasped through the wheel; a pale, closed-eyed Smethwyck was still pinned by the darkwhisper, which wrenched its claws up from the deck. Then she saw Arthur, who was on his knees, wrestling to unclip the safety harness, tears glistening on his cheeks.

Yelps and moans sounded from below deck as the rest of Eudora's crew began climbing their way out.

Maudie scrambled across to Arthur and threw her arms around him. "Where's Welby?"

Arthur couldn't speak. He was taking in gulps of air as though parched of water.

She stood up and called for Welby, looking around the area of rock where they'd come to a standstill.

A darkwhisper landed on the deck, and another. Maudie bent down and yanked Arthur to his feet.

Suddenly she saw Welby on the rocks close by. She thrust a hand over her mouth to stop herself from yelping, then saw his chest rising. "Arthur, he's alive!"

With a glance over her shoulder to check that there were no darkwhispers close, she clambered over the side and urged Arthur to follow.

Arthur looked back to see at least five darkwhispers on the deck, one with its eyes set on Eudora. The sight kicked his legs into action, and he climbed over and ran with Maudie to Welby.

With his eyes fluttering, and his skin pale as snow, a heavy wheeze escaped from Welby's mouth.

"Welby!" Arthur said urgently.

But Welby merely groaned.

"It'll be all right; Harriet will be here soon," Maudie said in the most confident voice she could muster, but as she glanced out to sea, it was clear that the water-wings still had some distance to go, and without sails they wouldn't be as fast as Florian's. The fire-bird, with its red-orange wings beating wide as a house and its sweeping scarlet tail flowing across the sky, was flying close to Florian, protecting him from a nearby darkwhisper, although the creature was doing its best to get to them.

A sense of crippling dread came over Arthur as he knelt beside Welby. "You saved me," he whispered, his voice trembling.

With that, Welby's eyes opened a little, and he gave a strained smile. Then he closed his eyes for the last time.

One of the darkwhispers was watching from a crag above, unseen by the twins in their moment of desolation. With a swift soar it landed next to the old man.

Arthur fell back and let out a cry. "Get back, leave him alone!" he roared.

But the darkwhisper fixed Arthur with its cloudy eyes.

✳ ✳ ✳

He was back, knocking on number four Archangel Street. Welby opened the door. It was the moment Arthur and Maudie had first met Welby, when they'd arrived to be interviewed for the expedition to South Polaris. Welby stared at him with judging eyebrows and spoke in his well-to-do Uptown accent, and Arthur could once again feel all the emotions of the moment: desperation, nerves, burning hope.

Maudie turned to see the darkwhisper staring at Arthur, but looming over Welby, its feelers around Welby's head, tiny electric sparks rippling the length of them. She called out and looked for anything she might use as a weapon, and Valiant passed her a large stone, so she hurled it at the darkwhisper.

It hit the creature on the body and bounced off as though it was made of rubber.

Arthur was sitting back, a strange, dazed look in his eyes.

Maudie threw another rock, then another, and Valiant did too. With a glance behind, she saw that Florian and the fire-bird were nearly there, and relief swept through her. The fire-bird shrieked and the darkwhisper looked up and screeched back.

But the darkwhisper wasn't moving. Why wasn't the darkwhisper flying away?

Both creatures' eyes were locked intensely, and for a split second Maudie was reminded of the thought-wolves. Was this how the fire-bird challenged the darkwhisper?

Then the fire-bird bowed its head to the dark-whisper, almost as though submitting—or giving its approval? Maudie stared in disbelief, every muscle paralyzed in naked fear.

The darkwhisper lifted its head and moved toward Arthur.

"What are you doing? Stop it!" she shrieked at the fire-bird. She noticed Parthena had landed close by. "Parthena, do something!" But Parthena seemed frozen too. Even Florian had become very still. "Florian, help me!" She tried to reach out to him, to pull him to help her, but he didn't move. Although there was no glazed look in his eyes, he was shaking with terror. He must've been reliving what had happened to his sister.

The darkwhisper was now staring into Arthur's face.

* * *

The door closed on number four Archangel Street as they stepped out from the interview. Rather than stepping into daylight, it was pitch dark. He reached for Maudie beside him, but his hand simply flailed in the air because she wasn't there. He knew this place. He was now in the Slumps of Lontown, the poorest, most deprived area. He looked around, half-expecting the Begginses to appear, but the more he looked around, the more he realized that this wasn't the Slumps as he knew it; the houses were a little different, not as old.

He was in the past.

This wasn't his memory.

A woman hobbled down the street, crying. Her stomach was swollen; perhaps she was having a child? Then he saw she was clutching a tiny, naked baby to her chest. She knocked on a door; someone opened it and then shut it straightaway. She tried another, and they yelled at her. It was a perishingly cold night, and that poor baby would freeze and die if someone didn't help.

Arthur took off his jacket. "Hey," he called out. "Hey, I'll help you."

But the woman didn't even turn her head, because he wasn't there, not really. He was in a memory.

Thick fog rippled down the streets; an unnatural, dense, dream fog that swallowed him in an instant, then was immediately broken by fierce sunshine. He was still in the Slumps, but there was a young boy, skinny as his own bones, and the boy was begging in the streets, bruises on his face and arms.

"Spare a sovereign for a boy? Spare a sovereign for a boy?" he asked over and over, from one uninterested stranger to another. The boy, who couldn't have been older than six, eventually sank against a wall.

"Someone help him!" Arthur yelled. But again, his voice was not there.

The boy stared into the air as though he was already a ghost, like he wasn't there either. There was something familiar about his face, his eyebrows.

Like a lightning bolt to the chest, Arthur realized the boy was Welby. He felt it with all certainty.

Some children ran down the street past him, then one told the others to stop. They went back to the boy and started pushing and shouting things at him.

Suddenly there was a fire in the boy's eye, and he leaped to his feet and began kicking and chopping with his hands. He was clearly outnumbered, but he was giving it everything his tiny body had. Arthur found himself shouting, "Go on, Welby! Clout them on the nose!"

A figure appeared at the end of the street, strolling up confidently. She stopped in front of them and stood with her hands on her hips.

The gang took one look at her and fled.

Again, this woman looked familiar somehow. She reached out a hand to the reedy-limbed boy, now lying on the ground.

Wait, there it was on her arm: the Culpepper swallows! But this wasn't Harriet. Who was it? If this was a young Welby, then it must be Harriet's parents? Or Octavie? No,

*that still wouldn't fit . . . her grandparents? No, still not
quite.*

*She spoke to the boy, and Arthur couldn't help but
move closer, so that he could take in every word.*

"You have no parents?" Her voice was kindly.

Young Welby shook his head.

"And no home?"

"Never, Miss."

"You've never had a roof, or a bed?"

He shook his head.

"Is there anyone at all who will miss you from here?"

"No, Miss."

"Not a soul?"

"No, Miss."

*"Well, we simply can't have that. You've clearly lived a
thousand lives in your short years, and that just won't do
at all. Young man, it is time for you to be a child. Such a
strong young person deserves a home. Will you come with
me?"*

He looked at her apprehensively.

*Crouching down to his level, she put a hand on her
heart. "I promise you will come to no harm and I will keep
you safe and warm."*

*The glint of a smile sat in the smallest corner of Welby's
lips. It was almost too scared, too disbelieving, to show itself.*

She offered her hand. "Do you have a name?"

He nodded.

"Then might you tell me?" she asked in a whisper.

"William, Miss."

"You don't need to call me Miss, William. My name is Argentia."

CHAPTER 33

SAYING GOODBYE

ORE MEMORIES FOLLOWED: Welby starting school and trying to fit in by speaking in his best Uptown voice like the other children, his first time in a sky-ship with Argentia, getting into trouble and fights at school, graduating from the universitas, holding a baby Harriet when her parents were called away on business—and all with the undying friendship and loyalty he felt for the Culpeppers.

The fog cleared and Arthur blinked several times quickly, as though not sure if he was still in a memory or back in reality. Then he saw with a lurch that a darkwhisper was facing him directly, feelers resting on his temple, cloudy eyes fixed on his.

To his right was the fire-bird, but with a swish of its scarlet tail, it took flight.

Yet, for some reason, Arthur didn't feel afraid of the darkwhisper. Then it blinked, took a step back, and flew away.

As it did so, all the other darkwhispers took to the sky, spiraling up into the blue-gray. There was the distant rumble of thunder and they turned and flew toward the dark clouds on the horizon.

Maudie and Florian ran to Arthur.

Arthur looked at Welby's lifeless body, and a full range of emotions fueled every cell in him: deep sadness, regret, warmth, wonder. There was happiness too, somehow, somewhere among the grief that made him want to tear out his heart as he thought of Welby's life. And as he thought of Dad.

"Arthur, do you remember me?" Maudie stuttered, putting a shaking hand on his arm.

"Of course I do." He frowned and watched the darkwhispers disappear into the distant storm. "They're not all bad," he said softly. He'd lost some of his fear of the darkwhispers.

"What just happened?"

"I think it chose to use its gift in this moment. It's as though they can read our past, what made us who we are and our intentions, and . . . I don't know . . . it gave me Welby's memories . . . and now I understand. I never took the time to think about it. I assumed so much and now he's gone and . . ." He buried his head in his hand.

"Excuse me? Can you tell me where I am?" It was one of Eudora's crew.

"Can't you remember?" Maudie called.

He frowned and narrowed his eyes. "Remember what?"

More crew members appeared from below deck, staring around confusedly. Then Eudora Vane peered tentatively over the edge of the *Aurora* at them. "Er . . . hello. . . This is rather embarrassing. I've ripped my dress and I seem to have forgotten where I am. You couldn't be a dear and help, could you?"

Arthur, Maudie, and Florian all exchanged open-mouthed glances. Valiant had jumped up on to Maudie's neck and was trembling at the sight of Eudora.

"Aren't you . . ." She squinted as though trying to place them. "I was planning an expedition, somewhere south, I think. Are we south? I thought it would be cooler than this . . ."

"She doesn't know who we are. The darkwhispers took their memories! I think she thinks she was planning to go south," Maudie whispered.

Smethwyck appeared and spoke in an urgent whisper. "Hello, I think these people may have kidnapped me, because I don't remember what I'm doing here . . . at all!"

Then a confused-looking Ermitage stumbled on deck. "Ah, my dear old thing. I wonder if you can point me in the direction of the . . ." He paused and scratched his beard. "Never mind."

By this point, the other water-wings had reached the shore, and Harriet jumped out and ran to Welby. She put a hand to his chest. Her shoulders heaved as she inhaled a slow breath. Felicity looked over the scene, then ran to the children and engulfed them in her warm arms. After a while, Harriet joined them, and they all hugged for a long time.

Eventually, they broke off and helped Tauria, Florian, and Cassea gather up the befuddled Vane crew. It was strange to see Eudora assume no authority at all. She'd lost her powerful posture, and although Arthur and Maudie found it hard to take in, there was even a glint of wonder as she looked around at this world, as though seeing it through the eyes of a child. Ermitage and all the Vane crew members seemed to have lost many years of memories.

The darkwhispers had all disappeared into the distant storm clouds of the south, and more water-wings and Erytheans arrived.

"The *Aurora* isn't too damaged," said Florian shakily. "I'm no expert on your mechanics, but the engine is intact, and the hull is just badly scraped. There are some holes, but they can be fixed."

Tauria nodded. "We'll head back to Tempestra, regroup, and organize any repairs you need to your sky-ship. And we'll help you remember this gentleman. In our world, when someone passes, we celebrate who they were and give them to the sea. Perhaps we can honor him in this way?"

Harriet nodded. "Yes, I think he would like that."

Some of the Vane crew were lying down and appeared to be falling asleep.

"Are they all right?" asked Arthur.

Tauria nodded. "They will likely be sleepy for several days. We have seen it before when people have lost memories to the darkwhispers." Then she began talking with Cassea in Erythean.

"What are they saying?" Maudie whispered to Florian. She put her hand on his arm; he was still trembling.

He listened for a moment. "She is regretful about the punishment decision; she thinks perhaps they were too harsh, but she is furious with Eudora about what happened to the water-bears, and she is unsure about letting them return with the Culpepper crew because it still might jeopardize the Erythean secrecy code."

They listened some more, then Florian said in a hushed voice, "They are deciding whether they will keep them here."

"We should take them back home with us," Arthur said, interrupting Tauria's conversation. "They're confused and have no memories. They're no danger to you now."

Tauria stared at him. She thought for a moment, then nodded. "I think it may be best if we . . . what would you say in Lontonian? If we washed our hands of her. They will remain dazed, and their new memories will be unreliable for a while, so when you return you can ensure that they believe they have only been to the Stella Oceanus."

Harriet nodded.

"However, Ermitage Wrigglesworth must remain here. As we discussed before, too many of your people think he is dead, and if he arrived back alive, too many questions would be asked. His actions have led to many wrongs this day. We will need to watch him closely, to find a way for him to give back."

Arthur looked across at Ermitage, who was sitting on a rock looking confusedly at the sky. He felt so many emotions coursing through him. He wanted to rush over and shake him, to demand he tell them why he helped Eudora Vane and her crew escape, even though it was useless because he wouldn't remember. Arthur moved to stomp forward, but a gentle hand from Harriet stopped him.

He looked at her. "Why did Ermitage do it?" he said in despair.

She shook her head. "I guess he just missed Lontown too much. He was blind to the possible consequences of his actions."

Arthur thought of Ermitage back in the jungle, longing for "dear old Lontown." He sighed. Ermitage would pay the ultimate price for his decision. He wouldn't ever go back.

Maudie held up the loose strand of her ribbon, and together they tied it in her hair.

Afterward, Tauria led them back to the waterwings. "We'll return to the city and rest. The storm may shift and bring another deluge, and we should get ahead of it."

* * *

This time the storm remained in the south and the rain decided to stay away, as though somehow it knew that they had all taken as much as they could handle for one day. Back in their quarters, no matter how hard Arthur willed it, or how tired and bruised his body and mind felt, sleep refused him. So he decided to take a short walk outside.

The night remained as still as the moment between breaths, and clouds petered out to mere wisps of dove-gray in the vast midnight blue. Arthur sat on the edge of the jetty and watched the reflection of the sky ripple on the surface like a secret mirror version of the real world. In that world, maybe things were different and Welby lived on. A tear trailed down his cheek.

Losing Welby had hit them all hard, and Arthur all the harder for the memories he now had within him. Yes, he was lucky: he was back with Maudie, back with Harrie and Felicity; Parthena was here, they were safe, the rest of the crew was safe. Yet . . . yet he'd never felt so empty and alone, not since the moment he'd heard the news about Dad.

He didn't want to go back to Lontown. He didn't want to go anywhere.

A voice, as though carried on the wind, whispered his name. He looked around, but there was no one else on the jetty.

Then it happened again. This time louder. And he

recognized the voice, although it was utterly impossible. Wasn't it?

"*You are stronger than you know, cub.*"

"Tuyok?" Arthur breathed. Again, he stared into the indigo night and searched for the great white shape of the thought-wolf. But then Maudie was calling to him, walking up the jetty with Valiant on her shoulder.

Arthur blinked. Of course he'd imagined Tuyok's voice.

"Are you all right?" asked Maudie gently.

He shrugged. "I feel like the universe has broken, and I don't think it can ever be fixed. And part of me thought that somehow we would get justice for Dad. Now this has happened to Welby, and really it's all her fault again. Everything comes back to that woman, and I'm trying to be angry with her but . . ."

"I know," Maudie said.

"It doesn't matter how far we explore, where we go, I just feel so . . . lost."

They heard a flapping sound and looked up to see Parthena flying toward them. She landed on Arthur's shoulder. Her wing brushed Arthur's arm.

Then the voice was there again, but it sounded clearly inside of him.

"You are never alone. No matter how far from home, we walk beside you . . . you are never truly lost."

Convinced he was losing his mind, he looked to Maudie, but her mouth was wide in amazement.

"Was that . . . ?" She shook her head.

"You heard it too?"

"Tuyok? Tuyok!"

But there was only silence in reply.

And although Arthur and Maudie still felt sad and wounded in their hearts, they now also felt a spark of hope, and warmth, and wonder.

* * *

The following day, they sailed on the water-wings: Maudie with Arthur and Felicity with Florian. Harriet traveled with Tauria and Cassea on a larger boat.

They sailed along the riverway to the estuary where Erythea met the southern coastline.

There was a separate boat for Welby's body, pulled by the main boat of the Professus Excelsis.

When they had traveled a short distance into the open sea, the water-wings gathered in a semicircle. Arthur and Maudie positioned their water-wing close to Florian's.

Harriet stood on the prow of the boat and inhaled

a long breath before speaking. "William Welby was my second-in-command for as long as I have captained a sky-ship. He was the most loyal and true person I could have hoped to sail with, not only to me but to my family and to my crew."

Felicity sniffed into her handkerchief.

"I can't imagine sailing without him, but as he said to me when I captained my first expedition, 'Leave the shadows behind, and always look to a new dawn on the horizon.'"

She glanced over at Arthur and Maudie as she spoke the words, and neither of them could breathe for a moment.

Harriet closed her eyes for several seconds, then opened them and said, "Goodbye, dear friend."

Next, Tauria stood and spoke in Erythean.

Florian looked across to Arthur and Maudie. "She is saying that those who leave a mark on the Wide are never truly gone. Given from the water of life, returned to her arms."

They looked on in reverent silence as Welby's boat was released to the sea. Arthur tried his best to imagine that Welby was just setting out on a new adventure into unknown waters. "Adventure awaits . . ." he said in the mildest of whispers.

Back in the city, as they walked along the jetty, Harriet put a hand on Arthur's shoulder. "He had a good life . . . in the end . . ." Her voice drifted off.

"I think I understand the darkwhispers now."

She looked at him curiously.

"I think I understand Welby now too. I mean *really* understand him."

"What happened on that island, Arthur?"

"The darkwhisper did something. I think. . . .

I think it took Welby's memories and gave them to me. Somehow it knew that they needed to be passed on. We thought they were bad, the darkwhispers, but they're not, not really, they're . . ." What were they? He couldn't even begin to think of the right word. He frowned. "I don't know what they are. They're complicated." There was so much in the Wide to explore, and the more he explored the more it amazed and enthralled him, yet for every question answered, more were asked, and he felt at that moment that he didn't really understand anything at all.

"What does your heart tell you?"

"That they aren't good or bad. That they need an energy source to live, just like me, or Parthena, or the thought-wolves." He shrugged. "A bit weird that it's storms and memories. But they don't mean to hurt people, I don't think."

Harriet gave a small smile. "It's all just energy to them. And it's all right not to understand things, Arthur. The acceptance of not knowing, saying you don't know, is what opens the path to new knowledge."

He suddenly felt bad. Here he was trying to make sense of things for himself, when Harriet was facing a heritage that, up until a week ago, she hadn't known existed. And she'd just lost a friend who had held her in his arms when she was a baby.

Harriet gazed out across the plateau. There was still a peacefulness about her, despite everything they'd all been through, and she still had that look of strength, of knowing who she was and what she stood for.

"I'm so sorry about Welby," he said.

She smiled at him. "Thank you. He was very fond of you, you know."

"I know," he said softly.

CHAPTER 34

A SECRET WORTH KEEPING

THE NEXT DAY, Harriet and Felicity went with the Erytheans to collect the *Aurora*. Satisfied from the previous storm, the darkwhispers remained peacefully on their rocky crags, but the fire-bird flew above them regardless. They mended the propeller and succeeded in getting liftoff, flying back to the mainland of Erythea. Repairs recommenced, and the following morning they prepared to set sail for home.

Tauria, Cassea, and Florian came to see them off. They settled memory-less Eudora and her crew on the *Aurora* and told them they were heading back home, although none of them were entirely sure where that was.

Maudie stood facing Florian.

"I've arranged for Ermitage Wrigglesworth to stay in Althuria so that I can keep an eye out for him along with my sister," he said.

"That's kind of you; I'll let the others know." She stepped a little closer. "Thank you for everything, and I'm sorry I was . . . well, you know, a bit dismissive when I first met you."

He smiled, green eyes sparkling. "Maybe one day you can come back?"

"Maybe one day you can come to Lontown."

Florian glanced at Tauria, who was talking with Harriet. "I would like that," he whispered.

"Do you think they'll change their minds about the secrecy code?"

He shrugged sadly and looked at the ground. "I will miss you, Maudie Brightstorm."

She felt a strange pulling in her chest. "And I'll—"

Arthur, who was helping Felicity load the last of the supplies that the Erytheans had gifted them, looked over and coughed loudly. "Do you think you could help with this crate?"

"Er, yes," said Maudie quickly. She took her ribbon from her hair and pressed it into Florian's hand. "Now you'll have to come to Lontown one day to return it." She hurried away.

Harriet turned to Tauria and Cassea. "If you

ever need help from us, you need only ask. And if things change, you will always be welcome to visit us in Lontown."

Tauria dipped her head in thanks.

"Time to go," said Harriet.

"One last thing," said Tauria.

She handed them each a fire-bird ring.

"Our secret is in your hands."

"We respect your wishes and we won't let you down," Harriet said solemnly.

When Maudie tried to put the water-bear down, he whimpered. "I can't take you back; you're too different, and it'll look suspicious. We have to keep the secret."

Tauria smiled and winked. "I'm sure you can come up with something. A new species on Nova, perhaps?"

Valiant took her hand and made the action for *yes*. Maudie's face exploded with a grin.

"Looks like you've got yourself a sapient friend, Maud!" Arthur said.

"Speaking of sapients, poor Queenie will be worried, and so will the rest of the crew. Let's get going," said Harriet.

With one last look back at the emerald landscape of Erythea, the city of Tempestra a tiny spec in the distance atop a glistening plateau, they waved to

Tauria, Cassea, and Florian, then took to their posts and fired the engines.

Under the protection of the fire-bird, the *Aurora* sailed past the darkwhispers, and they continued on to Nova without it. Within three days they were reunited with the rest of the crew. They didn't reveal the secrets of Erythea, not even to their crew, although Gilly kept glancing at Maudie and the water-bear with a knowing smile. Harriet told them that they found the *Aurora* nearly sinking in the sea with the Vane crew dehydrated and suffering mental strain with a suspected permanent damage, and that Welby had lost his life saving them. They left it in Gallus's hands to dispose of the *Victorious* in whatever way he saw fit and set off again.

As they journeyed home, the shock of losing Welby weighed heavily within the sky-ship. Arthur kept expecting him to appear in the doorway, looking at him from under those eyebrows. But the Vane crew kept them busy, mostly with endless questions as they all tried to figure out what they were doing in a sky-ship above the Stella Oceanus.

Weeks later they arrived back in Lontown. Eudora Vane and her crew were taken into the care of the Geographical Society Hospital. Harriet and her crew met with the Society and gave their account of what had happened, confirming that Ermitage Wrigglesworth had lost his life at sea outside Nova.

After that, they went to Octavie's house. She apologized for not being able to tell them the full story about Erythea, but she was incredibly relieved that they had been allowed to return and share in the secret with her.

"Part of me hoped you would find Erythea when I gave you the ring. I couldn't say, of course, because it would've broken the Erythean secrecy code, but I suspected that Ermitage had found a way. I didn't want to lead you to danger, but I knew that the firebird would watch over you. What I didn't suspect is that that Vane woman would do what she did."

"No one seems to be able to predict the lengths she will go to," Harriet sighed.

"At least it's safe now that she's lost a great chunk of her memory," said Maudie.

"We'll have to keep checking on her and the others to be sure," said Arthur.

* * *

"Hello. You're the nice children who helped me, aren't you?" Eudora said, sitting forward and running her hands over her pink satin eiderdown. Eudora's room in the Geographical Society Hospital had high ceilings and crisp, white walls. "How wonderful. Are your parents with you?" She tilted her head as though expecting more visitors to appear behind them.

A knot yanked tightly in their stomachs, and Arthur bit his tongue for fear of what might come out. He saw Maudie's fist clench and he put a hand on her arm. He told himself for the umpteenth chime that this wasn't the same Eudora. She had no memory of what she'd done to their father.

"No, they're not with us," he said.

"Pity. I would have liked to have thanked them." She smiled sweetly. "I'm an explorer!" Then she whispered, "And this strange insect seems to follow me everywhere." She nodded to the windowsill, where Miptera sat quietly gnashing her mandibles. "I think she belongs to me. She's on my tattoo, would you like to see?"

She lifted up her sleeve before they had a chance to answer. "Isn't it glorious?"

Then she sat back. "It's strange, though—I still don't know what I was doing in the Eastern Isles."

Arthur and Maudie exchanged an awkward glance.

"We'd better be going," Maudie said.

"But you've only just got here. I'd love to find out more about you."

"You must be tired, and we've got to, er . . . to do some studying and . . . stuff. Maybe another time."

They stood up and hurried to the door.

"Come again," Eudora called.

Under her breath Maudie said, "Not likely."

Arthur glanced back at Eudora. She smiled sweetly.

Then she winked.

He blinked. Was it just a twitch of her eyes? Was he seeing things? Yet there was something in her smile that unnerved him. He looked back again.

"Yes, *do* come again," she said, and once more her smile unsettled him.

The door clicked shut behind them.

He shook his head as though to get rid of the thought.

"Are you all right, Arty?"

"Yes, I think so."

"Let's go home."

As they rounded the corner they jolted to a stop; Thaddeus Vane was walking up the stairs toward them, his footsteps acute on the marble steps. He paused and rested his hands on his diamond-topped cane, and looked first at Maudie, then at Arthur with his razor-sharp glare. He was lower down on the stairs yet seemed to rise above them and fill the space. His eyes were probing and Arthur felt utterly transparent, strangely weak in the presence of this immaculate man.

"The twins," Thaddeus said, matter of factly, but there was meaning in there too, as though he was contemplating. Arthur wished he could work it out, but instead he took Maudie's arm and swiftly pulled her past their grandfather and down the staircase.

✱ ✱ ✱

Harriet and Felicity were waiting for them outside.

"I have some news for you," Harriet said, handing the twins a thick folder. "Welby was working on this before we left. It's the reason he kept disappearing for hours when we were rebuilding the *Aurora*."

Arthur felt dreadful, having accused him of sneaking away.

Maudie held the folder and Arthur flipped it open.

"It's the deed to Brightstorm House," Harriet said brightly.

Arthur and Maudie stared, mouths wide. A rush of elation filled them both. They glanced at each other, barely able to believe it. *Home*, Dad's home, the place they'd grown up and shared so many memories. They both looked back down at the deed.

Home.

Their eyes met once more, and the question they suddenly both felt was reflected.

"Oh! You don't *have* to move out of Archangel Street!" said Harriet quickly.

Felicity's brow was wrinkled, but she smiled. "That is, if you don't want to, of course." Then she spoke in the quietest voice Arthur and Maudie had ever heard her speak in, as though trying to hold something inside that was threatening to burst. "We'll always be your family, twinnies, wherever you are."

Arthur pulled Maudie to the side and whispered intently. After a moment she nodded, then began whispering back. They turned to face Harriet and Felicity.

"We've made a decision. We'd like to make Brightstorm House a home."

Harriet and Felicity both nodded solemnly.

"We totally understand—" Harriet started.

"But not a home for us. We're not sure how, yet, but we'd like to make it somewhere for the homeless children of the Slumps. A safe and warm haven for those who need one."

Harriet's mouth dropped open. "Wow . . . er . . . that's pretty incredible!"

Felicity rushed and hugged them so tight that they gasped for breath when she eventually let go.

Harriet kissed them both on the cheek then stepped back. "It won't be easy. It will need funding. I'm afraid we've nothing to show for our expedition, so reserves are rather on the dry side."

"We've thought of that," said Maudie. "We'll help fund it with my sky-ak invention."

Arthur nodded. "And we're going to . . ." The sudden tightness in his chest stopped him speaking.

Maudie placed an arm over his shoulders. "We're going to rename it '*Welby House.*'"

Harriet bit her lip and took several breaths before she spoke again. "Well . . . you two continue to both surprise and amaze me."

They turned away from the hospital and began walking down the street.

"It looks like we've got some work to do before we set off on our next expedition."

"Good. My feet could do with a rest," Felicity said.

"But not *too* long." Arthur could already feel the pull in his stomach, the one that wanted him to keep moving, to discover more of the Wide, to discover more of himself.

Harriet squeezed his shoulder. "No. Not too long. Come on. Let's go home."

They walked back through the busy Lontown square, everyone rushing about on whatever important business they each had.

"It's strange," said Maudie. "All these people in Lontown, totally oblivious to the fact that you-know-what exists."

Arthur nodded and hooked her arm. "It is. But do you know what? I reckon some secrets are worth keeping."

ACKNOWLEDGMENTS

I'm so delighted that the *Brightstorm Adventures* are continuing with *Darkwhispers* in North America. Thank you to Norton Young Readers for your continuing belief in me and the crew, with special thanks to my wonderful editor Kristin Allard and fabulous publishing director Simon Boughton. You continue to be a total joy to work with and, once again, your editorial suggestions have brought some extra magic to the *Brightstorm Adventures*. Continued thanks to the wider teams at both Norton Young Readers and Scholastic UK—all hugely important cogs in the wheel—and also to my brilliant editor in the UK, Linas Alsenas, and my second-to-none agent, Kate Shaw.

George Ermos and designer Jamie Gregory have created yet another stunning cover. Thank you for your artistic magic, and George, extra thanks for bringing the world of *Darkwhispers* to life so amazingly in the internal illustrations. They make the US edition really special.

Thank you to all the booksellers, librarians, and educators who have adventured with the Brightstorms so far. I hope you've enjoyed escaping to the Wide and that you didn't get too wet in the jungles of Erythea— do keep in touch to let me know!

Lastly, as always, my thanks to the lovely young readers who have become part of the Brightstorm crew in North America—it's great to have you on board for another adventure! Well done for surviving the Darkwhispers. Dream BIG—your imagination is limitless. You know you're all hired for the crew, right? Where to next, I wonder . . .